"Just lead the posse," said Fogarty.

McGregor and Pepperdine exchanged a look before Joe Fogarty continued. "It's a long chance but I saw one of 'em as plain as I see you right now. If he's who I think he is, he's one of those young marauders. . . ." Fogarty paused, eyeing the older men in the doorway. "The long chance is that they'll draw you posse men off, make a big circle, come back and bust them kids out of jail."

At the blank looks he got from the men Fogarty made a gesture. "Go on. They'll be gathering down there. Damn it — go!"

Pepperdine spoke. "One of us could stay here, Joe. There's two of 'em and from the looks of things they shoot first and fast.

"Just — damn it — go!"

Also by Lauran Paine:

ASSASSINS' WORLD

BANNON'S LAW

DAKOTA DEATHTRAP

GERMAN MILITARY INTELLIGENCE
   IN WORLD WAR II: The Abwehr

THE MARSHALL

SKYE

TANNER

WITCHCRAFT & THE MYSTERIES: A Grimoire

THE HORSEMAN*

THE NEW MEXICO HERITAGE*

THE GUNS OF SUMMER*

Published by Fawcett Gold Medal Books

THE YOUNG MARAUDERS

Lauran Paine

FAWCETT GOLD MEDAL • NEW YORK

A Fawcett Gold Medal Book
Published by Ballantine Books
Copyright © 1989 by Lauran Paine

Library of Congress Catalog Card Number: 89-91903

ISBN 0-449-14632-4

Manufactured in the United States of America

First Edition: February 1990

CHAPTER ONE

A Bad Night

Not much was known about the old fellow except his name, which had been Caulfield Randolph, and that he had been a Secesh soldier. Folks around town told Dr. Pohl some of the other old gaffers might know more, but as Henry Pohl told his wife Eleanor, it didn't make much difference. There was an entire row of grave markers in the cemetery with nothing more than a name on them. If there were no kin or heirs that anyone knew about, it was customary to simply bury people.

Infrequently, usually long after some of those people had been buried, a stranger would arrive in Sheridan seeking information about someone whose name was on one of those stone markers, but that happened very rarely; when it did occur, Dr. Pohl referred them to Town Marshal Joe Fogarty who kept burial records.

Dr. Pohl "laid them out," which in the case of those old men who lived in shacks below town to the south, usually meant washing as much of them as would show above their clothing, having the local carpenter go out back across the alley to his embalming shed for coffin measurements, and letting the liveryman, Reg Lee, know when to hitch up his hearse for the drive to the graveyard.

Henry made no secret of his wish that a regular undertaker would set up shop in Sheridan. His normal practice took all

1

of his time as it was; caring for the dead he usually did after supper in the evenings, which left precious little free time. And the pay wasn't very good. Most of them, like old Caulfield Randolph, died with little more than the clothes on their backs. If they had nothing, the town council anted up, but there was grumbling about that too. Henry Pohl's usual fee for laying out was four dollars. The town council would not go a cent over two.

After supper Henry listened to the wind against his house, watched Eleanor carry empty plates away, and reflected upon a particularly difficult delivery he'd made at a ranch six miles from town earlier in the day. The baby had come through well enough, but the woman, a little slip of a thing, hadn't. Henry would drive out there again tomorrow, and that was something else that annoyed him. In some towns there were hospitals where women could go to have babies. Sheridan not only had no hospital, it wasn't really large enough to support one. So Henry had three rooms in his home set aside for patients, but trying to get some damned cowman to bring his wife to town to give birth was like peeing in the ocean. A total waste of effort.

Eleanor returned from the kitchen with a glass of watered whiskey. She was a buxom, handsome woman with a complexion like fresh cream, large blue eyes, and taffy-colored hair. At thirty-five, she was ten years younger than her husband. They had been married—and childless—for fifteen years, long enough for Eleanor to know her husband's every mood, his every expression. She put the watered whiskey in front of him and resumed her position at the opposite end of the table. She knew how his thoughts were running, so she said, "Let it go until tomorrow, Henry. Another day won't make any difference. Not to Mr. Randolph, and it's not warm in the shed anyway."

Dr. Pohl's cheeks acquired a nice color as he sipped, his eyes losing some of their tired look. He smiled. "It's all right. It won't take long. And I've already notified Reg and the carpenter. They'll be by for him tomorrow." He downed the last of his drink. "That was a rough delivery today. Four hours, Ellie, not to mention six miles out and six miles back." As he rose, Dr. Pohl continued to smile. "Be back in fifteen minutes. Keep the coffee hot."

The embalming shed was across the alley, a short distance by any measurement, but he buttoned up his coat, put on his hat and gloves, tugged the hat down, and braced into the bumbling wind of a pitchblende night.

Stars were arrayed indiscriminately like diamond chips, the scimitar-shaped moon looked pure white, and dust was everywhere as Dr. Pohl headed for the shed.

With nothing to impede it, the wind hit him hardest in the north-south alley where the dust had stinging force. He remembered something Hugh Pepperdine, the saddle and harness maker, had said one time. "When it's hot, a man can get in the shade. When it's cold, he can make a fire. But what can a body do about the damned wind?"

He clung to the shed door so the wind wouldn't slam it inward, then closed it after himself in pitch-darkness and groped for his coal-oil lamp. The smell of embalming fluid engulfed him as it always did.

The shed was not windproof. He smoked up the place lighting three sulfur matches before he got the lamp lighted, and straightened to hang it aloft from its hook. Then the doctor settled back on his heels to remove his gloves as he gazed in the direction of his embalming table. He had one glove off. The sheet was in place over the corpse from poll to heel, but old Caulfield Randolph had been a tall man, lean as a hound, and the sheet was now clinging to a shorter form which was thicker. Protruding at the lower end was a pair of spurred, booted feet. Old Caulfield had been barefoot.

Dr. Pohl removed the second glove, remained over by the door as he stuffed both gloves into a pocket, finished his cursory study of the shrouded figure and approached the table. He lifted the sheet, shifted slightly to one side for the light to fall, and did not move for a long time.

The face was young and weathered. There was a hint of

rusty-colored beard stubble. Dr. Pohl had no idea who the man was as he placed three fingers on the side of the tanned neck. He lifted the hand, rolled up the eyelids, hesitated for one startled moment then went to work with abrupt, grim intensity.

He did not see old Caulfield Randolph lying on the floor until he moved to the far side of the table and nearly stumbled over him. Of one thing he was certain, Caulfield hadn't got down there by himself, and the young man on the table hadn't put him there. But neither had the young man climbed atop the embalming table by himself, either, because, although he was not dead, he was so close to being dead he couldn't in God's green world have come here without help.

It was a gunshot wound, hot to the touch and badly swollen where the slug had entered and where it had exited. Despite the cold, Henry sweated as he worked. When he'd done as much as he could, he returned to the house, told his wife to open one of the sickrooms, and hastened back to the shed. He hoisted the young man, who was heavy, and carried him across the alley into the warm kitchen, and with Eleanor big-eyed and motionless, staggered with his burden to the room with the open door. He eased the man onto the bed and slowly straightened up with back pain.

Eleanor did not say a word. She went to the far side of the bed and began removing stained, worn clothing. When she saw the badly inflamed wounds, she paused to exhale a rattling breath before continuing her work.

Henry had his back to her at the cupboard and counter where he laid out instruments before scrubbing with carbolic-acid-scented water in a blue-rimmed basin. When he turned, Eleanor stepped back slightly and looked around. "Where did you find him, Henry?"

"On the table in the shed. Old Caulfield was on the ground. Someone had to do that, Ellie—put this one on the table and old Caulfield on the ground."

"Who?"

Henry's temper slipped a notch. "How the hell would I

know? I lit the lamp and there he was. My guess is that whoever left him thought he was dead."

"He very nearly is, Henry."

Dr. Pohl nodded. "Rinse the instruments and bring them over on the tray."

Ellie moved to obey as she said, "Blood poisoning . . . ?"

Henry was leaning over the stocky young man's naked upper body and said nothing as he probed, but when his wife brought the tray, he shook his head. "Not a chance in the world." Then he swore. "Goddamned ignorant cowmen anyway. That injury is at least three days old. If they'd brought him in when it happened, he would have had a chance."

Eleanor studied the frail rise and fall of the wounded man's chest. "He was shot in the back."

Again Henry said nothing as he went to work. He had no difficulty opening the swollen punctures to drain, nor did he have any trouble cleansing each wound. Beyond that there was nothing he could do. His wife suggested laudanum. Henry shook his head. "No need. He doesn't feel any pain."

"But he might regain consciousness."

Henry put a solemn gaze upon his wife. "Not unless you believe in miracles. I should go hunt up Joe Fogarty. Shooting someone in the back is down his alley, not mine. I'd guess it was murder, Ellie."

They went through the man's pockets and came up with no more then Henry expected; a clasp knife, some crumpled greenbacks, silver money, a stiff blue bandana handkerchief, a half-empty sack of tobacco with wheat-straw papers, and half a handful of ammunition for a handgun. There were indications on the trousers that the dying man had worn a shell belt and holster, but there was no sign of either.

One thing registered in Henry Pohl's mind. The shell-belt sag had been from right to left, which meant the dying man had been left-handed.

He returned to the bedside, gazed a long time at the weathered, sun- and windburned face, and made a little flapping gesture of helplessness with both arms. Henry walked out of

the room to retrieve his coat, hat, and gloves across the alley
and go looking for Town Marshal Joe Fogarty.

He would not have bet a lead *centavo* that before he returned the wounded man wouldn't be dead.

Nothing had changed since he'd had his watered whiskey
except for the dying man; the wind was still gusting from
different directions, maybe a little colder than it had been an
hour earlier. The stars were still in place and the sickle moon
did not appear to have moved much, if at all.

Sheridan's main thoroughfare was empty except for a few
humped-up saddle horses at tie racks. Near the lower end of
town the carriage lamps out front of the livery barn guttered
inside their smoked-up glass housings. Up at Pepperdine's
Harness Works old Hugh was working late, with two
reflector-model coal-oil lamps burning.

Joe Fogarty had just dumped an armload of firewood into
the battered box near the jailhouse office stove when Henry
Pohl walked in. Joe was a big man in his thirties, wifeless,
like others around town, chewed tobacco and could hit a
knothole at twenty feet. He was capable of cleaning out Rusty
Morton's saloon, and in fact had done it many times, mostly
on Saturday nights, but he was a good-natured man—usually,
anyway—well-liked in town and on the ranges beyond.

When the medical practicioner walked in, Joe looked up,
nodded, and waited for the door to close against the cold
wind which had come in with the doctor. He and Henry Pohl
had known each other since the doctor had first appeared in
Sheridan. Fogarty pointed to a rickety chair whose under-
pinning had been reinforced with wire and said, "Nice night,
isn't it?"

Henry sank down on the rickety chair to remove his gloves.
"Yeah. If you're a Valkyrie."

Joe continued to gaze at his visitor. "A what?"

"Never mind. Is that coffee hot?"

"No. I just got the stove fired up."

"I had old Caulfield on my embalming table, went over

there after supper to finish up with him, and there was a younger man on the table with the old gent on the floor."

Joe Fogarty leaned with clasped hands on his table.

"He wasn't dead, Joe. He'd been shot through the body from in back, maybe three days ago, maybe longer. I've never seen him before and there's nothing in his pockets to say who he is."

"Is he conscious?"

Henry gazed at the big man. "No, and he wasn't when whoever put him on the table brought him in. And he most likely won't be before he dies."

"I'll go back up with you. Maybe he'll say something. You're sure he'll die?"

"As sure as I am of that damned wind out there. If they'd brought him in after the shooting . . . The slug went through his intestines and out the front. Without blood poisoning he might have hung on for a while, but internal bleeding would have taken him off eventually."

Marshall Fogarty leaned back off the desk. Wind was scrabbling under the eaves of the jailhouse roof, and somewhere nearby a length of corrugated roofing was noisily slapping.

Fogarty made an understandable but inaccurate guess. "Got into an argument in a bunkhouse maybe, or out behind someone's barn. Cowboy, is he?"

"Looks like one, but he hasn't been riding very high. His clothing was filthy, old and patched, his boots were run over and cracked."

"Have money on him, Henry?"

"Three paper dollars and sixty cents in silver."

"Weapon?"

"No. He'd been wearing one, though. The marks are clear enough on his pants. Shell belt and holster. Whoever brought him in must have taken them."

Fogarty fished for his plug of molasses cured and said nothing until he'd carved off a slice and got it properly pouched in his cheek. Joe was a genuine chewer, almost never expectorated—that was for boys trying to be men. "I guess," he said in a voice lacking enthusiasm, as the wind continued to howl over the front of the building, "what we need, Henry, is the identity of whoever brought him in and put him in your shed. Maybe they figured he was dead."

Henry crossed to the stove to feel the coffeepot. It was only lukewarm so he returned to the chair. "Not 'we' Joe—you. But I've had some time to think, and it came to me that whoever put him in my shed had a reason for not hanging around."

"Not if he was the man who shot the feller in the back."

"It wouldn't be that one," Henry said. "If it was murder, I can't imagine the murderer going to all the trouble of putting his victim in my embalming shed."

For the first time in several hours the doctor smiled; the expression on the big lawman's face showed disgust, bafflement, and annoyance. Fogarty saw the doctor's smile and wagged his head. "He's goin' to have a head start on me, Henry, because even if I could see in the dark, I'd never find him on a night like this."

Dr. Pohl departed without getting hot coffee, but the man left alone in the jailhouse office got some. He took a cup to the barred window to sip while he gazed past steel bars into a night as wild and capricious as any he'd seen in a long time.

If Henry's wounded man wasn't going to regain consciousness and wasn't going to make it until morning, then there wouldn't be much point in bucking the wind from one end of town to the other to see him. Eleanor was worth that much effort, but a dying cowboy wasn't. Or was he?

He finished the coffee, shrugged into a sheep-pelt coat, pulled his hat down hard and left the jailhouse to walk northward. The wind really didn't hit him until he was abreast of Pepperdine's Harness Works, then it almost took his breath away.

He used the lights in Henry Pohl's residence as a guide, kept his head down so the hat brim would deflect some of the eye-stinging dust, and kept on plodding.

Across from Pepperdine's place the saloon was doing a fairly lively business. Otherwise, at this end of town there was almost no sign of life.

CHAPTER TWO

The Stranger in the Shed

They sat around the table in Eleanor's warm kitchen, Fogarty and Henry Pohl sipping watered whiskey, Eleanor with a coffee cup surrounded by both her hands.

Fogarty's powerful shoulders were hunched as he gazed at the far end of the table. "Henry, how old would you make him?"

The doctor did not even hesitate. "Sixteen, seventeen. At the most, not a day over eighteen."

Eleanor was thinking of something else. "Joe, surely some of the range men could identify him."

Fogarty studied the contents of his glass. "Eleanor, every spring they come like locusts. Some get hired, some keep on riding, and a few hang around hoping." Joe raised his eyes. "I'll ask around, but you got to realize that when a stranger dies in Sheridan without anything in his pockets, the chances are high he's going into the ground near Caulfield Randolph as an unknown."

She straightened in the chair. "He's just a child, Joe."

Fogarty went back to considering the contents of his glass as he dryly said, "Well, young, but hardly a child."

"I don't believe he shaved yet."

Fogarty replied to that in the same tone of voice. "Eleanor, I don't know where folks got the idea that shaving makes a boy into a man, because it don't. Carrying a gun and using it seems to me to be a better way to make that kind of a judgment."

Eleanor's next remark came directly from what was really troubling her. "A sixteen-year-old has a mother, Joe. Maybe a sister and a father. Somewhere."

Fogarty inclined his head as he returned his attention to Eleanor's husband. "Is there anything you can give him that'll bring him around long enough for me to talk to him? Just for a couple of minutes?"

Henry Pohl shook his head. "He's too far gone, Joe. Even if he wasn't, even if I brought him around, there's no guarantee he wouldn't be out of his mind if he spoke. I'm sorry but it's hopeless."

Fogarty drained his glass, put it down gently, and leaned back away from the table. He had seen the dying youth, had examined his clothing inside and out and looked for scars, birthmarks, anything that might aid an identification, and had come up with nothing.

He sat slumped in thought until Eleanor offered to refill his glass. He roused himself to smile, shake his head, and push up out of the chair, saying, "Well, at least the wind's stopped."

Henry went with Fogarty out to the front porch, where the cold hit them. Sheridan was almost completely dark and silent now that the wind had died. Henry said, "He'll be gone by sunup. Anything special you want me to do?"

"No. Just let the carpenter and Reg know," replied the town lawman, squinting at the flawless heavens. "Maybe he could be buried the same time as old Caulfield."

Dr. Pohl thought that was possible. "As soon as he takes off I'll take him to the shed and get him ready. Reg'll be surprised. He's expecting to tote just old Caulfield out there. Knowing Reg, I'd guess he'll charge another dollar for hauling the young one too."

Marshal Fogarty ambled up to the roominghouse, went to his cold room, and bedded down without bothering with a light. He'd had an idea back in the kitchen. He still had it when he climbed between flannel sheets, and shortly before daybreak, when he awakened, he still had it. Only in the morning his mind had fleshed it out until it seemed much more plausible than it had in Eleanor's kitchen.

After tidying up at the wash house he went southward in the predawn chill, crossed over to the cafe, with its frosted window, and entered a large room where food fragrance and stove warmth offered a pleasant contrast to the roadway cold.

Fogarty found an opening, sat down and nodded around. When a gingery-haired, pale-eyed shorter man who'd neglected to shave that morning turned a craggy face and said, "Good morning," Fogarty repeated the greeting without either one of them smiling or taking the conversation any further.

The cafeman was also an unsmiling individual, but with him the condition would not be altered by hot coffee and breakfast. He brought platters of food, refused to be drawn into any of the conversations along the counter, and raised his eyes only when another customer walked in.

The newcomer was tall, rawboned, gray, and grizzled, with alert, lively, shrewd little eyes. His age was somewhere between old and damned old but he moved without stiffness and spoke loudly without inhibitions, addressing the cafeman as though he were blind to the sullen look across the counter.

"Horace, last night there was a big dog curled up out front. This morning there's no sign of him. Are we havin' spuds and ground meat this morning?"

There was laughter, but the cafeman did not join in. He reddened, his jaw muscles rippled, and he turned to stamp back beyond the old curtain to his cooking area.

The rawboned newcomer pushed in beside the other older man, the one with carroty-colored hair and whisker stubble. He looked at the shorter man's platter and said, "What is it, James?"

James McGregor turned a sour face. "Beef hash with spuds, and it's pretty good. Why'n'ell do you always have to come bouncing in here before anyone's had coffee an' spoil Horace's day?"

The lanky man leaned around to address the town marshal. He winked at Fogarty. "It's got to be that way, don't it, Joe? Someone's got to do it. We couldn't have Horace actin' normal, could we? It'd give Sheridan a bad name."

Fogarty went on eating, but McGregor dug the other man with an elbow as he growled at him. "Don't lean like that. It's crowded enough as it is." As he reached for his coffee cup, he also said, "They'll bury Caulfield today. Reg told me last night at the saloon. You goin' out there, Hugh?"

Pepperdine settled back on the bench. "Yes. Are you?"

"I oiled my boots last night and got my good pants out of the box." James paused to swallow before continuing. He was a dour man, in contrast to rawboned, lanky Hugh Pepperdine. They were as different as night and day but remained very close friends. "I don't like to see them leave. After Caulfield there aren't many left."

The harness maker gazed at the gunsmith. "Aren't many left? Who?"

"The old-timers," McGregor replied. "When they're all gone, then it's our turn to be the old-timers, and you know where that ends."

Hugh Pepperdine saw Joe Fogarty looking at the gunsmith. Hugh addressed the lawman. "He hasn't had his second cup of coffee yet. He gets better after that, but not a hell of a lot better."

The surly cafeman brought Pepperdine's breakfast, put it down with unnecessary force, glared and stamped back behind the curtain. Farther down the counter Rusty Morton, who owned the saloon, called up to Pepperdine, "Don't be surprised if it tastes of wolf bait."

Laughter echoed beyond the steamed-up front window.

When Marshal Fogarty had finished, paid up, and departed, he went no farther than an overhang upright, where he leaned to glance up and down the road. So far, into the new day, there was no traffic. He was still leaning there when Pepperdine and the gunsmith came out. Hugh was sucking his teeth and McGregor was chewing a toothpick. They both nodded at the marshal and were turning northward when Fogarty said, "If you got a minute." They stopped. Fogarty approached closer and smiled. The moment the harness maker saw the smile, he said, "No sir. Not on your blessed life."

McGregor turned irritably on his friend. "He hasn't said anything yet. What's the matter with you?"

Pepperdine remained silent, but his eyes bored into the town marshal's as Fogarty spoke. "It's cold out here. I got a fire in the office and I'll make a fresh pot of coffee." He jerked his head and stepped off the plankwalk.

Neither of the older men moved. McGregor said, "Joe . . . ?"

Fogarty turned, smiling again. "Just a little talk among old friends. What's wrong with that?"

They followed him across to the jailhouse, where it was not only warm, but coffee aroma contributed to the pleasantness. Marshal Fogarty went behind his table, sat down, dumped his hat and motioned. "Set, gents. The coffee needs a little more boiling."

They sat, Hugh Pepperdine as wary as a bitch wolf and James McGregor sitting like a stone plinth, expressionless, motionless, pale eyes fixed on the big town marshal.

Fogarty smiled broadly, interlocked fingers atop the table, and told them about the dying man at Henry Pohl's place. "Shot from behind maybe two, three days ago. By now he's dead. Someone carried him to town and put him on Henry's embalming table last night."

Neither of the older men moved nor made a sound.

"He had nothing on him to say who he was or where he came from. Young, not much more'n a boy. Henry figured he was about sixteen, no older than eighteen." Joe Fogarty studied the expressionless faces on the bench against the far wall and sighed. "Coffee's ready by now," he said, and leaned to arise as dour James McGregor spoke.

"And you want to make something out of this, Joe?"

"No. No, except that a sixteen-year-old's got a mother somewhere, James. I'll get the coffee."

"Never mind the coffee," McGregor exclaimed. "Joe, every time you've dragooned us into some kind of a mess, you started out just like you're doin' now. I've had enough coffee anyway. Just spit it out so's we can tell you to go to hell and get to work. I'm so far behind at the shop it'll take me—"

"All right," Fogarty exclaimed, settling down in the chair. "I want to know who he is—or was."

Hugh Pepperdine snorted. "What difference does it make? If he's dead, he won't care, and neither will—"

"Hugh, let me finish," the lawman said a little sharply. "The reason I want to know who he was is because, sure as hell, whoever shot him in the back didn't bring him to town, and whoever did bring him didn't even knock on Henry's door to say a wounded man was in the shed. What I particularly want to know is—why did someone bring him after dark when they could have done it any time over the past couple of days in daylight and maybe saved his life?"

Fogarty carved off a plug and settled it into his face as McGregor watched and said, "All right. It's a mystery. Now just tell us flat out why you told us all this."

Fogarty put away his clasp knife. "Old Caulfield's going to be buried this afternoon."

"We know that."

"And, the young feller's going to be buried at the same time," Fogarty explained, and paused. But when both the older men sat there staring at him, he also said, "Just about everyone in town knew Caulfield. In fact, just about everyone in Sheridan knows everyone else. Is that right?"

Both the older men nodded.

"Well, whoever carried this young feller to town had to like him to go to all that trouble. So, I told you boys the whole story because if you're going to the graveyard today, you can sort of watch for a stranger, someone who takes more interest in the young feller's passing than in Caulfield's passing.''

Pepperdine's eyes widened slightly. ''And you'll grab him. By golly, Joe, that's pretty clever. And he can put a name to the young feller.''

McGregor asked, ''After you grab whoever shows up to see his friend off, then what?''

Fogarty scowled. ''Hugh just explained it, James. I'll be able to identify the young feller.''

''Why is that so important? Hell, we bury unknowns and unclaimed around here every month or so . . . Joe, you want to know what I think?''

Fogarty did not say he wanted to know or didn't want to know, he simply sat across the room, hunched and expressionless.

McGregor was not the least intimidated. ''You want to catch this other one because you think maybe the dead one was an outlaw and his friend will be one too. Why? Because he brought his friend to town after dark and snuck away without a word.''

Fogarty shifted his cud, leaned back, gazed around the little, dingy office, and returned his gaze to the gunsmith. ''Anything wrong with that, James? If the surviving feller is an outlaw, you want him running loose in our territory?''

''No, but all you had to do was explain the whole damned rigamarole. There are times, Joe, when you're as devious as one of those Spaniards down around Santa Fe.''

Fogarty smiled. ''All I'm asking is that you mingle in the crowd and watch for a stranger who's lookin' sad around the second grave.''

Pepperdine nudged his friend. ''No harm in that, James.''

McGregor grimly nodded his head at the marshal. ''All right, but you mark my word, Joe, that's the end of it. The last couple of times you got us to help you, we ended up—''

''That's all there will be to it,'' Fogarty hastily said, and arose to get the coffee. With his back to the older men as he filled three tin cups, he also said, "You were going out to the cemetery anyway, weren't you?"

The other two agreed that they were, declined the coffee, and walked out into a warming, sunbright morning. On their northward stroll Pepperdine's earlier wariness appeared to have vanished. "It's a pretty good plan, James. For a fact a stranger out there will stick up like a sore thumb, 'specially at the young feller's grave."

McGregor would not dispute this, but once his suspicions had been aroused, being dragged behind wild horses would not have made him relinquish them. "Just think back," he mumbled. "Fogarty's got us shot at, horse-kicked, half starved, worked over, and every time we swear never again. Why did you agree with him, Hugh?"

"Because, you old haggis eater, all we got to do is sort of move around and look out for a stranger, tell Joe, and go back to town. Now how can that get us used up?"

They halted in front of the saddle maker's store. McGregor's gun shop was diagonally across Main Street, one door north of the saloon. McGregor watched three rather threadbare rangemen walk their horses down Main Street from up north as he said, "Do you know what time the buryin' is to take place?"

"Two o'clock."

McGregor nodded curtly. "Meet me over at my shop when you're ready. Hugh, it's a damned mile walk to the graveyard."

Pepperdine wasn't worried. "There'll be wagons and buggies. We can get a ride." He watched McGregor cross the dusty roadway and disappear inside his store, then turned to pick up where he'd left off to go down to the cafe a couple of hours earlier. He'd worked late last night, and if necessary he'd do it again tonight to complete the *la jinetta* bronc saddle he'd been making; not for anyone in particular, but to put in the window.

The last seven saddles—and one set of handsome black

California light harness—that he'd made for display had sold out of the roadway window within a couple of weeks, which was better than sitting around twiddling his thumbs waiting for a rangeman or a rancher to order a custom-made rig. Rangemen would have come in often, but they rarely had the kind of cash that was required for a new rig. Ranchers might own ten thousand acres, run two thousand mammy cows, live in a two-story house, and have silver slathered over their bits and spurs, but they'd ride the same old rig until it fell apart. Then they'd use wire to keep it together before they'd appear on the range riding a new rig.

Hugh was bending over his big worktable, positioning tin patterns on both sides of the spine of the tanned hide, when weasely little Silas Browning, who owned the stage company and the mail franchise in the Sheridan country, walked in. Making that little sniffing sound which annoyed the hell out of a lot of people around town, Silas stopped at the counter to squint as Pepperdine painstakingly outlined the skirt patterns with a pencil. Silas said, "I got a story to tell you you won't believe. Last night someone put a dyin' man in Henry's shed across the alley and—"

"Yeah, I know," Pepperdine said without looking up from his work. "Is he still alive?"

Silas raised his oversize hat, vigorously scratched, lowered the hat and said, "No. He was dead when Miz Pohl looked in on him about breakfast time. And how did you know? I only just heard myself."

Pepperdine finished tracing, straightened up to examine what he'd accomplished, then faced the small, wiry old man under the huge hat. "If you'd get down to the cafe at a decent time for breakfast instead of lyin' in bed until after sunrise, you'd hear things. . . . Who told you?"

"Reg Lee. He was complaining over breakfast about having to wash his black team and get 'em dry before time to hitch up the hearse. He didn't say who the young feller was. Do you know? Was he from town or maybe on the range somewhere?"

"Nobody knows," stated Pepperdine, who had few pleasures in his life, but one was to tease the stage-company owner. Hugh approached the counter, leaned down like a conspirator and lowered his voice almost to a whisper. "But there's a sort of secret goin' around that he was one of the James boys."

Silas Browning reared back, indignant and sniffing. "Where'd you hear such a damned lie? There was only Jesse and his brother. Jess got himself killed, and Frank James went to prison, got out, and went out to California to go into the hotel business."

Hugh leaned lower and squinted. "Silas, there was another brother. Most folks never heard of him. His name was Moses, Moe James. He escaped after the Northfield raid and sort of disappeared."

Silas stood at the counter for a moment looking incredulous, then red as a beet. "Hugh, you're makin' this up. You're sayin' this to get folks all stirred up. There never was no Moe James and you know it!"

Silas swung around and marched out of the harness works looking incongruously diminutive under the huge hat he was rarely without.

Hugh was so tickled, he rummaged beneath the counter for his bottle of old popskull, tipped it, swallowed twice, rehid the bottle, and went back to work.

CHAPTER THREE

Springing the Trap

Marshal Fogarty stopped by Henry Pohl's place on his way to the hotel. Eleanor met him at the door, looking solemn. "He died sometime in the night," she told the lawman. "When I went to peek at him about dawn, he was dead. Did you want to see Henry?"

"No. Just wondered about the lad is all."

"He had the carpenter in this morning and saw Reg Lee at the livery barn."

Joe nodded. "Gravediggers?"

"Yes. Henry took care of that too before he had to go to a ranch six miles southwest of town to look in on a baby and a new mother."

Fogarty continued on his way northward, past the abstract office, the harness works, and was out front of the corral-yard gates with only a short way to go when Hank Dennis, who owned the big general store, hailed him from across Main Street. The marshal walked over looking solemn as an owl. Where they met in front of the log gates, Hank said, "I just heard from Rusty at the saloon about the young stranger who's going to be planted this afternoon alongside old Caulfield Randolph."

Joe nodded, waiting for the rest of it. Hank was a nosy individual. Not as bad as his wife, but still nosy.

"He was put on Henry's embalming table in the night, Joe?"

"Yes."

"No identification on him?"

"That's right. Henry, I got to clean up, get ready for the burials."

"Yeah, me too. Shot in the back, was he?"

"Yes. Blood poisoning set in and he died in the night," the marshal said, nodded, and resumed his walk in the direction of the hotel. The building was more nearly a big old roominghouse, but the sign said HOTEL and the waspish proprietor liked calling his establishment a hotel and did not like having it called a roominghouse.

Fogarty got trapped in the dingy hallway in front of his room and again had to answer questions about the dead rangeman, or whatever he'd been. But this time the inquisitor had already made up his mind about the dead youth. "Outlaws, sure as hell," he told Joe at the doorway. "That's how they do. Bring someone in who got shot, leave 'em in the night and skedaddle."

Joe reached for the doorknob. "Maybe," he said, opened the door and closed it.

The proprietor went in the direction of his windowless kitchen, wagging his head and muttering. He'd been a widower thirteen years and had been a suspicious, brusque individual at least three times that long.

Fogarty had one window in his room. It faced southward. He had a fairly good view of Sheridan from the north end to the shacks below Reg Lee's livery barn and corrals at the south end of town. There appeared to be less activity today than there normally was, probably because folks were closing shops and preparing for old Caulfield Randolph's funeral. Sheridan had no resident minister, but twenty miles south at Bordenton there was a Baptist parish. The preacher from down there usually officiated at burials in Sheridan, and in a case like this, Hank Dennis usually paid him the five-dollar fee. Hank too was a Baptist. Hank hadn't mentioned sending for the preacher, but Fogarty was confident he had. Hank was, above all else, a believer in order and custom, and as probably the most well-off merchant in town, he could afford the five dollars.

By the time Joe had cleaned up out back at the wash house and was dressing for the funeral, the sun was slightly off center. Now the sidewalks were empty and most of the stores, including Rusty Morton's saloon, had been padlocked. The procession out to the graveyard would begin shortly. The signal for this exodus would be Reg Lee in his black stove-pipe hat and black coat—which he'd been unable to button for five years—sitting in front of his elegant black hearse with the side windows, tooling his pair of black horses at a slow walk the full length of Main Street before turning eastward and bumping over open country to the cemetery.

Fogarty brushed his hat, rubbed his boots, put on his white shirt, his black Prince Albert coat that was only a little darker than his britches, looped his gunbelt, buckled it, and tucked a fresh plug of molasses cured into a pocket.

As he was leaving, the roominghouse proprietor came out of the rearward gloom. He too was dressed for a funeral, but hadn't bothered to shave nor comb his hair. When Fogarty looked around, the older man said, "Well, we wasn't real close, but we played toothpick poker a few times."

Fogarty held the door for the older man to step forth into afternoon sunlight, pause to squint and make another comment. "The town's quiet, Marshal. Look yonder, there's Pepperdine and McGregor ridin' on the tailgate of Hank Dennis's wagon. . . . First time I've seen them two lookin' respectable."

Joe watched the wagon pass, met the gaze of the gunsmith and harness maker, and left his companion to cross the road toward the saloon. The spindle doors were chained and locked and Rusty Morton was pocketing the key as he turned, nodded to Fogarty and said, "You look like you're runnin' for office."

Fogarty, like everyone else in town, always admired Rusty's brocaded vests. The saloonman owned about eight of them, every one different, each one more resplendent than the others. Fogarty nodded. "If I ever get married, I'd take it kindly if you'd wear the vest with the purple roses and the fat cherubs on it."

They turned northward, walked together until the plank-walk ended, then joined the straggling long line of people walking among the ruts of the hearse. It was a hot afternoon, the grass was tall, the ground dry and dusty. There wasn't a cloud in the sky, and Rusty had to lift his hat twice to mop sweat off a pallid forehead. Halfway to the slight mound that bristled with stone and wooden grave markers, he said, "Did Reg have one coffin atop the other one?"

Fogarty had reached the roadway after the hearse had passed. "I don't know."

"He said it'd cost the town council less if he didn't have to make two trips. I heard that young feller didn't even have a gun or a saddle or a horse that could be sold to cover the expense."

Joe was watching the hearse swing broadside below two squared, deep graves. As the liveryman set his binders and climbed down to open the back, Joe said, "Folks liked old Caulfield. That's quite a crowd."

He did not hear the saloonman's answer. He was searching among the faces for a stranger and was sure there would be more than one. Attendance at a burial ensured that mourners or even strangers were welcome to the big supper the town ladies would lay out on trestle tables in the firehouse after no one was left up yonder but the men who'd spend eternity there.

It was hot on the little knoll. By the time Joe and Rusty arrived, some of the men who had made the trip in rigs could be seen standing on the far side of their buggies, facing away from where the boxes were being positioned at graveside.

Fogarty nodded, paused to say a few words here and there until he got over to where the gunsmith and harness maker were standing. Pepperdine said, "Everyone's here. I had no idea so many folks knew Caulfield."

His shorter, grizzled friend sniffed. "You got to more'n just know a man to walk this far, Hugh. You got to have liked him. Caulfield was a friendly person. I don't think he had an enemy in the world."

The minister appeared among the dark suits, took a position at the east or upper end of the graves, and stood with the Book clutched to his chest as he solemnly gazed out over the crowd. Silence gradually settled as bonneted women nudged their men and hats were pulled off. The minister offered a preliminary prayer, blessing everyone in sight, commending them for their presence, and paused a long time before beginning his reading.

His sermon was in the singular, but everyone understood it to include the nameless youth in the box at his feet. Where he had difficulty was in his eulogy. But he was capable. After speaking of old Caulfield's virtues, he nodded at the second coffin and did the only thing he could do—he prayed for the soul of the unknown, offered his personal opinion that the youth had been brought low by a murderer in the flower of his life and should rest at peace knowing the Good Lord would exact full payment because "vengeance is mine saith the Lord and I will repay."

Fogarty had picked out the unknown faces. Of about eight, he selected three who could have been companions of the dead youth. They were rangemen and, although their hats had been brushed, their clothing was stained, worn, and not very different from the clothes the dead youth had been buried in.

But there were other rangemen in the crowd. Most of them Joe had seen around town since early spring, when they'd been hired on at the cow outfits.

While everyone else solemnly watched the coffins being lowered by ropes, Joe Fogarty watched the people. He had just about made his solitary selection—a lean, tousle-headed young rangeman who held his hat in both hands, watching the second coffin being lowered—when McGregor spoke softly from behind him.

"There's a kid over there I've never seen before, with a bitter look on his face."

"Which one?"

"See that tall one holdin' his hat low in both hands? Look to his left past Eleanor and Hank Dennis's wife—that young one with the old ivory-handled Colt. See him?"

Joe nodded without speaking for a moment. "He's some-one's chore boy, James. He's too young."

McGregor snorted softly. "That gun's no child's toy, Joe. I could sort of ask around. See if anyone knows who he is."

Fogarty and the young boy were separated by about three hundred feet, and people were beginning to move now as the preacher drew his sermon to a close. The boy stood like a pillar with people passing around him. McGregor walked away in search of Hugh Pepperdine, and Fogarty swung his attention back to where the tall youth had been. The range-man was no longer there.

For a moment Fogarty forgot the youngster and searched the crowd for the other one. Reg turned his hearse and led the exodus back toward town exactly as he had an hour ear-lier. Buggies and wagons began moving. Mourners on foot cut off Fogarty's view until he passed in the opposite direc-tion, stepping out to one side of the people heading back toward town. Then he saw the tall youth standing beside the youngster, both regarding the second grave.

Fogarty increased his stride, but before he reached the pair, the two youths had separated. The tall one was drifting with the crowd in the direction of town, the youngster with the old ivory-handled Colt was only now beginning to turn away from the grave to join the last stragglers down off the knoll.

Pepperdine and McGregor saw Joe aiming for the young-ster and also veered in his direction. The boy didn't notice the two old men until they succeeded in blocking his pro-gress, cutting him off from the last stragglers.

The youngster stopped, expecting them to walk past, raised a grimy cuff to his face, and when the two older men did not walk past but stopped within fifteen feet of him, the boy's arm came down. His eyes widened, and from behind he heard someone say, "Just stand still, son, and nothing'll happen."

The youngster didn't stand still. He whirled on Joe Fogarty with his right hand moving. McGregor caught him from behind, pinning both arms. When the lad fought and tried to kick, McGregor lifted him off the ground as Hugh put out a hand, yanked away the hawleg revolver, and made a little clucking sound as he positioned himself so that his back cut off the view of anyone on the slope who might look back. "Settle down," he told the youngster, and looked at Marshal Fogarty. "No more'n thirteen or fourteen."

Fogarty spoke to the struggling boy. "I just want to know who you are, son. That's all."

McGregor loosened his bear hug, put the youngster down and waited for another outburst, but none came.

Fogarty tried again. "What's your name?"

The youngster was red-faced. He had slaty eyes that glittered as he snarled his answer. "My name's Billy Smith an' you ain't goin' to believe it an' I don't give a gawddamn whether you do or not!"

All three men regarded the youngster, with McGregor showing the most disapproval. "You're goin' to get your mouth washed out with soap," he growled, and that brought another outburst.

"Gimme back my gun an' I'll show you!"

Fogarty turned to watch the distant people on their straggling course. One person down there was standing slightly apart, looking back up the slope. The middling heat haze and the distance was too great for a positive identification, but Joe thought it was the tall one who'd held his hat in both hands.

He turned back to the youngster. "Billy, you got a partner?

There's a feller down the hill a ways watching up in this direction.''

The youngster swung his head, looked hard, then faced Marshal Fogarty as he said, ''Ain't no one I ever seen before. Gimme back my gun.''

Fogarty took the old gun, examined it, shucked out the loads and dropped it back into the youngster's holster as he said, ''Billy, we're going to walk back to town. You in the middle. Just walk, you understand?''

McGregor released his grip but stood poised to lunge. The youngster looked around at the gunsmith. ''You liked to cracked my ribs, you old—''

The thick, callused hand moved with the speed of a striking snake. Billy's old hat flew and he staggered. He reached for the old gun, gripped it with white knuckles, but did not draw it. McGregor's hand had stung his face but hadn't done anything more; the youngster glared as Pepperdine spoke quietly to him.

''Take your hand off the gun, Billy. . . . Now then, you better learn that when folks say something, they mean it. *Take it away from the gun!*''

The youngster's blue gaze fastened on Hugh with an icy glaze. ''Three to one,'' he snarled. ''All of you biggern'n me. If there was slugs in my gun, I'd teach you how kids is equal to old bastards no matter how big they are.''

Pepperdine looked to Marshal Fogarty and made a little helpless gesture. The marshal spoke quietly. ''I told you, boy, we're going to walk back to town without any trouble. You see those folks down there? You wouldn't want me to have to bend you over my knee and warp your backsides with them looking on, would you? That's what's going to happen if you even look like you're going to run . . . Billy?''

The youth's lips curled, his eyes flashed. Pepperdine got a fistful of dirty old shirt, lifted the youngster a foot off the ground, and smiled fiercely. ''Listen to me, you pint-sized ringtailed roarer. You're going with us one way or another, so why not just do it peaceable, then we won't tan your butt an' you won't get hurt.'' He put the youngster down. ''Just back to town. Hell, boy, that's where you were goin' anyway, isn't it?''

Billy pulled down a big, ragged breath, let it out, shot a furtive look down the hill to where the tall one was standing. The boy looked at Joe and spoke in a voice that sounded genuinely tired. ''All right. An' after we get down there, what?''

Fogarty shrugged heavy shoulders. ''First off, maybe we'd ought to eat, then we could talk.''

''I didn't do anything.''

''I believe you. Just slack off and give us a chance, Billy.''

McGregor turned, saw the tall youth still standing down yonder, and said, ''Your friend's worrying, Billy. Maybe we should talk to him too.''

The youngster picked up his hat and frantically wig-wagged with it. Down the distant slope the tall one lingered a moment longer then turned and went hiking in the wake of the stragglers heading for the firehouse and the laden trestle tables.

The youngster walked with the men. Nothing was said until they were well away from the cemetery, then Hugh smiled as he asked the youngster how old he was. The answer was fiercely defiant. ''Old enough, an' it's none of your damned business. How old are you?''

''Seventy-one.''

The boy's eyes widened. ''You're pretty strong for someone that old.''

Hugh continued to smile. ''You'll be even stronger when you get to that age, boy, but you got a long way to go from thirteen to—''

''Fourteen, damn it!''

Hugh's smile lingered. ''You got some growin' to do.''

The youngster's reply was short. ''I never got to grow another inch. That's a seven-inch barrel on my gun. A man don't have to be no more'n seven inches tall, does he?''

The men exchanged looks and said no more until they

were on the outskirts of town. Fogarty looked for the other one, the tall one, but did not see him. He did not believe that the youth would abandon Billy, but as they turned south on Main Street in the direction of the jailhouse, search as he might, Joe saw no sign of the tall one.

As they entered the jailhouse Billy snarled at Fogarty. "Yeah. You're a damned liar too. You said we was going to eat."

Joe looked at Hugh and James McGregor. "You could set here with him until I get back from the cafe."

McGregor looked up. "Is it open?"

Joe nodded. "It's open. I saw Horace stumping around in there."

McGregor pointed to a bench, told the youngster to sit down, and faced the marshal. "Yeah, it'd be open wouldn't it? Everyone was up yonder but that damned cafeman. Joe, he wouldn't even go to his own funeral."

Pepperdine thought he would. "That's one he can't avoid goin' to. Go on, Joe. I got work to do."

After the marshal had departed, the older men leaned on the wall gazing owlishly at what they thought had to be the youngest prisoner ever to be locked up in the Sheridan Township *calabozo*, and the child looked just as steadily back at them. Pepperdine said, "That big gun on that little kid puts me in mind of that old hat Silas wears. Too damned big for the size of him."

This time the youngster simply turned his head so he would not have to look at them, but there was no defiant outburst.

CHAPTER FOUR

A Lawman's Best Laid Plans . . .

Marshal Fogarty'd guessed about right. When he handed the youngster two pails—one of stew, the other one of coffee—his prisoner did not ask about eating utensils, he tipped the stew pail and made noises like a pig caught under a gate.

Hugh and James watched, shook their heads, and departed. Joe sat at his table examining the youngster's old firearm. It fired six rounds, but to reload it required at least fifteen minutes. When that kind of a gun had been the best available, every town—no matter how small—had at least one gun shop where a man could leave his pistol to be recharged.

Joe put the gun on his table, shed his hat, watched his prisoner use a shirttail to wipe his face, and wanted to smile. He'd had his share of prisoners, but not very many as prickly or as young as this one.

Billy was sipping coffee as Joe said, "Feel a little better?" When he was ignored, Fogarty added, "That tall feller who was with me? He said this morning he thought that was dog stew."

The reaction was instantaneous. The youngster held the coffee pail away from his face and looked steadily at the town marshal. "What kind of gawddamn town you got? I'd throw up if I could."

Fogarty continued to eye the youngster whose outburst had provided him with the answer to a question that, if he'd asked it point-blank, would have got back one of the lad's defiant retorts. "What kind of town you got" meant Billy Smith had never been in Sheridan before.

Joe set another trap. "Nice town, with the same kind of folks you'd find in any other town, and we got a doctor folks come to from a hundred miles around. Given half a chance, he can save lives other doctors lose, but not if someone's let go until they're full of poison."

Billy's gaze went to his scuffed old boots. He said nothing. There was a spasmodic twitch of his jaw muscles.

"You got enough to eat? I can get more stew."

"Plenty," the prisoner replied without looking up.

"Billy . . . ?"

"What? Marshal, I ain't goin' to tell you anything. You can whup me an' I still won't."

Joe nodded about that. "All right. You don't have to tell me anyway." Joe watched the youngster's face. "I just wondered if you knew the name of the feller we buried out yonder this morning. It don't matter a lot. We got other unknowns out there, but it sort of bothers me that a feller goes into the ground without so much as his name on the headboard. Anyone deserves better'n that, wouldn't you say?"

Billy was struggling again, his jaw locked hard, his hands interlaced in his lap. When he refused to look up from his boot toes again, Fogarty could see his jaw muscles ripple.

The marshal stood up, took down his ring of keys, opened the cell-room door and said, "Come on. You got it all to yourself."

Billy looked up while dragging a filthy cuff across his face. "You can't lock me up. I ain't done nothing. You got to have a charge."

Joe nodded. "I got a charge, Billy. Resisting a peace officer. Get up."

Sheridan's jailhouse had one large strap-steel cage and three smaller individual cells. Fogarty put his prisoner in one of the small cells, locked the door, and leaned on it as he said, "You're likely to be here awhile."

He got a snarl from the caged youngster. "Lawman! Gawddamned badge-wearin' murderer!"

Joe returned to the office, locked the cell-room door, and draped the keys from their wall peg. Then he put the old gun in a box behind his table, picked up his hat, and left the jailhouse. He normally locked the roadway door when he had a prisoner. This time he didn't.

He walked northward as far as the corral yard, cut directly across the road, and entered Morton's saloon. He nodded to Rusty as he walked on through, past the storeroom to the alley doorway, then let himself out and turned southward. Morton followed Joe to the doorway, looking completely baffled. Someone banging the bartop for a refill turned him back.

Fogarty went down the alley to a dogtrot between Horace Dagget's cafe and Dennis's store. He walked through the narrow, gloomy, and strong-smelling little area, halted back a couple of feet in semidarkness and leaned so he could see the front of his jailhouse.

For midweek, Sheridan had considerable roadway traffic. None of it bothered Fogarty until a huge freight rig with a six-mule hitch came ponderously up through town from the south. By the time it had passed and he could again see the front of the jailhouse, several minutes had passed.

It was late afternoon. Customers of the cafe came and went, mostly preoccupied with their private thoughts, but one man who passed the dogtrot turned, blinked, and would have halted if Joe hadn't snarled at him. "Keep walking, James."

The gunsmith obeyed, but by the time he was abreast of the saloon, he veered across Main Street to the harness shop and told Hugh Pepperdine what he'd seen. He also said, "He was watchin' the jailhouse. You want to know what I think? He figures that tall lad'll be watchin' for Joe to leave so's he can sneak in there and get the little kid out."

Hugh turned that over in his mind for a moment before speaking. "Assumin' you're right, which will be a damned miracle, he won't just plain ride right up in front with a led horse for the little kid. He'll sneak down the back alley an' leave the horses tied while he breaks Billy out. You got a gun, James?"

"Not on me, but I can get one real quick."

Pepperdine scowled as he turned toward the back of the shop and the lean-to shed that was his residence. Back there he handed McGregor a battered old six-gun and shoved another one in the front of his britches, then opened the alley door and jerked his head.

They stood a moment, making sure no one was out there, closed the door and started southward. Midway, James pointed. "Movement in the woodshed across from the livery barn."

Hugh had seen nothing, but he began moving to the west side of the alley toward a dilapidated little cow barn. They stood in there watching the woodshed until a horse lustily blew its nose and Hugh spoke triumphantly. "Hid the horses in the woodshed."

McGregor's retort was sharp. "That means he's down there, or maybe already over at the jailhouse. Fogarty keeps the alley door barred from the inside."

They continued southward, wary and mostly silent until they were near enough to the woodshed to hear horses, then McGregor brushed the harness maker's arm. "Sure as hell Joe set some kind of trap. Like leavin' the front door unlocked. We better stay out here an' not get between Joe and the front of the jailhouse."

Hugh was less interested in speculation than he was in entering the woodshed, where someone might be hiding. He made a gesture. "Stay here. I'm goin' to saunter on past like someone who's usin' the alley as a shortcut. I'll get set on the south side of the door, you get set on the north side, and James, one time you damned near shot me in a mess like this, so you—"

McGregor hissed. "Get on with it, an' I didn't even have my gun cocked that time. Now, get along."

Pepperdine sauntered, his lanky frame moving with careless ease. He did not turn his head until he was out of sight of anyone inside the shed. Where he moved swiftly toward the south side of the woodshed, there was a huge manure pile from the livery barn with enough blue-tailed flies to make life miserable for anyone within their flight pattern. Hugh used his hat to keep them away, made a gesture with his drawn weapon for McGregor to get closer to the doorless, wide opening. When McGregor was poised and ready, gun up and steady, Hugh stepped around the wooden wall. He got inside the shed, where flies would not go because it was dark, and crouched with his weapon moving.

McGregor came in from the north side with a gun cocked and ready. Two startled horses, fully rigged and tethered, stopped switching their tails and rolled their eyes from one intruder to the other one.

Pepperdine saw nothing but horses. He began moving carefully until he was well inside. McGregor hissed at him from the far side of the animals. "No one here, Hugh."

Pepperdine straightened up, let the cocked revolver hang at his side and studied the saddled animals until McGregor reached him. Then he said, "If he's not here, that means he's around front somewhere, because he sure as hell wasn't in the alley."

McGregor pushed his weapon into his waistband. "Joe'll get him out in front." He looked around. The shed was almost empty, but six or eight rounds of dry red fir indicated that at one time, probably last autumn, the shed had been full. He said, "Plenty of hiding space, Hugh."

Pepperdine ignored McGregor, approached the nearest horse, branded H.E. on the left shoulder, and with McGregor watching, used his clasp knife to sever all but one strand of the cinch.

McGregor approached the second animal, also docile, and did the same, but because McGregor wanted positive results, he cut halfway through the remaining strand. As he moved back toward his friend he said, "We probably ruined two good cinches, because Joe'll nail him around front."

Someone was hurrying southward out in the alley, making no attempt to be quiet about it. McGregor would have moved closer to the opening if Hugh hadn't grabbed his arm and hissed. "He got inside from out front. Don't ask me how, with Joe watching, but sure as hell, there's two of 'em coming, an' they're close to running."

McGregor led off among the unsplit rounds of red fir, hoisted one atop the other and ducked down behind them. Hugh tried to lift a thick round, couldn't budge it, and with those hastening footfalls drawing closer, dropped flat on his stomach behind just one big round of fir firewood. He pushed his six-gun out and could hear his heart pounding. He did not look over at McGregor. He had no time.

The smaller, younger boy ran in first. Behind him the tall youth appeared with a six-gun in his hand. He holstered it as the youngster yanked loose the tied reins. Both of them moved with frantic haste. They both swung the animals, toed in, reached for the saddlehorns and yanked to get the lift they needed to get astride. The tall youth's half-severed cinch broke as his left foot was in the stirrup, his right one coming up off the ground.

His startled horse shied and snorted as the youth and saddle struck the ground. The younger boy made it into the saddle and might have made it out into the alley but his horse, frightened by the shying of the other animal, swung abruptly to see what was happening, and the second cinch tore loose. But this time the rider felt the saddle going and yanked hard on the opposite stirrup, which straightened the saddle on the animal's back. But when he aimed for the opening and dug in his heels, the horse gave a bound toward the alleyway, and the rider, still with the saddle between his legs, went backward over the horse's rump and fell, hard.

Both horses fled up the alley with reins flying.

The gunsmith stood up from behind his fir wood and aimed

a cocked handgun at the two figures thrashing in the dust, trying to get free of their saddles.

"Hold it! Stop squirming! Keep your damned hands out in plain sight!"

The tall youth was free of his saddle but was using both hands against the ground to push upright when the gunsmith spoke. He hung there like a gut-shot bear, looking up where another man with a cocked weapon came up out of the gloom. For five seconds he did not move, then he audibly groaned and let his head hang.

Billy Smith extricated himself, looked at the armed men, and sat up. His unloaded old six-shooter was in its hip holster.

Hugh walked over, leaned to pluck away both handguns, then stepped back as he said, "Stand up! Now keep facin' me and walk backward until I can see you better . . . Billy! You run an' I'll make a hole in you a pair of oxen could walk through."

Both boys shuffled backward until daylight from the alley made them clearly visible. McGregor said, "Stop. That's fine. Now both of you set down. *Set!* That's better." McGregor risked a look at Pepperdine. "You watch 'em, I'll go find Joe."

When Hugh was alone with the captives, he moved to a red fir round, sat down with the cocked gun dangling between his knees, and stared without saying a word for a long time. When he was ready, he said, "What in hell's wrong with you? You act like bronco In'ians, skulkin' around tryin' folks' patience."

Neither of the lads made a sound. They sat looking stonily at the harness maker.

Hugh sighed and spoke to the tall youth. "If you do much of this kind of thing, boy, you'd better learn to do it right. Never—you hear me?—never in broad daylight. You two are goin' to get killed someday."

Billy's shock had passed. He glared at Hugh. "If you hadn't cut them cinches, we could have made a run for it."

Hugh almost answered that, but he didn't. He just sat there looking at Billy, and was still sitting like that when James returned with the marshal. McGregor said, "A freight wagon went by. Probably about the time Slim here snuck inside from out front."

Pepperdine gazed at Marshal Fogarty, whose angry gaze was fixed on the prisoners. Pepperdine said dryly, "Joe, next time get on a roof." Hugh stood up to ease off the dog of his six-gun and carelessly shove the weapon into his waistband.

Fogarty growled at the lads to get to their feet and herded them up the alley toward the wide-open rear door of his jailhouse. The door-bar had been pitched aside by the tall youth so he and his companion could escape by way of the alley.

Pepperdine and McGregor brought up the rear, silent and grim all the way. McGregor would have departed while Fogarty was locking his prisoners into cells, but Hugh shook his head and patiently waited until Joe returned. The marshal was hesitant to look at either of the old men as he tossed his key ring aside and shoved back his hat.

Pepperdine spoke quietly. "Care to hear what I think, Joe?"

Fogarty's sulfurous gaze raised to the tall, older man's face. "Yeah, I know. But it would have worked if the damned wagon hadn't gone by like it did, slow and heavy."

Hugh shrugged. "That's not what I meant." The other two men regarded Hugh from expressionless faces. Pepperdine said, "When I was watchin' them in the shed, Billy said they could have made a run for it."

"What of it?" Fogarty growled.

"Well, the one we buried today had been shot in the back. That's what of it. Maybe it wasn't murder. You understand what I'm saying?"

Fogarty moved slowly to his table, sat down and dumped his hat. McGregor moved to a wall bench and also sat down. Hugh remained on his feet as he added a little more to what he'd said.

"That's a guess. But Billy would have tried it. Even with

us behind him with guns in our hands, if the horse hadn't jumped out from under him an' his saddle, he'd have tried to run for it. He could've got shot in the back doin' that.''

McGregor slapped his legs and stood up. "I got work to do . . . Joe?"

"Sure. I'm beholden to both of you." Fogarty raised up a little. "I thought you said you wouldn't get pulled into something like this."

McGregor nodded. "We did. What was we supposed to do when I saw you hidin' in that dogtrot? It was plain as the nose on your face what you was doing. An' remember, we helped bring that little whelp down here from the graveyard. We had an interest in him."

Fogarty sighed, leaned back off the desk, and ruefully smiled. "Like I said, I'm beholden."

As McGregor passed out into late-day sunshine, Pepperdine turned to close the office door behind himself and said to Fogarty, "Next time get on a damned roof where no wagon'll cut off your view."

He closed the door, turned to catch up with the gunsmith, and McGregor was standing in the middle of the plankwalk, glaring. As they started northward the gunsmith said, "Now, why in hell did you have to say somethin' like that for? He got humiliated enough without you rubbin' salt in it."

"Because it's the danged truth, James."

"Is it? You ever been atop a roof in a fix like that?"

"Yas, you old screwt, more'n once. Joe's a good lawman. He figures things in his head real good. Like expectin' someone to show up when they buried that lad shot in the back. But James, you'n me bein' about the same age, we know something fellers Joe's age haven't learned."

"What do we know?" challenged the gunsmith.

"That sly, experienced old gaffers'll beat out fellers who do it all in their heads every blessed time."

McGregor, unable to refute this, said, "The same age. Hugh, you're at least five years older'n I am."

They were in front of the harness shop when Pepperdine

stopped in his tracks, looking at the shorter man. They'd been through this before, and while Hugh didn't give a damn who was the eldest, he could not allow this opportunity to pass with his old friend any more than he could have kept from roiling the surly cafeman. He said, "If anyone's older, it's you, James," and proceeded to bolster this with a bald lie and a straight face. "I met a freight swamper last winter who knew you back east. He said someone you was related to told him for a fact you was seventy-two."

McGregor reddened but held his temper until he was in the middle of the road on the way to his shop, then he turned. "You didn't meet any swamper who told you any such a thing, because I never had any relatives back east or any-where else. And you know what I think? I think the reason you was on those roofs was because the law was probably lookin' high and low for you."

Hugh waited until his friend had gone into the shop and slammed the door before entering his own place of business. As he shed the six-gun and picked up his stained apron, he had a sudden thought and stood a long time considering it before walking around behind the counter to resume his work on the bronc saddle.

Outside, Sheridan was slackening off. Evening was close, with suppertime to follow, and another day would end shortly. Down at the jailhouse Marshall Fogarty got pails from the cafeman, gave them to his prisoners, did not say a word to them, and returned to the office.

If it hadn't been for McGregor seeing him in the dogtrot, his humiliation would certainly have been a lot harder to bear than it was. Because if that hadn't happened, he'd have lost his prisoner sure as hell.

CHAPTER FIVE

Two Old Men and a Candle

After supper Hugh went over to Rusty's saloon, saw James nursing a whiskey at a distant table and took another jolt glass and a bottle over there with him. He sat down uninvited, and McGregor spoke as though they hadn't insulted each other this afternoon. He said, "There's the one that got buried, and the youngster, an' the tall one—could there be more of 'em?"

Hugh poured a drink, refilled the gunsmith's glass, and then raised his own, thoughtfully considering his friend. "Maybe. Joe can thrash it out of 'em. We did our part and a little more."

They downed their jolts and relaxed. The saloon was moderately full. More men would arrive, mostly local drinkers, but perhaps with a few truant range riders sprinkled around. Hank Dennis arrived for his one drink before going home to supper. He was wearing a dark coat, a vest with a gold chain across it, and an expensive-looking black derby hat. In that getup he looked more like a politician than a storekeeper.

Without looking away from the storekeeper, James said, "You know who he sets me in mind of?"

"Nope. Who?"

McGregor's craggy features came around completely bare of humor as he said, "Moe James, the one that got away.

You ought to be ashamed of yourself tellin' Silas a story like that.''

Hugh made a little lopsided self-conscious grin, then got the conversation onto the idea that had occurred to him shortly after he'd returned from the jailhouse.

"You reckon Joe's got the boys to talking yet?"

McGregor considered his whiskey glass as he replied. "Well, there's sure a foolproof way, y'know."

"How?"

"Remove their boots and socks and hold a candle to their feet."

Pepperdine leaned back and stared at the gunsmith. Before he could remonstrate, the gunsmith looked across at him and smiled. "Just hold it, not burn 'em."

The harness maker was not appeased. "You cold-blooded old billy goat. There's a lot easier way'n that."

"Is there? If that tall one's as stubborn as the young one, Joe'll sweat blood an' they still won't tell him anything."

"Not him," exclaimed Pepperdine, leaning forward again, still scowling. "Eleanor."

McGregor considered the harness maker for a long moment, then sat straighter in his chair. "I wouldn't have her listen to the language those boys use."

"They wouldn't use it in front of a woman."

"Wouldn't they? I'd hate to bet my life on that."

"Joe'd knock their heads off," Pepperdine said, and sat poised to leave his chair. "The young one's barely more'n a child. He'll remember his maw, an' right now he's got a big knot in his belly. I'm goin' over there and see what Joe thinks about gettin' Henry's wife to talk to the youngest one."

"Wait," grumbled McGregor, downing a drink. He made some elaborate motions of taking out his long leather purse with the rawhide pucker string and trying to reach some coins at the bottom. Pepperdine watched, made a sour face, then dropped two bits on the table and turned to depart. To the best of his recollection, McGregor hadn't paid for more than maybe one or two drinks since Hugh had known him. Damned old haggis eater was tighter than the bark on a tree.

Marshal Fogarty had just returned from the cafe when Pepperdine and McGregor arrived. He nodded and disappeared down into the cell room to look in on his prisoners. When he returned, his visitors had helped themselves to coffee and were comfortably settled.

Pepperdine explained to Fogarty how it just might be possible to get his prisoners to talk. As he was enthusiastically explaining his idea, Joe Fogarty went to the stove and filled a cup from the pot. He took it to his table, sat down and smiled at the harness maker.

"It won't work," he said, raising his cup.

Pepperdine scowled. "How do you know until you try it? Hell, the youngest one's no more'n a button. He—"

"Because I tried it a couple hours ago. Even let her use the office while I went down to the cell to talk to the other one."

Both the older men looked blankly across the room. Marshal Fogarty put the cup down and gently wagged his head at them. "Not only wouldn't he so much as tell her his name—kept insisting his name is Billy Smith—but you know what the connivin' little devil did? He cried in her lap and moaned and groaned, and when I came back, she was madder'n a wet hen about me keeping a child in my filthy jailhouse. Filthy? I sluice it out with water every week whether I've had drunks in here or not, and sweep it out too. She stormed out of here, and when I turned away from the door, that measly little bastard was standing by the cell room door, grinnin' from ear to ear."

Hugh and James exchanged a glance before the gunsmith spoke. "Take off their damned boots and socks and hold a candle to 'em, Joe."

This time Pepperdine not only did not dissent, he nodded his head at the town marshal. But Fogarty's reaction was the same as Pepperdine's had originally been. He looked horrified. "You cruel old devil," he exclaimed. "You'd ought to be ashamed of yourself."

McGregor was unperturbed. "How are you going to get anything out of them, Joe? An' there's somethin' else to think about. Now we know there's three of 'em been partnering together. The dead one and them two in your cells . . . How many more you think there might be? For all we know, there's a band of renegades out yonder. A gang of young marauders."

Silence settled in the jailhouse. Fogarty drank his coffee, clasped big hands atop the table and studied his knuckles. McGregor and Pepperdine sat with legs thrust out, watching the marshal right up to the moment when Fogarty said, "The tall one won't talk at all. He wouldn't even say his name. Nothing. I got blue in the face, and he sat on his bunk lookin' at the wall. I might as well have been talkin' to a rock. But just in case, I'm going to ride out tomorrow. Cover the range and scout up the foothills. If there is a band of them, there'll be signs."

McGregor and Pepperdine agreed that might be a good idea, but neither of them volunteered to accompany the marshal. They got all the way up to the saddlery before McGregor halted, touched his old friend's chest with a thick finger and said, "He'll leave early. Before sunup."

Pepperdine nodded about that. To cover much territory on horseback Fogarty would indeed have to be well beyond town before sunrise.

"We'll meet at the cafe like we usually do. We'll have all day."

Hugh's brows knit. "For what?"

"To persuade them youngsters to talk. Good night."

Pepperdine stood watching his friend across Main Street. Somewhere up in the vicinity of the roominghouse, but on the far side of the road, a dog started raising hell and propping it up.

Hugh barred his front door and went through to his lean-to where he kicked off his boots then tossed his old hat aside.

He fumbled in a barrel for a bottle of Taos Lightning and sat on one of the two rickety chairs, sipping a nightcap by lamplight.

As sure as the Lord made little green apples, if he let McGregor talk him into what the old devil had in mind, and Joe Fogarty or anyone else found out what they'd done, they'd be lucky if all that happened was that they'd get ridden out of town on a splintery pole.

Hugh went to bed in a troubled but relaxed state, slept like the dead, and rolled out ahead of daylight to cross the alley to his outhouse. He returned to wash and shave, still thinking, with even more certainty, that even if they succeeded in McGregor's enterprise—if the youngest lad ever got turned loose—the boy would go bawling all over Sheridan about being tortured. After all, Billy had been sneaky enough to use Eleanor.

Pepperdine entered the cafe and went to sit down beside the gunsmith, who was already eating. For the first time within decent memory Hugh did not even look at the disagreeable cafeman.

McGregor paused between mouthfuls to glance around and slowly lower and raise an eyelid. Then he'd go back to spooning up his mush before tackling the breakfast steak and grease-fried spuds.

Hugh's breakfast arrived with a snarl from Horace Dagget, the cafeman, but Hugh did not even look up as he went to work on the meal. Other diners exchanged glances. One man, the town blacksmith, was dribbling small coins atop the counter beside his empty plate when he said, "Hugh, you feelin' all right?"

Others paused to glance at Pepperdine, awaiting his answer. No one was smiling, they were genuinely concerned.

Hugh looked around and nodded. "Feel fine."

"You're awful quiet this morning," the blacksmith said, moving away from the counter on his way toward the door.

Hugh lied. "Didn't sleep real good last night, is all."

When the cafe got noisy again he leaned toward the gunsmith and hissed at him. "You're crazy."

McGregor looked up. "Why?"

"Because it'll get all over town. Fogarty'll find out. James, we'll be lucky if we don't get lynched."

McGregor finished his meal, arose, put down some silver, and without a word walked out front to lean on a post, eyeing the jailhouse.

When the harness maker appeared, James said, "They already been fed. Horace took food over to them, and Joe left town an hour ago."

Hugh had a hopeful thought. "The door'll be locked."

James wagged his head without taking his eyes off the jailhouse. "No. It'll be open so's someone can take grub over there." He looked up and down the roadway. There was no horse traffic and only a few people were in sight, heading for their places of employment. James grunted and started across Main Street. Hugh ambled in his wake, head turning, eyes sweeping both sides of the road right up until James opened the jailhouse door.

Inside, the place smelled of coffee and the little iron stove was warm. McGregor got the key ring, stopped at the cell room door and pointed. "Fetch that candle," he said. "They got to believe it's going to happen."

Hugh brought the candle. As McGregor approached the cells jangling the keys, both prisoners arose from their bunks, looking hopeful. The light was not very good as James unlocked the doors. He growled for the tall youth to go into his friend's cell, then followed him inside. When Hugh closed the door, McGregor pointed to the boys as he said, "Take off your boots an' socks."

He got big-eyed looks from the youths. They stood like statues. McGregor, who was a burly, rugged individual, handed the key ring to Pepperdine, took two forward steps, and repeated himself. "Take off your boots an' socks. Set on the floor." When the boys continued to stare, McGregor grabbed a handful of shirting and flung the tall youth down, pointed a rigid finger and said, "Don't get up! Off with the boots!" He turned for the younger lad, but the boy was finally untracked. He dropped to the floor and began kicking out of his boots. Neither boy had socks.

Pepperdine lighted the candle, met the horrified stares of the prisoners and started toward them. McGregor walked up behind the youths. Finally the youngest lad found his voice. "What d'you think you're doing? Where's the marshal? Get away from me, you bastard!"

McGregor got a fistful of hair and held the lad still as Hugh sank to one knee with the lighted candle. When the youngster jerked his foot away, Hugh caught him by the ankle, wrenched the foot around and brought the candle closer. The youngster started to scream. McGregor jammed the boy's head forward and downward. The scream sounded like a choking sob.

The tall youth was white as a sheet as he watched the younger boy struggle as the candle moved to within inches of the sole of his foot. He suddenly said, "Leave him alone."

The old men acted as though the tall boy hadn't spoken. Hugh had to grapple with the cringing foot, but he was capable enough. When the heat touched the youngster's sole he tried to cry out again, and this time when McGregor pushed his head downward a little farther, the only noise was a wheezing gasp.

The tall boy lunged, and Hugh straightened his free arm, knocking the tall boy backward. As he rebounded, he yelled at Hugh. "Leave him be. He didn't do—"

Hugh raised a ferocious scowl. "I'll ask you just once. If you lie, you'll get it worse than he's going to. What was that boy's name we buried yesterday?"

"Paul Dagney," the tall youth blurted out.

Hugh continued to hold the writhing leg and the candle. "What's this lad's name?"

"Billy Smith. It really is."

"You got a name?"

"Matt Hampstead."

Hugh did not move the candle. The youngest boy had tears on both cheeks as he continued to struggle. McGregor spoke to the oldest boy. "Matt, you fellers have a camp somewhere?"

"Yes sir. Northeast in a forest of oaks near a creek."

"Who's out there?"

"Josh an' Sam'l."

"Who else?"

"That's all. There was just the five of us."

McGregor released his grip on Billy Smith's head and stepped back. "Get up an' set on the bunk." As the boys obeyed, James looked triumphantly at Hugh.

Hugh still held the candle, but he moved back where he could lean on the wall as he eyed the white-faced, badly shaken youngsters. James, still looking menacing, spoke to the tall youth.

"What happened to the lad we buried?"

When neither of the youths answered McGregor stepped in front of them, fists at his sides. Matt Hampstead, the taller boy, said, "He got shot in the back."

"Where?"

"Southwest of here a fair distance."

"How?" James growled, and this time when the boy hung fire, James leaned for a handful of cloth. Matt Hampstead rocked as far back as he could, which was not far enough, so he pushed his words out in a rush, making them run together. "Damned old man with a horse camp heard us tryin' to get fresh horses, come bustin' out of his camp . . . We was already ridin' away when he commenced firing. He hit Paul in the back."

McGregor stepped back. "Horse thieves," he growled at them, and for the first time the youngest boy spoke, spat his words at the older men as he wiped tears away with a dirty sleeve.

"We couldn't buy 'em. We had no money. Our horses was rode out. That old bastard didn't give us no chance to—"

"Damn horse thieves," James said again. "He should have hung you."

". . . To offer to work it out for him. He just bawled like a bay steer and commenced shooting," Billy Smith yelled at McGregor. "We ain't horse thieves!"

"You were ridin' stolen horses when you reached Sheridan, weren't you? If that don't make you horse thieves, I don't know what does."

Hugh cut in. "Where are you boys from?"

"Different places," Billy snapped.

"Where are your folks?"

"Ain't got any. My paw went off after my maw died. Matt's folks died of the cholera. Paul run off from a workhouse back east somewhere." Billy had to pause long enough to pull down a big breath before continuing. "We come together down in New Messico, a town called—some damned Mex name—made a camp, stole some chickens and whatnot, and decided we'd go north an' maybe get hired on as riders or chore boys or something."

Hugh nodded. "Stole horses in New Mexico and rode them down gettin' up here?"

"What was we supposed to do, mister, set down an' die? We couldn't get work in New Messico and didn't have no money until—"

"Shut up!" Matt snapped at the younger boy.

McGregor crossed to the door and leaned there, studying the boys, then jerked his head at Hugh, locked the cell from the outside and led the way up to the office, where he pitched the key ring atop Joe Fogarty's untidy table. "Blow out the candle," he said dully, and watched Pepperdine blow it out and put it back on the shelf where he'd found it.

When Hugh turned, James was staring at the wall. Hugh said, "There's two more."

James nodded without speaking, until he was over by the roadside door. With a grip on the door handle, he said, "Any of that familiar to you?"

Hugh nodded.

"Let's go up to the saloon," McGregor mumbled, and led the way.

Daylight made the world beyond the dingy jailhouse seem brighter than usual. Up at Rusty Morton's place there were no horses at the rack out front, and in fact Rusty had just returned from the cafe when the harness maker and gunsmith walked in. He stared at them. "What you two been up to? You look like you seen a ghost."

McGregor leaned on the bar. "Bottle an' two glasses, an' don't be askin' questions."

Morton, whose brocaded vest for the day had brilliant yellow California poppies against a flourishing background of green shrubbery, set up the bottle and glasses, then hovered.

Both the older men had one jolt, settled down at the bar and looked stonily at the backbar shelves. Morton refilled the little glasses, but neither of his customers touched them, not even after Rusty said, "On the house. What's eatin' you?"

McGregor's pale eyes went to Morton's face. "I said don't ask questions."

The scanty-haired, moon-faced saloonman was undaunted. "I heard you. How long we been friends, James?"

McGregor eyed the refilled glass and shifted position against the bar. He ignored the question when he finally spoke. "You ever hear of a fourteen-year-old horse thief, Rusty?"

Morton waffled. "Well, I suppose age wouldn't have a hell of a lot to do with it if someone was afoot, would it?"

"That lad we buried beside old Caulfield yesterday . . ."

Morton's smooth forehead puckered. "What about him?"

"He got shot in the back ridin' away after stealin' a horse."

Morton's brows shot up. "Who told you that?" When neither of his only patrons replied, he continued to stare at them. He finally said, "Joe got that out of them? I saw him ride out of town before daylight when I was out behind the saloon."

"Noooo," Hugh mumbled. "James an' I just come from talkin' to his prisoners. They told us."

Now the saloonman's expression slowly changed, until his face was smoothed out as he regarded the older men. When he finally spoke again, his voice was very soft. "That youngster was defiant as a boar bear yesterday. . . . You two went to the jailhouse after Joe left town?" Morton did not get an answer, and may not have expected one. He rolled his eyes, made a sweep of the bartop with a sour rag, and leaned looking at James and Hugh. "You whupped them into talking? Joe'll skin you alive."

He got no response this time either as McGregor pulled out his pouch of a purse, groped for two silver coins, placed them atop the bar and jerked his head as he started for the roadway.

Hugh followed along up to the gun shop, where McGregor took an oily old apron and tied it into place. He didn't say a word until Hugh had pouched the first chew of the day into his cheek.

"Well, now I wish we hadn't done that, Hugh. Except Joe wouldn't have had the guts, an' those boys know enough about adults to be *coyote*."

Hugh's conscience was not that much perturbed. He'd been against McGregor's plan from the beginning while simultaneously feeling in his heart it was about the only way anyone was ever going to make the boys talk. He said, "Somethin' I've learned by livin' as long as I have. I learnt it from breakin' horses. Scare the pee out of them right off. Let 'em know you *can* do it, whether you ever really do or not. I never could figure out whether fear was another name for respect, but I do know for a fact you'll have a lot less trouble with green colts if they respect the hell out of you. An' the best way I know to get that respect is to use a shot-loaded quirt once, maybe twice, and chances are you'll never have to use it again."

McGregor leaned on his worn old wooden counter, looking out where brilliant sunshine shone. He'd never broken horses, but he had been orphaned as a youngster. He knew something about *that*.

CHAPTER SIX

An Angry Town

When Horace Dagget brought breakfast for Hugh and James the next morning, he leaned to make himself heard above the noise of his cafe. "Them boys over yonder had one hell of a tale to spin last night when I took supper over to them." Horace paused, unsmiling dark eyes like stone. "Joe got back to town before I'd finished up last night. I figured he'd be hungry, so I killed time, but he didn't come out of the jailhouse for damned near an hour, an' I gave it up an' went home." Dagget straightened back a little as someone farther along called for more coffee. Before departing, Dagget said, "He's goin' to be after you two like a buck in ruttin' season."

Pepperdine finished eating and was sluicing the food down with black java when he leaned, brushed shoulders with Mc-Gregor, and said, "I got an idea."

McGregor spoke around a mouthful of food. "It's in a strange place."

Hugh leaned to arise. "I'll be out front," he said, paid up and left.

While waiting in the dawn chill, Pepperdine watched the hotel at the north end of town. By rights the town marshal should have appeared by now, but it wasn't uncommon for him to get his sleep if he'd been up most of the previous night. Pepperdine was relieved that there was no sign of him, and when McGregor appeared, also looking apprehensively northward, the harness maker said, "That young one lies when the truth'd fit better."

McGregor thought about that, then wagged his head. "He'd know us on sight, Hugh. He could describe us."

"I know that, but like I just said, Joe knows how sly and devious the lad is. All we got to do is say it wasn't us."

The gunsmith drew a toothpick from a pocket, studied it briefly, then popped it into his mouth and spoke around it. "Hugh . . . let's not make it worse. We got what we went for, Joe needs that information, an' as for the lads—all Joe's got to do is look at the bottoms of their feet. We scairt hell out of them but we didn't hurt 'em. Joe's not goin' to like that, but . . ." James spat out the toothpick and led off across the road to the far plankwalk and turned northward with Pepperdine at his side.

The inevitable occurred out front of the abstract office, which was one door south of the harness works. Joe Fogarty had seen them from the hotel porch and had set his pace to make the interception about where it happened. He did not smile, nod, or say good morning, he simply stopped, blocking the way, hooked thumbs in his shell belt and gazed steadily at them.

McGregor gave look for look. "You find anything?" he asked, and as Fogarty's smoldering gaze locked on to the gunsmith's face, McGregor spoke again. "Didn't think so. Their camp is alongside a creek in a stand of oaks northeast of town. There's only one creek over there."

Hugh made a dry comment. "Just as well you didn't, Joe. There's two more of 'em. Most likely at that camp. Among other things, they're horse thieves."

Finally Fogarty loosened. "Is that what they told you when you burnt their feet?"

Hugh scowled. "We didn't burn their feet. Go look at 'em. Make 'em take their boots off. All we did was scare 'em into giving us the information you need. We didn't burn 'em."

Hugh eyed the lawman thoughtfully. "What did they tell you?"

"How you tortured them."

"I don't mean that. I mean what did they tell you about how the one named Paul Dagney got shot, about themselves and the ones that are still runnin' loose?"

Fogarty looked away for the first time, glanced southward down Main Street, then across at the cafe's steamy window and back. "We didn't talk about those things. They was cryin' and cringing in the back of the cell when I came along with a lantern, scairt to death. They begged me not to torture them."

Pepperdine looked thoroughly disgusted. "For crissake, Joe, they were using you. Especially Billy. That little devil's been stayin' alive by lyin' an' schemin' and usin' folks so long, I just don't believe he could change if he wanted to. They got you all upset over somethin' that never happened."

McGregor nodded his head. "You look at their feet, did you?"

"No."

"Well, go down, give 'em their grub, an' make 'em take their boots off. Come along, Hugh." McGregor edged around the big lawman, walked into Pepperdine's shop, and halted at the counter with smoldering eyes. When Hugh went behind the counter his friend said, "I told you I was sorry we did that, but right now I'm not sorry at all."

Pepperdine's reply was different. "The trouble is, James, you'n I know we didn't hurt those little weasels, an' Joe'll figure it out, but I doubt that folks around town will believe we didn't."

McGregor was preparing to respond when one of Silas Browning's old stagecoaches rattled past with chain traces slapping. The bundled-up man on the seat waved at the figures he could discern through Pepperdine's front window and got back two matching salutes. Then the driver warped his four-horse hitch to the far side of Main Street in order to be able to enter past the corral-yard gates without brushing his wheel hubs.

The stagecoach usually blocked roadway traffic, but this morning there was none as the driver cleared each gate with inches to spare and set his binders in the middle of the yard. He tossed the lines to a waiting yardman and climbed down hand over hand to open the near-side door for a handsome woman and two dandified drummers with their display cases. He ignored the peddlers but watched the handsome woman until she'd left the yard, heading northward in the direction of the Sheridan Hotel.

As the driver shucked off his gloves and unbuttoned his blanket coat, Silas came around from the boot, huge old hat shading his face and even his shoulders. He did not smile nor greet the whip, he simply said, "If we don't get more passengers from down at Bordenton, it's not goin' to pay me to send stages down there."

The driver shot a look at Silas and without a word walked past on his way across to Morton's saloon. Silas watched for a moment then turned, made his sniffing sound, and spoke fiercely to the yardman, who was bending over, freeing the traces.

"Barleycorn! That's all they think about. Whiskey, the devil's potion, for a fact."

The yardman neither stopped unhitching nor looked up until Silas was stamping back toward his office. Then he spat amber, wagged his head, and addressed the near-side wheeler. "Nothin' worse in this world than a hard-shell Baptist." The horse did not even flick its ears.

Silas was out front, glaring in the direction of the saloon, when Pete Donner, head of the local bank, came along, stopped and followed old Browning's line of sight. "Something happen at the saloon?" he asked.

Silas sniffed. "Jack Carpenter just come in with the north-bound out of Bordenton. He didn't even speak, he just hiked over there to swizzle Morton's soul-corroding rotgut."

The banker was a dark man with a mouth like a bear trap

and not one drop of humor in his carcass. "Did you hear what those two old fools did last night?"

"What old fools?"

"Pepperdine and McGregor. They broke into the jail-house, dragged those two prisoners out, and burnt the bottoms of their feet to make them talk."

Silas's small eyes widened beneath the oversized brim of his hat. He was speechless.

Pete Donner relished the small man's expression. "The way I heard it, those lads'll have trouble with their feet for the rest of their lives."

Silas's initial shock passed. He looked over at the front of the gun shop, then craned his neck south toward the same side of the plankwalk before he said, "I believe it," and gave a rattlingly loud sniff. "I ain't the least bit surprised. Them two old devils, always with a bottle to hand and all. Who told you, Pete?" Before the banker could reply, Silas continued, "They was drunk, sure as hell. But now they done it. Folks'll be after them like the devil after a crippled saint."

Donner smiled with obvious satisfaction, then slapped the smaller man lightly on the shoulder and continued southward toward the bank. He crossed Main Street on an angling course, passed Morton's saloon without looking in that direction, and threw a wave to Marshal Fogarty, who was locking the jailhouse door before striking out northward.

The sun was well up, morning chill had yielded to new-day warmth, and visibility was excellent. When Marshal Fogarty turned in at the harness shop, the sky was flawless blue in all directions, something folks in town would appreciate and the rangemen beyond town would not.

Hugh was dampening the swell and seating leather before rolling them loosely inside burlap. He had his bronc saddle about half finished, and looked up at Marshal Fogarty with a smile. "Coffee's on the stove," he said, but Joe Fogarty settled against the counter without even looking toward the little iron stove.

Pepperdine's smile faded as he studied the large man. "Well? You see any burns?"

Fogarty gave a delayed reply. "They wouldn't take their boots off."

Hugh's eyes narrowed. "So you sat on 'em and pulled them off."

"Well, no. Billy said he'd scream if I touched him. They'd hear it over at the store and other places. Folks are already upset."

The lanky older man moved to the counter, where he could lean while looking the marshal in the eye. "They did it again, didn't they?"

Fogarty considered the little iron stove with the pot atop it, moved over to fill a cup and return to the counter with it while Hugh watched. When they were leaning again, old Hugh said, "Forty years ago I knew an old widow woman in Idaho who told me something interesting. She said when a fool looks in a mirror, he sees a fool."

Fogarty reddened. "Meaning?"

"They use the fact that they're kids to the hilt. 'Specially Billy. The story that we burnt their feet is probably all over town by now. To prove it's a lie, all you had to do was pull their boots off."

Marshal Fogarty tasted the coffee, which was as unhealthy as original sin, and set the cup aside. He looked interested only when the harness maker said, "Get Henry Pohl down there with you. Yank their boots off. If they raise a ruckus, sit on them. Everybody respects Henry an' believes him. But don't tell him why you want him at the jailhouse, because if he tells his wife, she'll be harder to handle than a porcupine."

Fogarty did not look happy. He might have said something, perhaps argued, if a customer hadn't entered the shop, catching the attention of both men.

It was a woman in a dark dress, with reddish-brown hair showing beneath her little hat. She hadn't been a girl for a while, but she still had a flawless complexion, large blue eyes the deep color of cornflowers, and the kind of tentative smile that could melt granite.

She nodded at Hugh but spoke to the large man with the badge. "A clerk at the general store said he saw you come up here, Marshal. I think you may be able to help me. I'm looking for the grave of my uncle, Caulfield Randolph. The only letter I ever received from him came from Sheridan."

Joe Fogarty let his breath out slowly. "He's buried about a mile easterly in the local cemetery."

Old Hugh watched them, and interrupted to say, "He'd be proud to get a rig an' drive you out there, Miss . . . ?"

"Randolph. Caulfield was my father's only brother. I never knew him, but before my father died, he told me stories about him. I wanted to meet him, but the proprietor at the hotel told me he died a short while ago."

Marshal Fogarty nodded gravely. "I'd be happy to drive you out there, Miss Randolph. It'll take a little time to get a rig ready. Will you be at the hotel?"

"Yes, but I really didn't mean to interrupt whatever you're doing, Marshal. I could walk out there, if you'll point out the way."

Hugh looked pained. "Heat's coming, ma'm, and it's a long walk."

Marshal Fogarty nodded and walked the handsome woman to the doorway. There, he paused as she moved slowly past and looked back. Old Hugh threw up both hands and rolled his eyes. As Fogarty was beginning to move again, Hugh said, "When you get back, take Henry to the jailhouse with you."

Thirty minutes later Pete Donner arrived at the harness shop with a reinforced bullion bag of heavy canvas to have repaired. Hugh examined the bag as the banker looked stonily at him, and said, "You and McGregor really stirred things up this time."

Pepperdine's eyes slowly rose to the dark man's face. He and Pete Donner had coexisted for years; neither cared for the other. In a voice dripping sarcasm, Pepperdine said, "I expect you know all about it."

"The whole town knows all about it," stated the swarthy man.

Hugh tossed the bullion bag aside. "The town don't know crap an' neither do you."

Donner reddened and his voice rose a notch. "Everyone's heard you tortured two lads in the jailhouse. What more is there to know?"

Papperdine shook his head. "How long you got to live before you know that you can hear anythin' about anyone at any time, and that mostly what you hear is either a lie or damned close to it?"

"You didn't burn those boys' feet?"

"We didn't burn anyone's feet, Pete. Now, I can't get to this mendin' job for a few days."

Donner ignored the mending job as he stared directly at the harness maker. "How did such a story get started if you didn't torture those lads? Hugh, everyone in town is talking about—"

"I just told you, folks in every town I've been in got tongues that hinge in the middle and wag at both ends. Come back next week, I'll have the pouch finished by then."

Hugh turned his back toward the counter and went to work on the bronc saddle. When he looked up, Pete Donner was briskly crossing Main Street on the way to the bank, which was located south of Morton's saloon.

Because of his encounter with the banker, he missed seeing one of Reg Lee's rental top buggies pass. But with the sun setting and shadows beginning to appear, he saw the rig return to town, heading toward the lower end where Lee had his livery business. The handsome woman had a shiny nose from the heat, but she was smiling, and Marshal Fogarty, also shiny-faced, allowed the buggy horse to amble along on slack lines as though Joe were in no hurry.

Jack Carpenter, Silas Browning's top driver and an old friend of the harness maker, drifted in wearing a whiskey blush as he jerked a thumb over his shoulder and said, "Marshal Fogarty don't waste no time, does he?"

Hugh was groping beneath the counter for the bottle he knew the stage driver expected, when he replied. "We buried an old man not long ago named Caulfield Randolph. She's his niece and came lookin' for the grave. Joe got a rig to take her out there and back."

Hugh set the bottle on the counter and made a face. "If Silas walks in, he'll fire you and never bring me any more repair work."

Burly Jack Carpenter held his hat with one hand, tipped the bottle, swallowed twice, then put the bottle down before he said, "I wish someone would tell me why I work for that silly old son of a bitch."

"Because you got a wife and kids down in Bordenton, and Silas's got the only stage company in the country."

Carpenter turned to gaze out into the mellowing late afternoon when he spoke again. "Sure heard an interestin' story at the saloon, Hugh."

Pepperdine sighed. "I'll bet you did. Did you believe it?"

The burly man faced Hugh as he replied. "Naw. I told 'em if you'n McGregor had done anythin' like that, Fogarty would have you chained to a wall an' locked up for life."

"Anybody believe you, Jack?"

Carpenter shrugged powerful shoulders. "Maybe Rusty. The others stood against the bar like a herd of storks lookin' down into their glasses . . . Hugh? Any truth in it?"

"Maybe a mite. Joe couldn't get anything out of those lads, so James an' I went down there, scairt the whey out of them, and got a lot of answers."

"You burnt their feet?"

"Never touched them, Jack, except to make them believe we'd do it unless they talked."

Carpenter moved his head up and down very slowly, then grinned, winked, and reached for the bottle again. By the time he was ready to go up to the corral-yard bunkhouse, he was moving with the exaggerated slow dignity of a person who was convinced no one would recognize his gait and bearing for what it was, and he could therefore pass as being stone sober.

Fortunately, when he arrived in the corral yard, three yardmen were on hand but old Silas had gone down to the cafe for supper. The yardmen steered Jack to the bunkhouse and left him there.

Hugh missed James at the cafe for supper but found him a little later sitting relaxed in shadows out front of his shop, smoking a foul little pipe. When the harness maker sat down on the same bench, James said, ''I think maybe someone's sick down at the jailhouse. Henry went hiking down there carryin' his little satchel.''

Hugh eased back, shoved out long legs, and smiled in the gloom as he explained why the doctor had gone to the jailhouse. McGregor tamped the pipe with a callused thumb pad, spat, and made a thoughtful remark. ''That part of it will come out all right, then. Joe and Henry'll know what a pair of lyin' kids we got. But I keep wonderin' about the other two, the feller called Sam'l and the one called Josh.''

Hugh continued to sit in comfort. ''If I was in their boots, by now I'd be fifty miles away and still riding.''

McGregor plugged the pipe back between worn teeth and spoke around it. ''Unless you wanted to rescue your friends.''

''From the town jailhouse? It'd never work, James.''

''Wouldn't it? It damned near did, and sure as hell would have if you'n I hadn't hid in that old shed where their horses was tethered.''

CHAPTER SEVEN

A Dead Man

Marshal Fogarty awakened to the sound of Jack Carpenter's stagecoach making its wide turn past the corral-yard gates to line out southward down Main Street. It was early and Sheridan was just beginning to stir. The air was as clear as glass, and the sound of chain-harness tugs made a discordantly musical sound until the horses picked up the slack.

Fogarty rolled out, stepped into his britches and boots, slung an old gray towel over one shoulder, and went out back to wash.

By the time he was ready to walk down to the jailhouse, he looked as solemn as a judge. South of the corral yard Hugh Pepperdine had fired up his woodstove and was unlocking the roadway door when Joe Fogarty came abreast. They exchanged a nod, Fogarty paused, then gave his head a little wag and turned in.

The coffeepot wasn't hot, otherwise Hugh would have offered him a cupful, but Fogarty did not miss this commonplace act of cowtown hospitality. He said, "I don't know what to do about Billy."

Hugh was tying his apron and said nothing.

Fogarty's gaze was fixed on the bronc saddle. "The other one, Matt Hampstead, he lies in self-defense, but Billy lies when there's no need for it."

Hugh leaned on the counter. "You pulled their boots off?"

"Yes. I never believed you'n James did that, but I think Henry wasn't convinced until he saw their feet."

"Eleanor'd believe it, Joe."

"Yeah. She hasn't spoken to me since Billy put on his act and cried in her lap."

"Henry'll take care of that."

The marshal shrugged. "I reckon. I got to turn 'em loose, Hugh."

"All right."

Fogarty looked Pepperdine in the eye. "I know what you're going to say—that I'm not their mother—but if there was a decent home where folks would want to take on a kid to raise and make something out of him . . ."

Hugh's dead-level eyes did not waver. "Billy? Joe, you ever own a bucking horse?"

"Sure."

"Well, then you know once a horse learns to buck a man off, he never forgets it. If a man catches him real young when he first tries it and whales hell out of him so's he understands not to do it, chances are he won't. But let him get a little age on him . . ."

"Hugh, he's only fourteen."

Pepperdine's gaze did not waver nor soften. "You've seen him; he's learned how to use folks. He lies as naturally as he breathes. It's his nature. You saddle some decent family with that lad and you'll be pilin' a lot of heartache on 'em. I know he's only fourteen, but nothing is going to change him now. It's too late. Turn him out, run him off, and forget it."

Marshal Fogarty leaned on the counter gazing into the dawn-lighted, chilly, and empty roadway. A weathered old ranch rig pulled by a pair of unmatched, twelve-hundred-pound horses plodded past on their way down to Dennis's store. Fogarty straightened up off the counter as he said, "You had breakfast?"

Pepperdine hadn't; but before doing so he wanted to inspect the dampened swell covering and seating leather. "I got some work to do first. . . . Joe? You showed her the grave?"

Fogarty's troubled look faded. "Yeah."

Pepperdine nodded gently. "She's pretty as a spotted pony."

Fogarty considered his friend's response. "More'n that. She's easy to be around, nice and all, and when she laughs, it sounds like . . ."

"Angels playin' harps?"

Fogarty saw the suppressed smile on the old man's face, reddened, and walked out of the harness works without another look. Hugh waited past a decent interval then laughed aloud.

By the time Hugh got down to the cafe, the place was almost empty. A grizzled, bitter-faced stockman was noisily slurping hot coffee, and he and the blacksmith's helper, a tousle-headed youth of medium size, with bulging muscles in places where most folks didn't even have the places, were along the counter when Pepperdine sat down. He exchanged traditional glares with the cafeman and said, "Horace, if you don't upend a plate over that pie, there'll be so many flies on it, it'll look like it's been sprinkled with pepper."

That cafeman was ready. "Maybe. But I never held no candle to the feet of little kids." He went after a cup of coffee, and Hugh's gaze followed him.

The vinegary-faced old stockman looked at Hugh for a moment before continuing to noisily sip coffee. The blacksmith's helper kept his head down as though he hadn't heard anything.

When the cafeman brought Pepperdine's breakfast, he slammed down the platter and stamped back into his kitchen. While Hugh was eating, the grizzled stockman arose, put coins on the counter, and departed, spurs ringing with every step. Hugh, who knew them all, had never seen this one before, so he twisted on the bench to look into the roadway, and got a surprise. The stockman was crossing toward the jailhouse. He entered and closed the door after himself.

Later, when Hugh was on his way northward and passed the emporium, Hank Dennis's old clerk was adjusting his black sleeve protectors after manhandling a barrel of dried apples up against the front of the store on the plankwalk. He nodded at the harness maker and said, "Fine day. Not a cloud in sight."

Hugh, who had known Dennis's clerk for years, paused to glance upward. The old man had a prominent Adam's apple which now, in his sundown years with the skin slack, bobbled more noticeably than it had when he'd been younger. He had faded, watery-blue eyes, very little hair, and the complexion that went with being a storekeeper. His name was Arthur Jackson. Once, Caulfield Randolph had told Hugh the old store clerk was a relative of Stonewall Jackson, but that could have been a fabrication since old Caulfield, a former Rebel soldier, wasn't always reliable about things like that.

Not that it mattered. The war had been over a long time now. Hugh smiled. "Good weather's just right for old bones," he said, and they both laughed as Hugh continued his walk back to the shop.

Shortly before noon one of those high-wheeled freight wagons, loaded to the axles, ground its ponderous way down Main Street behind eight Mexican mules. The driver was a massive, bearded, beetle-browed dark man who sat hunched, trailing lines through thick hands. Beside him on the high seat was a turkey-necked, weathered, scrawny individual of indeterminate years who hadn't been near a pair of shears in a long time and did not seem to have been close to soap and water for even longer.

Joe Fogarty's roadside door was open to let in some fresh air and midday heat. Joe heard the huge old wagon coming before he saw it.

After his earlier experience with a freight outfit cutting off his view of the jailhouse and coming within an ace of letting a prisoner escape, he was not favorably disposed to freight rigs using Main Street. In fact there was an ordinance against that kind of traffic through town. Big wagons, emigrant rigs or freighters, were supposed to go through Sheridan either on open plain to the east or the west. All the docks where freight was delivered were behind the stores. In most places, not just in Sheridan, freighters used alleyways.

Joe left his table, reached for his hat, and was in the doorway as this particular wagon moved slowly past. He and the beetle-browed driver exchanged a look, neither of them nodding or speaking. The swamper, though, fidgeted at sight of the big man with the badge and muttered nervously to his companion. The driver was looking steadily at Fogarty and ignored his helper.

Henry Pohl was coming up from the south in his top buggy and had to rub wheels against the plankwalk because the freighter made no move to yield.

Fogarty walked across the plankwalk into the road, grabbed the near-side mule's cheekpiece and yanked him to a halt. The freighter did not move. The man was still hunched and expressionless, but both large hands closed tightly on the lines.

Fogarty said, "You ever been in Sheridan before, mister?"

The driver's reply was slow coming. "Yeah, but not lately."

"There's a town ordinance against big rigs using Main Street."

The gorillalike driver considered Fogarty's statement before speaking again. "Is that a fact? I didn't see no sign at the north end of town about that, an' since I ain't a mind reader . . . Take your hand off'n the cheekpiece, mister. We'll just drive on through."

Fogarty released the mule, but the driver did not flick his lines, he continued to sit up there studying Joe Fogarty. His swamper was grinning from ear to ear, not from amusement, but from a bad case of nerves.

Joe stepped back. The driver still did not flick the lines. In fact, he let more slack through his fingers. "Y'know," he said in a rumbling tone of voice, "I'm a law-abidin' person, but I sure don't like havin' someone grabbin' one of my animals, ordinance or no ordinance."

Fogarty recognized all the signs. In his line of work a man learned to see them early in his career. He said, "You're blockin' the road. Drive on out of town. If you got deliveries, use the alleys."

Still the driver sat up there, dark beard making it impossible to see his expression. He finally straightened up, heaved a sigh, handed the lines to his swamper, and without another word started climbing down.

There were spectators on both plankwalks. Down at the livery barn Reg Lee stood in his broad doorway watching. His dayman was also standing there, leaning on a manure fork.

Marshal Fogarty moved down the side of the mules and reached the near-side front wheel as the massive driver touched the ground with one boot. When the driver, still with one foot on a wheel hub, turned his head, Joe tapped the man and put his entire body behind the blow, which caught the larger, more massive man squarely on the jaw.

The driver went down like a tree. Dust spurted when he struck, and the scrawny swamper leaned over the high seat making strange sounds in his throat. He stared at the face-down, unconscious driver at the town marshal's feet. "You never give him a chance," the swamper shrilled. "You never—"

"I gave him all the chance he needed," Fogarty replied. "I told him to drive on through."

The swamper was fidgeting with nervous agitation as he leaned over, looking down. "You never let him get his guard up. He couldn't protect his jaw. He can't take a hit on the jaw. Anywhere else, but not there."

Reg Lee was approaching from the middle of the road.

From over in front of the cafe, Horace Dagget yelled to Fogarty. "You better chain him before he wakes up, Marshal."

The blacksmith and his helper came over, glanced at the unconscious man, then looked at one another. They took hold of the driver by the ankles and shoulders, hauled him around back, let down the tailgate and heaved him into the wagon.

Fogarty spoke to the agitated swamper. "Drive on out of town, and unless you got a delivery, keep right on going. When furry face wakes up, tell him any time he's got deliveries in Sheridan, if he don't go around town, I'll lock him up and give the key to a pack rat."

The swamper talked up the mules before the big old rig began to creakily move. Henry Pohl drove on as though nothing had happened.

The blacksmith and his apprentice threw Fogarty a wave and returned to their shop. Other spectators turned away. Up near Dennis's store, where two horses were tied, no one had appeared during the freighter interlude, even though every other store in town'd had people standing out front watching.

Joe returned to his office with a sore and bruised set of knuckles. He was holding the injured hand in a bucket of cold water when he thought he heard a board breaking, or maybe it was a limb off one of the trees that were unevenly interspersed along Main Street.

He dried the hand, which was beginning to swell, thought he'd better get some food for his prisoners and had reached the doorway when two riders raced past in a belly-down run. The rider on Fogarty's side turned. Joe distinctly noticed the face before he saw the fist coming up with the gun in it.

He was flattening sideways when the horseman fired, and this time there was no mistaking the sound of gunfire. This time it was not muffled by distance and the confines of a store's interior.

Fogarty swung forward, reaching for his holster with the swollen hand. Several people across the road squawked and ran. Joe had the gun raised and cocked, but the speeding horsemen were already south of Lee's barn, down among the scattering of old shacks where men like old Caulfield Randolph had lived.

He tried one steady shot, knowing perfectly well the range was too great for accuracy. When the gun bucked, pain ran from his injured hand all the way to his elbow. He cocked the gun again, but by then the speeding horsemen were even beyond accurate carbine range.

They passed the big old freight wagon so quickly that it looked as if it were tied to a tree. Beyond that, with the rig between town and the riders, they could not be seen.

Fogarty holstered his weapon and struck out for the far plankwalk. By the time he got up to Dennis's store, there was a small crowd hovering out front. He shouldered through, got inside where sunlight did not reach, and saw the old man sprawled on the floor with blood under him.

As he knelt, he spoke over his shoulder. "Someone fetch Henry Pohl."

Hank Dennis, white to the hairline, spoke from behind a counter he was leaning on for support. "He's dead, Joe. Raise his head. Look at the back of it."

Fogarty did not lift the old man's head. He felt the side of his throat, then removed his hat, leaned to listen for a heartbeat, and straightened up as people began crowding in from out front. He pushed them aside and crossed to the counter where Dennis was leaning. Hank had the appearance of a man who was going to be sick any moment. Fogarty deliberately stepped squarely in front to cut off Dennis's view of his clerk as he spoke.

"What happened?"

The storekeeper's eyes were glazed. He did not respond to Fogarty until he'd groped for a stool and had climbed onto it, one hand gripping the edge of the counter. "They walked in while I was showing bolt goods to a couple of ladies. Arthur waited on them. I heard one of them ask for a box of handgun bullets. Arthur put them on the counter. I saw one of them cut a plug off his chewin' tobacco, and they leaned on the counter watching the ladies. When the women finally left, I was goin' to go over there. One of the men pointed a gun at my belly. They didn't say a word. The other one went behind the counter and emptied the cash drawer. He stuffed the money inside his shirt. I couldn't believe it was happening. They went over near the door. One of them walked out and untied two horses at the rack, nodded, and the one with the gun started toward the door. When Arthur moved over to lean on the counter, the gunman turned and shot him in the head without any reason. We didn't have a gun under that counter. Arthur was just going to lean on something.''

Dennis got down off the stool, and with his back to everyone, walked steadily toward the back of the store where a thick door opened into the alley. He went out there as Joe Fogarty responded to a tug at his elbow.

Henry Pohl shook his head. ''He never knew what hit him,'' the doctor said.

Fogarty ranged a look over the silent, solemn crowd until he saw James McGregor's rugged features locked down in an expression of unrelenting bitterness. He asked James where Pepperdine was and got a negative head wag from the gunsmith, who did not look up from the dead man.

Henry Pohl dragooned the blacksmith and his helper to carry the body up to his embalming shed, and hiked along behind them. People began to leave the store. Two young boys who'd been peeking past the roadway opening were caught by the ears and dragged away by a large woman.

Hank returned from the alley looking no better than when he'd gone out there. Pete Donner entered from out front, noticed the blood, saw Hank and Fogarty and made a grating remark. ''Is everyone just going to stand around? Joe! It could've been the bank!''

Fogarty considered the swarthy older man with a cold stare and said nothing as he walked past out into the splendidly beautiful sunbright day.

McGregor came up behind him. ''I'll ride with the posse,''

he said. "Give me a few minutes to find Hugh. We'll meet you down at Reg's barn."

Fogarty nodded while staring across at the front of his jailhouse. After McGregor had departed, the banker came outside too. He teetered on the edge of the plankwalk, squinting southward where the big old freight wagon was distant enough to look like a toy. When he faced around, Joe was still staring across the road. The banker scowled. "You're going to take root there. How many was there?"

"Two."

"Just two, then for crissake what are you waiting for? Joe, if they escape, they'll sure as hell feel bold enough to return. I got a shipment of silver bars in my safe waiting to go to Bordenton."

Fogarty's gaze finally dropped to the banker's hostile, swarthy face. He seemed about to speak, but instead he brushed past and walked in the direction of the jailhouse.

The banker's anger increased until haggard Hank Dennis spoke from his doorway. "He's goin' to get up a posse."

Donner put a sulfurous glare upon the storekeeper and walked briskly up toward his bunk. As he was passing the harness shop on the far plankwalk, McGregor and Pepperdine emerged carrying booted Winchesters and wearing shell-belted sidearms. Donner glared at them too. He seemed about to speak, but McGregor's icily forbidding look changed his mind. He continued on up to the bank while Pepperdine and McGregor went southward.

They did not expect to find Joe Fogarty in his office, but the door was open as they started past. The marshal was leaning on his table, staring at the cell-room door.

McGregor halted, turned back, looked in the office and said, "You feelin' all right?"

Marshal Fogarty turned his head as he straightened off the table. He did not reply to the question, but said, "You two head up the posse."

Hugh and James were flabbergasted. Pepperdine said, "All right, if you're not feelin' good, but—"

"Just lead 'em," the marshal exclaimed. "I'm feelin all right. Go on, take 'em out of town, see if you can single out their horse tracks, and watch for when they leave the road."

McGregor and Pepperdine exchanged a look before Joe Fogarty added a little more. "It's a long chance, but I saw one of 'em as plain as I see you right now. If he's who I think he is, one of those young marauders, then I'm going to get Billy or Matt to describe their friends to me. And if the descriptions fit . . ." Fogarty paused, eyeing the older men in the doorway. "The long chance is that they'll draw you posse men off, make a big circle, come back, and bust Billy and Matt out of jail."

At the blank looks he got from the men in the doorway, Fogarty made a gesture. "Go on. They'll be gathering down there. Dammit—*go*!"

Pepperdine spoke. "One of us could stay here, Joe. There's two of 'em, an' from the looks of things, they shoot first and fast."

"*Just—dammit—go!*"

CHAPTER EIGHT

Toward the End of a Bad Day

The bitter-faced, rugged stockman entered the jailhouse about the time the town posse was riding south. His smile consisted of a baring of teeth. He and Joe Fogarty had met in the jailhouse office shortly after breakfast, before the stockman had gone up to the hotel to get a room.

He hadn't heard the killing gunshot, but like everyone else in town he'd heard the other ones. As he'd been walking southward from the roominghouse he'd seen armed men converging on the livery barn.

He hadn't seen the raiders nor talked to anyone, but when he sat down and tipped the chair back, he said, "Did you get a look at them, Marshal?" and when Joe nodded, the older man's unpleasant smile lingered. "See the brands on their horses, did you?"

Joe hadn't seen the brands, in fact hadn't paid any attention to the horses. "No."

"I'll make a guess," the rugged older man said. "They was the partners of the ones you got locked up. Too bad you didn't see the brands. They'd be my H.E. mark. H.E. for Homer Elmore. Hadn't been for them marks, I wouldn't have been able to track 'em up here. Folks saw 'em between my ranch and this place and remembered the brand."

Joe pulled out a cumbersome watch, opened the face,

glanced at the delicate little hands. Then he closed the watch, pocketed it, and stood up. He hadn't spoken to Billy or young Hampstead since the raid. He knew from experience that the fierce old stockman would want to accompany him into the cell room, and it wasn't his custom to allow things like that, so he said, "I got a little work to do."

The older man pushed the chair forward and shot up to his feet. He was probably in his sixties, but he had that unique youthfulness older men had whose lives hadn't been easy nor soft. "I'll go get somethin' to eat. Marshal, has it crossed your mind them boys raiding your town wasn't so much to rob anyone as it was to do somethin' that'd draw most of the menfolk away?"

Fogarty nodded. It not only had occurred to him, it was the reason he was still in town, but all he said was, "It could be somethin' like that."

Homer Elmore went clanking out of the jailhouse on his way to the cafe. Fogarty walked down into the cell room, looked in at his prisoners, who were now both in the same cell, and said, "There was a little trouble."

The boys were sitting together on a bunk, motionless, silent, and watching Marshal Fogarty apprehensively. Joe added a little to more to his statement. "An old man got killed. Store clerk who most likely hadn't had a gun in his hands for fifty years." Joe had their complete attention. "The gunman went hell for leather southward out of town. One of 'em shot at me, an' missed." Billy and Joe were barely breathing as Joe continued speaking in the same matter-of-fact tone. "They were riding horses with an H.E. brand."

Billy's tongue darted out and back like a tongue of a snake. Matt Hampstead locked his hands in his lap. Neither youth took his eyes off Marshal Fogarty until he made one more statement.

"Same brand, boys, on the horses you fellers rode into town on. Same horses we got down in the public corrals at the lower end of town."

It wasn't meant to be a lie, it was meant to be a bluff.

There wasn't a sound. Even the front roadway was quiet. Joe leaned on the strap-steel door, looking in. "Did either of you ever hear of a man named Homer Elmore?"

Billy shook his head without speaking. Matt did not even do that much; he stared steadily at the marshal.

Joe regarded the taller boy. "You've figured it out, Matt?"

The tall youth was mute and still, but Joe was sure he'd seen a flicker of understanding in his gaze. "H.E. stands for Homer Elmore, the feller whose horse camp you lads raided; the man who shot Paul Dagney as you fellers were making a run for it on Elmore's animals." Joe straightened up off the door as he added, "He's in town."

Finally, one of them spoke. Billy said, "No he ain't. That was 'way over east in New Messico. Even no In'ian could track like that."

"He didn't have to track," explained the lawman. "He hunted folks up along the way who remembered his H.E. brand and seeing kids on the H.E. horses. They'd remember four kids tryin' to hold the fifth one in his saddle."

Matt finally moved. He arose, stepped to the rear of the cell, and faced around with his back to the wall like someone facing a firing squad. He was a handsome lad, fair and slightly freckled, with blue-gray eyes and, when the sun was right, peach fuzz on his cheeks. When Billy looked at him and said, "He's lying, that old son of a bitch ain't here," Matt fired back a cold answer.

"Then how did he know the old bastard's name, Billy?"

For once Billy's big sack of glib answers was empty. He said nothing.

Joe watched them for a few moments more, then started away as he heard those musical spur rowels enter the office up front. He'd barely turned when Matt called to him. "Marshal. He can have his horses back."

Joe's eyes twinkled ironically. "That's real decent of you. I'll fetch some grub later."

Homer Elmore was perched on the same tilted-back chair he'd used earlier, but now, having eaten, he was chewing a toothpick. When Fogarty turned to padlock the cell room door, Elmore followed Joe's progress across to the untidy table. When the lawman sat down, Elmore tongued the toothpick to one side of his mouth before speaking.

"Hard bunch of folks you got in Sheridan, Marshal. But I sure agree. It's been years since I've known of it bein' done, but I agree, if you can't get answers by bein' decent, there's always a candle and bare feet, ain't there?"

Joe glanced out his barred roadway window in the direction of the cafe as he growled at Homer Elmore. "You been listening to fools. It didn't happen."

"Well, now, the town believes it did. Tell you somethin' else, Marshal—this is my idea, an' as far as I know, the town don't have any reason to suspect it. I believe them two older lads raided your town to draw off all the able-bodied men."

Joe swung his gaze back to the bitter-faced stockman.

Elmore said, "They'll be back."

Fogarty leaned on the desk. "Depends on how close they were, the five of them. I know two of them, the ones in my cell, was close enough to the one you shot to come into town for his burial. If the other two are like that too, you're maybe right, they'll come back."

Elmore smiled without a shred of humor. "They're close, Marshal. Fellers that ain't close don't hold a dyin' man on a horse for three days of ridin'. They leave him and don't look back."

There was no reasonable way to refute Elmore's words, so Joe simply leaned back in his chair, eyeing the older man. Elmore was one of those hardscrabble stockmen who'd spent half a lifetime battling odds no one in their right mind would even consider. If he'd ever had any tolerance, it had atrophied long ago, and that showed in his face. Even when he smiled there was no softness. He would use a gun at the drop of a hat, and the fact that he was still above ground meant he was probably pretty good with one.

Homer Elmore would not have been Joe Fogarty's choice for a companion even in a gunfight, but he was here and probably had no intention of leaving until he got his horses back, and there was an excellent chance he wouldn't even leave then. His kind rarely settled for recovery, they wanted to see horse thieves punished.

Joe arose, dumped his hat on, and said, "I got some chores to do."

Elmore continued to sit leaned back with his toothpick. "You go right ahead. I'll just set here. It'll likely be a long wait, an' if I know anythin' about renegades, they work best in the dark."

Joe went out into the sunshine, paused to watch the town blacksmith enter the cafe, then walked north up past the locked door of the harness works, where he had the misfortune to encounter old Silas in the gateway of his corral yard. Browning said, "Two of my yardmen went with the posse, so what'm I supposed to do if a rig comes in with busted grease retainers or a warped axle? Joe, how come you didn't ride with 'em?"

"McGregor and Pepperdine'll do the job as well as I could, Silas."

Browning's little close-set eyes remained on the big man, but whatever words of refute he might have used were left unsaid as he touched upon another topic. "Pete's sweatin' rocks. He always gets his wind up even when he reads about marauders in a newspaper. Them two'd be daft to come back here. That's what I told him, and might just as well been talkin' to a rock."

Fogarty left the older man in his gateway, went up as far as the doctor's cottage and turned in past the little picket fence.

Eleanor met him on the porch. Joe was braced for unpleasantness because of their last meeting when that little rascal had cried his heart out in her lap. But she surprised him by smiling as she said, "Henry's across the alley. If you'd like some coffee . . . ?"

"No thanks. I'm about coffee-ed out." He smiled at her and went around the side of the house, across the alley, and entered the embalming shed. Its odor of preservatives was unsettling.

Henry was drying his hands, his work completed. The old man on the table looked presentable, but his coloring was unmistakable as Henry spoke with professional detachment. "I've been trying to figure out how old he was. With a horse you can tell by the teeth until he gets smooth-mouthed." Henry hung the towel from a nail. "My guess is close to eighty."

Joe gazed solemnly at what had been old Arthur Jackson without the least interest in how old the man had been. When he said nothing, Henry looked around. "What's bothering you?"

Joe's reply was short. "What isn't? Those boys stole the horses they arrived up here on, and I've got a cold-blooded old stockman down in my office who owned them, and that's only for openers. I have a feeling they'll play fox with the posse and come larrupin' it back to town to get their friends out of jail."

"And you're worried that the old rancher'll start shooting on sight?"

Joe shrugged. "Maybe. If he does, if anyone does, Henry, there's going to be a bloodbath. If it's possible, I'd like to prevent it."

"Maybe they won't come back. In their boots, I sure wouldn't."

Joe shoved his hat back, still gazing at the corpse. "If you were one of them, I wouldn't worry. But you're not, and I've got a feeling about these two. They're older than Billy and Joe. The one I saw as they raced past the jailhouse looked to be well into his twenties."

Henry'd had enough gloom for the time being. "That lady you went buggy riding with yesterday—old Caulfield's niece. She's a professional nurse back east."

Fogarty turned slowly, looking mildly surprised. He'd spent the better part of yesterday with her and she hadn't mentioned anything like this. But then, she hadn't said a whole lot about herself.

Dr. Pohl was looking pleased. "She came by this morning. In fact the three of us were drinking coffee in the kitchen when we heard the gunfire at the other end of town. When they brought old Jackson up here, she helped me with him. Joe, I need a professional nurse."

"What about Eleanor?"

"She does it because there's no one else to help, but she's never liked it, especially this end of it. She hasn't stepped inside the embalming shed in over a year. It was her idea for me to hire Miss Randolph."

"Did you?"

Henry grimaced. "I can't possibly pay what she gets back east."

"Did you tell her that?"

"No, I didn't tell her anything, and I kicked Eleanor under the table when she talked about it. But if she'd settle out here . . . Why should she do that? She makes more money back east. They got inside toilets back there and piped-in water and real hospitals."

Fogarty smiled faintly at the rueful expression on his friend's face. "Tell her about the fishin' up at the mountain lakes, the fresh air, the good buck hunting and all."

Henry raised his eyes. "What the hell does hunting and fishing mean to a woman from the city?"

"I don't know."

"Let's go get some coffee," the doctor said, moving toward the door. But Joe only accompanied him as far as the alley, then declined the coffee and went southward toward the lower end of town.

Down there he leaned on the cribbed poles of the public corrals, looking in at the two H.E. horses who were lipping up remnants of their morning feeding. Reg Lee's dayman spotted the marshal and went up the runway to tell Reg, who hitched up his britches and went out back. He hooked a worn boot over the lowest pole to also look at the H.E. horses as he said, "There was a mean-lookin' rancher around here last night lookin' at what he claims is his horses, stolen in New Messico some time back."

Fogarty answered quietly. "Yeah. His name is Homer Elmore. H.E."

"You believe him, Joe?"

"No reason not to, Reg," the marshal said, and twisted to look at the other man. "Have you got a plan in case someone came along, maybe in the night, and tried to steal some of your horses?"

Lee turned a face screwed up into a worried frown. "That's why you didn't ride with the posse, you think they'll come back?"

"I think they might. I'd sure like to be wrong, but in case I'm not . . ."

"Well, that settles it. Sure I got a plan. Me'n my dayman'll take turns keepin' awake tonight. With shotguns."

Fogarty nodded his head. "That might work, Reg. My guess is that those two been at the raiding business long enough to know every blessed trick there is. Suppose you hobbled every horse inside the barn and padlocked the corral gates with heavy chain—and sat up with your scatterguns?"

Lee, whose paunch had a tendency to push his britches dangerously low, gave his pants a hard pull upwards and glared at the H.E. horses. After a long silence he said, "That's plain crazy, Joe. A posse's huntin' them, the whole damned town's upset."

"Maybe it won't happen. Most likely it won't, but I wouldn't want to bet my wages on it," stated the lawman.

He gave Reg a rough slap on the shoulder and turned in the direction of Main Street. He'd succeeded in worrying the only source of available saddlestock in Sheridan, and he'd done it the same way he'd convinced Matt Hampstead he'd seen the brands on the horses of the fleeing gunmen, by stretching the truth. If he'd tried to explain what he suspected rather than what he knew, his listeners would have been left with doubts, and under these circumstances doubting individuals were not what he needed.

On his way up to Morton's saloon he passed Dennis's store. The front door was padlocked. Next door at the cafe he encountered Horace Dagget, who was leaning in his doorway wearing a greasy apron, bedroom slippers, and a beard-stubbled face. Horace looked sullen but not openly hostile as he said, "There's talk goin' around they're goin' to take the posse to hell an' gone, then sneak back here after dark and bust out their friends."

Fogarty considered the beefy man for whom he had no great affection but did not really dislike. "You bed down early, do you?"

Dagget straightened up off his doorjamb—and smiled. "That's what I been tellin' folks. The reason you didn't head out with the posse was so's you'd have things organized when they come back."

Fogarty smiled back. "Did they believe you?"

"I don't know, but one thing I do know. It scairt the pee out of them. Look around, hardly a soul in sight. They'll be settin' behind windows the full length of Main Street. If those boys come back, whether they bust their partners out or not, no matter which way they go afterwards, they're goin' to look like sieves."

Joe did not glance around, he already knew the roadway was empty. He was about to speak when the cafeman stiffened looking southward, where two horsemen were coming into town from the lower end at a dead walk.

Fogarty turned, and when the cafeman reached behind himself for a Winchester rifle, not a carbine, the marshal said, "What in hell did they come back for?"

"Who, them raiders?"

"That's McGregor and Pepperdine."

The cafeman stepped clear of the doorway holding his rifle and squinted a long moment before loosening a little. Then he put the Winchester back out of sight inside the doorway.

"Got tired," he said uncharitably, and made a face. "You couldn't depend on them two anyway."

Fogarty said nothing, not even when the pair of riders came up the empty roadway as far as the jailhouse. They reined over to loop lines at Fogarty's rack and climbed stiffly down.

When the two men looked up, the marshal crossed over. Pepperdine spoke first. "Didn't find much."

Joe looked southward. "Where's the rest of the posse?"

"Still out there. There was tracks leading to the west. They're following them."

"What about you two?"

Pepperdine was fumbling for his cut plug when he replied. "Well now, Joe, if they'd run east or kept on south . . . But those tracks turned off west. James and I figured since they turned off in the only direction a man'd use if he was havin' sly thoughts about cuttin' out and around and returnin' to town, it wouldn't be a bad idea if a couple of us came back to sort of lend a hand. Just in case. So we told the other fellers to keep searching, we was too old for this kind of damned foolishness and was goin' back."

Across the empty, quiet roadway the cafeman threw back his head, and laughed. It was such a startling departure for him that all three men at the tie rack in front of the jailhouse turned and stared. He'd heard their entire conversation.

Pepperdine got his cud tucked comfortably into a cheek and grinned. McGregor simply stared at the cafeman, shook his head, and blew out a tired sigh. Part of what Hugh had said was sure-Lord true. His legs ached, he was thirsty enough to spit cotton, and his behind felt like someone'd been thumping on it with one of those newfangled wire rug beaters.

CHAPTER NINE

Different People, Different Attitudes

Marshal Fogarty was leaving Morton's saloon and didn't see old Caulfield's niece until she greeted him at the far plank-walk.

He'd been thinking about his various stops around town. He had one more to make, down at the blacksmith's shop, and so far he was satisfied. Everyone he'd talked to about possible trouble later on, probably after dark, was willing to lend a hand.

"Good morning, Marshal."

He stepped up onto the duckboards, turned, and nodded at her. Her dress was different today, some shade of pale violet color, and at this meeting she was hatless. But everything else about her was the same, and none of it could be improved on. He touched his hat brim. "Good morning, Miss Randolph. I'm sorry you had to be in Sheridan when the raiders came."

She stopped beneath the harness shop's overhang. "It was unexpected," she admitted. "It's such a pretty town, with shade trees and a rather sleepy appearance. I'm sorry about the old gentleman."

He nodded. "Dr. Pohl told me you are a nurse."

"Yes. Back east. It's really about the only occupation open

83

to women. Dr. Pohl is very good. He'd be very successful in a large city.''

Joe's eyes crinkled at the corners. ''If he got paid in money, he wouldn't know what to do with it. Out here he gets paid in vegetables, sometimes chickens, and for something real hard, he might get a couple of cows or maybe a horse.''

She smiled. ''But I get the impression that neither he nor his wife object, Marshal.''

He nodded about that, then said, ''The feller who runs the stage company might be grumpy today if you had in mind taking a stage back to the railroad.''

''Then I'll wait until tomorrow,'' she said very coolly, looking down the length of Main Street. ''It's awfully quiet, isn't it?''

''Yes. For the middle of the week, it is for a fact.''

Her dark blue eyes stopped on his face. ''Because of the killing?''

''Well, not altogether. There's a chance those raiders might come back and try to take two of their friends out of the jailhouse.''

Her eyes widened on him. ''Wouldn't that be foolish? On the same day they robbed the store and killed a man?''

''Yes'm, I'd say it'd be foolish, but with that kind you can't ever be sure of much.''

''I see. And that's why the town is so empty and quiet. If they return . . .''

He smiled again. ''Rough justice out here, ma'm.'' Joe saw old Silas emerge from his corral yard, step to the edge of the road, and peer southward. Fogarty was tempted to turn but he didn't. He continued his conversation with the handsome woman. ''If you're goin' to be here, might be a good idea to stay in your room.''

She put her head slightly to one side as she gazed at him. ''In broad daylight, Marshal, with the town waiting for them?''

He shrugged. ''I'd guess after dark, but like I said, with

their kind you can't be sure, and guessin' wrong could get someone hurt.''

Joe finally turned. What Silas had been peering at was no longer in sight, if it ever had been, and Silas had gone back into the corral yard.

When Joe faced back around, the handsome woman said, "Before I leave I'd like to talk to someone who knew my uncle. My father told me a little and I came a long way to . . . find his grave. Did you know him well, Mr. Fogarty?''

Joe had known the old Rebel. ''Yes'm, but he was closer to the gunsmith. That's his shop across the road. And right here, this shop belongs to the harness maker. You met him yesterday. He and your uncle were friends too.'' Joe stopped abruptly, recognized what he'd done—passed up a golden opportunity—and lamely tried to undo the damage. ''I could tell you a little.''

She started past toward the door on Joe's left as she said, ''I'd appreciate it. By the way, Marshal, my name isn't ma'm, it's Mary Ellen.''

She smiled sweetly and walked into Pepperdine's shop, where the proprietor was at work on the bronc saddle. He'd seen them talking out front and had been interested for a while, but had returned to work before the handsome woman spoke to him from the far side of the counter.

Joe Fogarty went back down to the jailhouse wondering if he'd missed his opportunity. He turned in at the doorway thinking that he probably had. Like many men west of the Missouri River, Joe Fogarty was almost totally without guile.

He went down into the cell room, found that Horace Dagget had brought the usual two pails of food, and without any preliminaries asked his prisoners for descriptions of Sam'l and Josh.

Billy started speaking too quickly. ''Josh is about my size, sort of In'ian lookin', like maybe he's a breed, and he's got some gold teeth in front. Sam'l's—''

Fogarty interrupted. ''Billy, once in your life try the truth.''

The youngster straightened to his full height in obvious indignation. "That is the truth."

Fogarty shook his head. "Both of them rode past the jail-house door where I was standing. I saw them as plain as I see you right now. Neither of them was undersized or dark . . . Matt, I'm going to describe one of them, and you give me a name. Pretty close to six feet tall, sort of mouse-colored hair, leaned down with a broken tooth in his lower jaw near the front, and shoots left-handed, like Paul Dagney did . . . Matt, which one was that?"

Billy spoke swiftly. "Wasn't neither of them."

Fogarty gazed in at the youngster without saying a word for a long time, then said, "When was the last time someone yanked you over their knee and warped your backsides? . . . Matt, which one was that?"

Billy's mouth was open when Fogarty leveled a stiff finger at him. "Not another word out of you! . . . Matt?"

"That'd be Sam'l, Marshal."

"What's his full name?"

"Sam'l Walsh. Him an' Josh sort of bossed things."

"How old is Sam'l, Matt?"

"Twenty-four he told us. Him and Josh are the same age. They been partners a long time."

Fogarty leaned back off the strap steel. "Tell me about that raid on the stockman's horses."

"What is there to tell? We had worn-out animals and had to get fresh ones. Something spooked the old man an' he come runnin' out shooting. He hit Paul in—"

"I know all that," Fogarty exclaimed. "Who scouted up the horses?"

"Me."

During this exchange Billy was staring at his companion. When there was a short lull, Billy snarled at him. "What're you doing? Remember what they told us when we first all ganged up to ride together?"

The tall boy turned on his cellmate with a growl. "Yeah,

I remember, an' what's it got us? They're loose an' we ain't. Those other times we was lucky. Our luck run out, Billy.''

Joe did not allow the youngster an opportunity to respond, but he spoke again, directly to the tall youth. "What other times?'' When Matt lapsed into a dogged silence, Fogarty tried a different tack. "You're not going out of here until I let you out. But if you want to help yourself, answer my questions. Otherwise I'll hold you until I've backtracked you, an' that takes a long time.''

Billy's lip curled as he said, "You can't keep us in here. You got nothin' to hold us on.''

Fogarty's gaze hardened. "Billy, you're a fool. I got no idea who told you that, but he sure was wrong. I got the horses you stole as evidence against you, so I can hold you until the circuit-riding judge comes to town. In some places stealing horses can get you hung.'' Joe paused, watching for a change of expression in Billy. When there was none, he made one more statement to the taller boy as he turned away. "Think on it, Matt. You're in maybe the worst predicament you'll ever be in. Those two fellers who let you get into this mess are goin' to leave you in it.''

As Fogarty started up the corridor, Billy called after him. "You don't know Sam'l an' Josh.''

Joe reached the office, closed the door, and turned to see Homer Elmore standing in the roadside doorway. The stockman's pale eyes were puckered into one of his humorless smiles. He'd heard some of the conversation in the cell room, but like many stockmen, he did not mention what was uppermost in his mind as he went toward a chair and sat down. He said, "You got a nice town, Marshal. A real nice saloon too.'' He got comfortable, shoved his legs out, and studied Fogarty with faded, nearly colorless eyes. "If them fellers who shot the store clerk come back, sure as hell they'll never leave here, will they? You got everyone pretty well cocked and primed. Now me, I don't worry much about the two that's free. If they're runnin' by now they're a hell of a distance away. If they ain't runnin' and try to sneak back in here after dark, like some folks seem to believe could happen, why then they're goin' to get all shot to hell. It's not them, Marshal; what I'd like to know is what you're figurin' to do with the other two, the lads you was talkin' to a few minutes ago.''

Fogarty's annoyance was noticeable. There was something about the stockman he did not like, and he'd just had a frustrating conversation in the cell room, so he dropped down at his table, returned Homer Elmore's gaze, and spoke plainly. ''I'm not going to do anything until the other two are accounted for, but I'll tell you what I think, Mr. Elmore. The two I got locked up and the one you shot have been led around by the nose by the older ones.''

''I see, and you can find an excuse for them because of that.''

''I'm not making any excuses,'' Joe retorted. ''Like I just told you, I'm not going to do anything until the dust settles.''

Elmore considered the scuffed toes of his boots and spoke matter-of-factly. ''Horse thieves are horse thieves, Marshal. It don't matter how young or old they are.'' When the stockman raised his eyes to Fogarty's face, they were as steady as stone and completely merciless. ''That's no different now than it was twenty years back. A man works hard to get an outfit set up an' going right. There's not a blessed thing he can do about fires and floods and droughts and whatnot, but—''

''Have you lost horses before, Mr. Elmore?''

''Lost? You mean stolen? Yes I have, and I'm here to tell you the thieves been taken care of. Couple of times I had to ride 'em down even farther than Sheridan.''

Possum-bellied Reg Lee appeared in the doorway, saw Elmore and would have turned away, but Fogarty told him to come on in, that Mr. Elmore would be leaving shortly.

Elmore did not take his dismissal in good grace, but he pushed past the liveryman and struck out for the opposite side of the road. Reg looked after him, shrugged, and used the vacated chair with the warm seat. "That's the feller who said those H.E. horses was his."

Fogarty nodded as he leaned back. "What's on your mind?"

"Peddler come in down at the barn a little while ago. One of them fellers who's got pans and whatnot displayed on the side of his rig. While we was talkin' he told me he seen two riders restin' their animals in a little shady draw about six miles northwest of town. He said he wouldn't have paid them any mind except that when he first saw 'em, they was brushin' out their tracks with sage limbs, and he turned off so's they wouldn't see him and followed an arroyo almost to the road before comin' up into town."

"How long ago would that be?" Fogarty asked.

Reg shrugged. "My guess would be maybe hour and a half. Maybe more. Peddlers don't travel fast, and this one, well, that old horse of his was born about the same time I was."

"Could he see them very well?"

"He said not. When he first seen 'em they was concentratin' on brushin' out their sign and had their backs to him. When he headed for the arroyo, he said they was too far away, but he guessed they was young. Joe, who else would be brushin' out their sign?"

Joe ignored the question to ask one of his own. "Did he see the posse?"

"Didn't mention it. He's over at the cafe if you want to talk to him."

After the liveryman departed, Joe leaned back and stared at the ceiling. He was still sitting like that when Jim Young, who ran a tannery at the extreme north end of town, walked in, bringing the odor of his tanning yard with him. Jim was big—not just tall, but thick and broad. He had trouble understanding a lot of things, and although he was probably in his fifties, in a conversation he left an impression of being about ten or twelve years old.

Town dogs had been digging under his fence and raising

hell with some green hides Jim had pegged out to cure. He'd tried to catch them but hadn't been successful, and wanted the marshal to see if he could do something because the dogs had ruined one hide and had gnawed on two others.

Fogarty agreed to help, but not this particular night. He suggested that the tanner load a shotgun with rock salt and try an ambush. The tanner smiled. He'd tried that three nights straight running and had fallen asleep each time. But as he turned to depart, he agreed to try it one more night if Joe would promise to help him if he were unsuccessful again.

The tanning aroma lingered long after Jim Young had departed. In fact it was still noticeable when another visitor walked in. It was Andy Dexter, who'd run the cafe for years, until his feet, which he'd frozen one time, became so troublesome he'd had to sell out to the present cafeman. His feet were a lot better now. He lived in a little log house behind Main Street on the east side.

He wrinkled his nose and Fogarty smiled. "Jim Young was just in here."

Dexter, a small, rather round and shapeless man, rolled his eyes. "He don't have to smell that way. I've known tanners all my life in one place or another and—"

"Andy, the smell goes with him, and nothing is going to change that. Coffee's hot if you want a cup."

"Swore off, Marshal. That's part of what Doc Henry's got me to doing. Along with goin' barefoot a lot and not lettin' my feet get cold, no coffee."

"How are they doing?"

Dexter looked down at his bedroom-slippered feet. "Pretty darn well. I don't know about when winter comes, but right now . . . I was just passin' by and on the spur of the moment thought I'd come in an' get your opinion about something. You remember old Caulfield Randolph?"

"Yes."

"Couple months before he died he gave me a little box to keep for him because he was always afraid his shack would catch fire. The flue wasn't very good. He said he'd come for it when summer arrived and he wouldn't have any more fires in the heatin' stove. This morning I heard there's a lady in town claims she's his daughter or—"

"Niece. His brother's daughter."

"All right, his niece. I asked around and was told she had a room at the hotel. I was on my way up there just now when I passed the jailhouse and thought about askin' you if she's really Caulfield's kin or maybe someone just claimin' to be."

Fogarty's reply was forthright. "I'd say she's his niece, and why would anyone pretend to be when they weren't? Caulfield didn't have anything but that old shack." Fogarty leaned forward. "What's in the box, Andy?"

"I never opened it. It wasn't none of my business. He was a friend who needed a favor."

"Where is the box now?"

"Over at my house. You want me to fetch it over here?"

"No. It's none of my business either. The lady's name is Mary Ellen Randolph. She'll be at the hotel until tomorrow."

The chubby older man stood up. "I'll go see her. It's sort of heavy, so she can come down to my place to see the thing. If she wants to haul it away, she'll have to hire someone to carry it."

Fogarty shook his head when he was alone again, stood up and reached for his hat. It was amazing how quickly a dead man was relegated to the past. Andy Dexter, who had known Dennis's clerk very well, hadn't even mentioned him.

From the roadway, where visibility was good, the sun took on a rusty-red sheen as it began its descent. There was a little more activity along the length of Main Street than there had been earlier, but Sheridan still lacked a lot of its customary bustle and noise.

Fogarty struck out for the cafe, but when he got over there the only diner was Pete Donner from the bank, and he only looked up long enough to glare at the marshal, then went back to his meal.

Joe asked about the peddler, and did not have to describe

him, which was just as well because he couldn't have. Horace Dagget said when the peddler had left the cafe he had struck out southward toward the lower end of town. Fogarty assumed the man had gone back down to his wagon, so the marshal headed in that direction too.

The last thing the cafeman said was that the peddler had tried to sell him a new cast-iron fry pan, and the man was badly in need of a shave.

CHAPTER TEN

Into the Night

The livery-barn dayman told Fogarty that Reg Lee had gone up to the saloon, and he offered to take him across the alley where the peddler had parked his wagon.

The vehicle was like a hundred other peddler wagons, with a high top and solid sides where samples of the peddler's wares were fastened for display. The cart looked to Marshal Fogarty as though it had probably covered more miles than most people traveled in their lifetimes.

The dayman said the peddler had been over here a while ago, but since he obviously was not around now, he must have gone up through town to try and rustle up some business.

Joe looked inside. There were worn old boxes with an assortment of wares in them; tin pots, iron kettles, knives, scissors, some washboards, rough chunks of dark soap wrapped in greasy paper that smelled of flowers, commode sets, tortoiseshell hairbrushes and combs for ladies, and much more. Joe stepped back as the dayman pointed to one of the public corrals where a horse with almost no chin and gray above his eyes was peacefully eating a flake of hay someone had tossed to him. Reg had been right; the horse was very old.

Joe left word with the dayman that he'd like to see the

peddler and walked back up the runway. Daylight was different now. There was less glare, a hint of diminishing heat and a faint aroma of wood smoke where women were firing up their ranges for supper.

At the upper end of town he saw Mary Ellen Randolph in Andy Dexter's company crossing to the east side just south of the tanning yard. Joe assumed Andy was taking her to his shack to show her the box he'd kept for her uncle.

There was less roadway movement now, but even at its peak on this particular day there hadn't been very much. Sheridan had used up its fear and anxiety, which could not be sustained indefinitely anyway. Nevertheless, Fogarty, who knew his town, could feel the reemerging tension as he strolled up to the cafe for buckets of stew and coffee to take across the road.

His prisoners greeted the arrival of food with the same interest Fogarty could remember experiencing when he'd been their age. Aside from the food they took little notice of Joe.

As they picked up the pails, the youths turned their backs on the man in the narrow little corridor, until he said, "They're thirty miles away and still riding."

Billy turned, slightly protruding upper teeth working on a mouthful of stew. He looked steadily at the large man before he swallowed and replied. "At least thirty miles. If they've got fresh horses, more'n likely twice that distance."

Billy had an occasional habit of putting his head slightly to one side when he spoke. Not always, but often enough for it to be noticeable. He had his head cocked that way now as the town marshal said, "You're in for a disappointment, boys. They're not coming back. Billy, I didn't come down in the last rain. I know what you're trying to do—convince me they're riding like hell to get as far from Sheridan as they can."

Billy was holding his pail on one hand, a spoon in the other hand. "I'm not tryin' to convince you of anything, Marshal," he said, turning his back to resume eating.

Fogarty put his attention on the other boy. "Matt?"

The taller youth did not turn when he said, "What?"

"Have you thought it over?"

"I don't know what you mean."

"Yes you do. Have you thought over answering a few questions in exchange for me talking to the judge when he gets here?"

Billy spoke. "He ain't goin' to answer no questions an' he don't want to talk to you."

Fogarty said, "Matt . . . ?" When the tall youth went on eating without turning, Joe gave it up and returned to the office.

Earlier in the day he'd hoped that Matt would not be influenced by the smaller and younger boy. But evidently in the hours when they'd been left alone, Billy had convinced his companion to have no more conversations with the lawman.

Joe tossed his hat aside in the office, sat down, and looked out past his partially opened roadside door, where the shadows were getting slightly thicker as time passed.

Reg Lee appeared in the doorway to block the view as he said, "That horse rancher's tryin' to talk up a lynchin' at the saloon."

Fogarty waited until the liveryman was seated before speaking. "The feller who owns those H.E. horses?"

"Yeah. He's pretty sly too, the way he alternates between sayin' those two that killed old Arthur Jackson an' the two you got locked up belong to the same band of raiders. An' that with you sittin' on your backsides while those killers get away, folks ought to take out the two that been caught and hang 'em not just for bein' part of the renegade gang, but also for bein' damned horse thieves."

Fogarty returned his gaze to the roadway as he said, "Where's that damned peddler? I left word with your dayman I wanted to see him."

Reg hadn't been back to the barn since going up to the saloon. All he knew about the peddler he'd already told the marshal. Right now the peddler didn't seem important, but a possible lynching did. "Maybe back down there by now. I don't know. Anyway, what difference does he make? I tell you, Joe, you'd ought to collar that rancher. He's goin' to stir up trouble sure as hell."

Reg left after failing to rouse the town marshal. Fogarty had kept turning his head, gazing out into the roadway. When Reg got down to the barn, he told his dayman he thought Fogarty was slipping, or something. He'd acted as though he were a hundred miles away.

While they were conversing in the gloomy runway, the hostler gave a little start and nudged his employer. Fogarty was across the alley near the peddler's wagon. He did not appear to be trying to locate the peddler because he did not call out; he stood between the shafts, reaching inside the old rig.

Reg said, "What's he doing?"

"There's a box just inside, behind the seat on the same side he's reaching, that's got scissors and all kinds of cookin' an' skinnin' knives in it. You don't suppose he's fixin' to swipe some of them knives, do you, Mr. Lee?"

Reg failed to reply as he began walking toward the alley. By the time he got back there, Marshal Fogarty was leaning on the near-side forewheel of the old wagon, looking at the ground. When Reg spoke, Fogarty raised his head. "Is he in the barn?" he asked.

"Who? The peddler?"

"Yes."

"He's not in the barn. I got no idea where he is. Why?"

Fogarty straightened up off the wheel and turned to go up the alley without another word. Reg and his dayman exchanged a look, went over to the wagon, and stood like a pair of oxen staring at it. The dayman, who was younger and with better vision, stepped closer, brushed against one side of the pair of shafts and scowled as he leaned to examine something on the warped wood of the side of the seat. As Reg came up, the hostler said, "Look there, blood. Serves him right, tryin' to steal one of them knives."

Reg shouldered the younger man away, gently extended a finger, pulled it back, and leaned for a closer look as he said, "Hell, it's bone dry. Couldn't be Joe Fogarty's blood. Must belong to the peddler; he maybe cut himself arrangin' things in there to show folks."

The hostler also leaned to feel the dark stain. He did not like abandoning his theory that the town marshal had been trying to steal some knives, so he said, "Maybe he cut himself when he was down here earlier lookin' for the peddler an' I showed him the wagon. He was gropin' around inside that time too."

Reg destroyed the hostler's theory as he leaned to look inside the old rig, pulled back and gestured. "Count 'em. There's twelve slots for knives, and there are twelve knives in the box. And that's not fresh blood by a long shot."

"I didn't say he actually got hold of one, Mr. Lee. I said maybe he was fixin' to—"

"Come on. We better feed early and get the chores done before dusk. I think we might have a busy night ahead."

He had no idea how busy!

By the time Marshal Fogarty had returned to the jailhouse, the lazy, pleasantly warm springtime evening was drawing to a close. It was suppertime, and that made Main Street seem even more deserted. Up at Morton's saloon Rusty was rinsing his mouth with a cup of java while reading a limp newspaper someone had abandoned at one of his tables. He hadn't yet fired up any of the coal-oil lamps, so he had to hold the paper fairly close to his face.

Pete Donner walked in, mouth pulled flat, dark eyes testy, and said, "What're you tryin' to do, go blind?"

Rusty carefully folded the paper, shoved it under the bar, and while showing no expression, set up a bottle and glass when the banker bellied up to the bar. Donner, whose disposition always had plenty of room for improvement, was particularly irritable this evening. He filled the little glass, downed its contents, shoved the glass away, and stared at Rusty, whose elegant vest showed a scene of lovers meeting in a bower. The woman had a flowing white gown. The man had lace cuffs and knee britches. The banker glared, then said, "That feller looks like he sets down to pee. I like the vest with the red sunset." Donner raised his eyes to the saloonman's face. "You know what that damn Fogarty's doing? Nothing. Absolutely nothing. Settin' on his backsides gazing out into the roadway like he expects those marauders to ride up, walk in, and surrender to him. I tell you, Rusty, next time the town council meets, I'm goin' to put in a motion that they fire him an' find a younger lawman."

Morton went wordlessly around the room lighting his lamps. When he finished, he returned behind the bar and asked the banker if he cared for a refill. Donner shook his head, then put a coin atop the bar and departed. Rusty dropped the sticky little glass into a tub of greasy water, shelved the bottle, and picked up the coin while looking in the direction of the roadway doors. He said, "You miserable son of a bitch," then put the coin in his cash drawer and brought forth the newspaper.

His second interruption was cause for less annoyance. The new customer was a beard-stubbled man wearing a suit coat that didn't match his britches—both of which looked like they'd been slept in. His hat was one of those curly-brimmed derbies usually associated with pictures of politicians or wealthy merchants back east. Except this hat had been dented, punched back into shape, but never brushed.

Rusty smiled expectantly while the stranger ranged a glance along his backbar before saying, "A jolt of that peach brandy."

Rusty dutifully filled a glass, then said, "Two bits, friend," and when the stranger seemed to recoil, Morton explained. "Whiskey's a dime, beer's a nickel, but that there liquor comes from Chicago at a hell of a price. I only stock a couple of bottles because it's too expensive for most of my customers.''

The ragged-looking stranger placed a quarter on the bar, tipped his head, and dropped the peach brandy straight down. His eyes popped wide, his breath came in a rush, he held to the bar and focused on Rusty. "Good Gawd'a'mighty!"

Morton's retort was a rebuke. "You're supposed to sip brandy, friend. Whiskey you can toss down, but that stuff'll scald your gullet and eat a hole in your belly. Just sip it. Care for another?"

"No! Why'n't you tell me before I drank it?"

"I figured you to be a brandy man since you asked for it. Brandy men already know not to drop it straight down. Want some water?"

"No," replied the stranger, passing a soiled coat sleeve across his face where tears were trickling. When he recovered, he nodded at a sawed-off scattergun leaning conveniently against the backbar wall. "You expectin' In'ians?" he asked sourly.

Rusty glanced at the gun before answering. "No, we got a pair of young renegades at the jailhouse an' there's talk their friends might try to break them out."

The stranger blew out a big breath, asked for a glass of beer, and while Rusty was drawing it, he said, "Yeah, I heard there was trouble in Sheridan. Dang near kept right on travelin'. I'm a peaceable man." He paused to half empty the beer glass and to beam on Morton. "Now that's more like it. You make your own, do you?"

"Yep. From an old German recipe."

"Sure. Every saloonman between here and Kingdom Come makes his batches from an' old German recipe. But this at least tastes good enough to be made that way."

Rusty leaned on the bar. "You a travelin' man?" he asked.

"Yep, A travelin' man." The stranger drained the glass and shook his head when Morton would have refilled it. "I'd like to," the stranger said, and thumbed his hat back. "But a man needs a clear mind."

"You got things to sell?" Rusty asked, since traveling men were invariably drummers.

The stranger nodded. "Got my wagon parked across the alley out back of the livery barn. Whatever you need, friend, I got, an' if I ain't got it an' you want it, next time I pass through I'll have it for you."

The stranger studied Morton for a moment, then broke into laughter. Rusty considered the man, who was much younger, trying to guess what had been said that was so funny.

As the man laughed, Rusty noticed a gap in the peddler's lower jaw where a tooth had been.

Rusty straightened up off the bar when several of his "regulars" arrived and went up to serve them. A little later when he looked down the bar, there were silver coins beside the empty beer glass and the stranger was gone.

Dusk settled with its customary stealth, lights glowed throughout Sheridan, and one of Silas Browning's sturdy but unpainted mud wagons came in from the east a mile above town, making a long-spending curve until it was poised for the run down to the north end. The whip let a little slack in the lines so the horses could ease over into a rocking-chair lope.

He hauled them down to a walk a half mile out, entered town up by the hotel where Marshal Fogarty was standing on the porch, and rattled past with the whip and the lawman exchanging a casual wave.

Down at the cafe there were the usual diners hunched over like buzzards, but with very little talk for a change. Everyone, even the blacksmith and his apprentice, were wearing guns.

Hugh Pepperdine, who had eaten earlier, was concentrating on warping the seating leather to the bronc saddle in such a way so that he wouldn't have to use his smooth old round of oak to press out wrinkles. He didn't see Joe Fogarty pass on his way to the jailhouse.

Hugh was turning to light a lamp when James McGregor

walked in puffing on his evil little pipe. Hugh grunted at him and stepped back from hanging the lamp when the gunsmith said, "Joe's worrying. He just walked past an' didn't even see me crossin' the road."

Pepperdine nodded about that. "Those posse men should have come back by now. You don't suppose they actually run onto them renegades, do you?"

McGregor knocked dottle from his pipe into the spittoon before replying. "More'n likely they're settin' out yonder somewhere passing a bottle around." He pocketed the little pipe. "Joe'd ought to set up some ambushes around town."

"He knows that, James."

"Then why hasn't he asked us to join 'em?"

Pepperdine gazed at the bronc saddle where it was cinched down on his workhorse. He began untying his apron. "Let's go down an' find out. You had supper?"

"No, maybe later. You?"

"Hour ago."

"I'll get my gun an' belt."

While the harness maker was gone, McGregor strolled to the doorway. The only person he saw was a rough-looking individual wearing a coat and britches that didn't match and a dilapidated derby hat, standing in front of Hank Dennis's store rolling a cigarette. He looked to the gunsmith like a cross between one of those old-time peddlers who traded whiskey to the Indians and a tramp. But the butt of his six-gun, exposed where his coat was hung up, had ivory handles, which was not altogether unusual; but in McGregor's opinion, men who carried that kind of a weapon were usually well-off stockmen or gun-handy professionals. The scarecrow rolling the smoke didn't appear to fit either category.

When Hugh arrived with his belt gun in place, McGregor led off through the settling dusk in the direction of the jailhouse. The peddler-looking individual hadn't moved, but now he was trickling smoke. McGregor said nothing as Pepperdine looked across Main Street, not commenting either.

They had passed before the peddler sauntered across to

the opposite plankwalk and turned southward too, cigarette hanging from the corner of his mouth.

There wasn't much visible life along Main Street. Most of the stores were closed and dark, but the jailhouse was lighted as Horace Dagget took pails of food over for Fogarty's prisoners. When he saw Hugh and James approaching, he hesitated long enough to put a sour look in their direction and say, "Well, what d'you know, the gummers is wearin' guns tonight." Then he entered the jailhouse and both older men stopped, too late to snarl an insult back.

No more than ten seconds elapsed before the cafeman came back out without the pails. His face was contorted, and this time he sounded different when he addressed the harness maker and his companion. "Empty, for crissake. Cell room door's open and ain't no one in there."

Pepperdine had the longest legs. He pushed past the cafeman and stepped into Fogarty's office. Behind him McGregor and the cafeman entered with a little more caution, but the cafeman halted in the doorway while the gunsmith advanced as far as the open cell-room door where Pepperdine was turning with an angry expression. He saw James and began to swear. "They done it! The prisoners are gone! Where'n hell is Joe? He was supposed to be in here."

Looking wild-eyed, McGregor stepped aside for his friend to pass back into the office. McGregor turned back, glanced at the gun rack, at Fogarty's untidy table, at the cafeman who was like a stone statue, and finally spoke to Pepperdine. "Lee's barn," he said, and nearly bowled the cafeman over as he led the exodus from the jailhouse.

Northward, in dark shadows out front of the abstract office, the scarecrow with the ivory-stocked gun and greasy old derby who had been watching, dropped his smoke, and stamped on it. The man moved quickly across Main Street to the dogtrot where Joe had tried to trap the outlaws, passed swiftly down through it and out into the eastside alley where a pair of rat-tailed dogs were foraging in some trash bins. Instead of tucking tail and fleeing, the mongrels turned with barking snarls toward the moving silhouette of the man with the derby hat.

The peddler ignored the dogs, hurried northward past Morton's back door, past McGregor's gunshop, and encountered three other men standing with saddled horses. There was a brief conference before two of the men swung astride and made enough noise to raise the dead as they loped down the alley. Then the riders turned back northward, making still more noise, and passed their acquaintances with a salute as they fled up out of town in a dead run.

The two on foot led their horses across the alley, into someone's carriage shed, and tied them there. They crept through several yards where more dogs barked, and faded from sight in the shrubbery around a house with a painted picket fence and no lights showing.

Someone yelled midway to the livery barn. The men down there turned as the yelling man ran to the center of the road, gesturing with both arms. "They're gettin' away. They was in the back alley. Didn't you hear 'em? They ran northward out of town!"

The small band of townspeople limned by Reg Lee's twin carriage lamps watched the yelling man approach in an agitated lope. Some of his contagious excitement took hold of Reg Lee, who bawled for everyone to get a-horseback, then led the rush down his runway.

McGregor and Pepperdine were not carrying saddle guns so they were able to rig out and get astride before most of the others, who had to waste time buckling saddlegun boots in place, were ready.

Hugh reined up short in front of the carriage lamps, looking northward, but there was nothing to be seen or heard up there. When McGregor came up beside him, Hugh said, "Where in the hell is Joe?"

McGregor had no opportunity to reply. Mounted men were jostling past, the agitated individual among them still yelling and gesturing. As McGregor joined the pack he leaned toward Hugh and said, "Stay clear of that crazy devil."

Only two people were standing out front as the riders charged past: Silas Browning and the young driver who'd recently brought in his coach. Silas yelled a question as the horsemen sped past, and did not get a reply. The young driver said, "What in the hell . . . ?"

Old Silas craned for a moment until the riders were out of town, then turned with a fierce scowl. "More damned foolishness. They'll be after them raiders, but anyone knows they went west an' there's already a posse out there trackin' em down."

His whip was bewildered. He hadn't been in Sheridan for several days. "Was Marshal Fogarty with them? I didn't see him, Mr. Browning."

Browning turned with loud sniff. "Him? He'll be settin' on his behind at the jailhouse, like he's been doin' since they shot Dennis's clerk."

The younger man's eyes widened on his employer. "Old Arthur Jackson? Why'd anyone shoot—"

"Go bed down, damn it. You got an early run tomorrow. This town's gettin' crazier'n crazier."

"Hadn't we ought to do something?"

"Yas. Get a decent night's sleep, like sane people," Silas snarled, and stamped back to his office.

Catty-corner across Main Street, Rusty Morton came out of his saloon too late to see the riders leave town but in time to hear them. He saw the young whip over in the gateway of the corral yard and called out. "What happened?"

The driver called back. "Darned if I know, but they sure was fired up."

As the driver turned back into the corral yard, Rusty remained in his doorway. His few midweek patrons came out to mutter, listen, and look in puzzlement at one another.

CHAPTER ELEVEN

"Now Get Up!"

An hour later, with the noisy posse men scattering out across the north country, the original posse, which had been out since early morning, came trooping into town.

Reg Lee saw them from his front runway and whistled to the hostler, who was hiding in a stall down near the alley with a carbine in his hand. The hostler hurried up front, expecting to encounter trouble, but Reg was standing in plain sight, his Winchester leaning against the wall. Reg jutted his jaw and said, "Look after them horses. They're as tucked up as gutted snowbirds."

The posse riders turned in and swung wearily to the ground. The hostler went quickly to work gathering reins to lead the tired beasts down into the runway as Reg spoke to the posse man nearest him. "You missed 'em, didn't you? Rode your tails off for nothing. Hour ago they busted their friends out of jail and headed north in a dead run. Some fellers from town went after them."

The man Reg had spoken to seemed impervious to the liveryman's implied derision. He was tall and thin, and right now he looked tired to the bone as he fixed a gaze on Reg Lee and jerked his thumb toward his companions who were bunched up in the gloom. "Lend a hand," the tall man said

and walked away. Reg followed until he was close enough
to see what the other men were crowding around.

A dead man tied belly down across a saddle.

Reg stood like a stone as the body was untied and lifted
down. Without a word being spoken, the posse men shouldered past and carried their inert burden down where a lamp
glowed in the harness room. They laid him face up on Reg's
floor and, still without speaking, watched the liveryman push
through to stare. An older and unkempt-looking rider said,
"We didn't find him until late afternoon. He was a peddler, an' there was a sign of wheels, so he must've had a
wagon, but by the time we got him loaded, it was too dark
to make out much."

The tall, thin man Reg had first addressed shoved his hat
back and shook his head. "Shot in the back. My guess is
that he was off the wagon, maybe fixin' to hobble his horse
for the night, when they caught him."

Reg scowled. "Who caught him?"

The riders gazed at him. One man said, "Who do you
suppose? Before it got too dark, we scouted up two sets of
horse tracks."

Reg turned his back on the corpse, saw his round-eyed
hostler in the doorway and said, "I was right. That dried
blood wasn't fresh. Gawddamn, that peddler—"

The tall man scowled. "What peddler, Reg?"

"He come in with the wagon, parked it out back an' turned
his horse into a public corral an' bought a flake of hay off
me." Reg turned slowly to stare at the tall man. All the riders
were looking steadily at him.

The hostler flapped his arms. "Mr. Lee, you don't suppose . . . ?"

Reg let out a ragged breath. "But if he was one of them,
where'n hell was the other one?"

The hostler had the answer to that. "Up at the jailhouse
bustin' 'em out while the one with a tooth missin' went
around town keepin' an eye on things."

A posse rider scowled. "Where's the marshal? He go with them riders you said left town headin' north?"

Neither Reg nor his hostler answered, so the posse man assumed their silence meant that Joe Fogarty had indeed left town in pursuit of the raiders. One by one they left the harness room, drifting through the dark night to seek their homes and their beds. It had been a grueling day.

Reg sank down on a bench outside his harness room while his hostler remained inside, looking at the dead man. The peddler was old. He was attired in none-too-clean red long-johns whose color was slightly lighter than the caked blood, which was dark and curdled where the slug had hit him high in the back. If there were any consolation to the killing, it had to be that the old man hadn't had time to feel anything.

Reg called, and the hostler went out into the runway where Lee was standing in front of the bench. "Toss some croaker sacks over him. I'm goin' to see who I can raise."

The hostler made a sound suggestion. "Doc Pohl. Won't be anyone else around."

Lee returned to his harness room, and without looking at the corpse, fumbled beneath a pile of salt-stiff, smelly saddle blankets and brought forth a pony of rye whiskey. He downed some of it, and ignored the hostler on his way toward the roadway.

Sheridan was deceptively quiet and dark, but as was always the case in these circumstances, there were a number of women behind locked doors who couldn't sleep and dared not go outside while their menfolk were on a manhunt. At least the manhunters had excitement and anger to occupy them. The woman had nothing but their fears. They did not even consider going back to bed.

Reg stopped out front of the jailhouse, looked in, approached the doorway, teetered there briefly, then entered. The building was dark. He went as far as the open cell room door before turning back. He continued on through Sheridan.

Reg hesitated out front of Henry Pohl's little picket fence, then turned in, marched up to the door, and knocked. The house was totally dark. He had to knock four times before he saw candlelight. When the door swung open he saw Henry Pohl appear in the opening attired in a bathrobe, his spiky hair and puffy face bathed in feeble light.

Lee wasted no time apologizing. "I got a dead man down in my harness room. Shot in the back. The posse brought him in. They said he was a peddler."

Henry eyed the liveryman with a gathering scowl. "Peddler? Didn't a peddler have a rig parked across the alley from your runway?"

"Yes. Doctor, didn't you hear the commotion a while back? Them two prisoners was taken out of the jailhouse, and a bunch of men from town went after them. Them renegades went north along with the sons of bitches that broke them out."

Pohl stepped out onto the porch with his candle, closed the door very quietly, and looked up and down Main Street. He hadn't heard a thing. It had been a long day and he hadn't gotten much rest the night before. "Where's Joe?" he asked.

Lee made an understandable guess. "Went with them riders, as far as I know." He stopped, then shook his head. "No. He wasn't down at the barn when they rigged out and rode up through town. Hell, I don't know where he is."

Henry said, "Give me ten minutes," and disappeared inside the house.

Reg perched on the porch railing, spat into a bed of geraniums then began fitting things together. As sure as the Good Lord had made little green apples, that peddler had been one of the renegades who'd shot old Jackson. Then they had led the possemen all over hell and left them out there while he, and probably his partner, came back to town in the peddler's wagon and busted those two youngsters out of the jailhouse. Where in the hell had Joe been? Where was he now, for crissake?

Henry Pohl managed to dress without awakening his wife. When he returned to the porch, Reg led the way back to the plankwalk and southward without opening his mouth until they were approaching the barn, where both carriage lamps were now glowing. "They was a sly pair, Doctor. The town was waitin' for 'em. Sure as hell they was comin' back for their partners in the jailhouse. Even Horace Dagget was packin' a gun." Reg paused in the runway entrance. "I wasn't plumb convinced they'd be crazy enough to come back. That's about the wrongest I ever been."

He took Henry to the harness room, pulled off the sacks the dead man had been covered with, and stood aside as Doctor Pohl sank to one knee to make his examination.

Reg's hostler came soundlessly to the doorway and said, "Now I know why he parked his wagon across the alley like he done. There's four animals missin' from the corral beyond the wagon. After dark we couldn't have seen 'em even with a lantern."

Reg gazed owlishly at his hostler then turned back. Dr. Pohl spoke as he stood up. "Right through the heart. In the morning see if you can round up some fellers to carry him up to my embalming shed . . . Reg, you need a drink. Good night."

They watched Henry Pohl return to the roadway and turn north. Not until he was lost to sight did Reg face his hostler. "Now you want to know whose blood is on the wagon?"

The hostler shook his head. "No."

"Which horses did they take?"

"Them three bay combination horses and that dappled mare who was always raisin' hell."

Reg went out to the bench and sank down. "That mare was a pain in the tail, but she was tougher'n a boiled owl."

His hostler agreed. "So was them other three. Good, tough animals. It looks like maybe that peddler with the tooth gone in front knew horseflesh an' most likely scouted up them four when we wasn't back there."

Reg continued to sit slumped until his hostler solicitously mentioned the bottle hidden under saddle blankets. Then Reg nodded without moving, and when the hostler returned, Reg swallowed three times before passing the bottle to his hostler. Later he arose from the bench and said, "I'm goin' home to bed." His hired man nodded without saying a word. After the liveryman was out of sight, the hostler emptied the bottle.

It was close to midnight, with most of those lighted windows around town which had come to life with the return of the posse men totally dark again.

A few light sleepers around town remained wide awake. One of them, Pete Donner, whose nerves crawled like snakes just at the mention of outlaws in the area, went downstairs to fire up the kitchen cookstove and put the coffeepot to heat.

The bank had been robbed twice in the last four years, and it did not help his nervous condition very much that last year, after six months of agonizing over the expense, he had imported a massive steel safe. The man who had arrived with the safe had said very candidly that there'd never been a safe built that someone couldn't open one way or another, but that the one Donner had bought came closer than any other safe to being impregnable. The man had been reassuring right up until Donner had paid him, accepted the receipt, and smilingly put on his hat. Then he said, "The weakest part of any safe is it's combination lock. By its nature, the lock couldn't be made of solid steel as thick as a man's wrist, and if someone knew how to use explosives, he could blow the lock off."

Donner drew off a cup of coffee, took it to the darkened parlor and sat down with unsteady hands. He'd heard the yelling over on Main Street, and later the thunder of riders busting out of town northward. He hadn't gone forth to find out what had happened, but he suspected Fogarty's prisoners had been broken out of the jailhouse, and that didn't mean anything to him. What did trouble him was that with those four outlaws loose and in the Sheridan township area, all that silver bullion in his safe—not to mention sixteen doeskin pouches of raw gold the bank was holding on deposit—would be a godsend, particularly to men who might come onto them by accident.

He finished the coffee and was padding back to the kitchen when a dog began to furiously bark in the near distance. Most of his neighbors kept dogs. Donner didn't. He did not like dogs. His house, like those of his neighbors, was east of Main Street, set well apart from the stores, the saloon, and the traditional Saturday night hoorawhing by rangemen who arrived full of vinegar once a week, religiously, to let off steam.

He listened to the barking dog, and while the sound tightened his scalp a little, rarely did a night pass that foraging raccoons and other varmints didn't sneak into town searching for refuse barrels, something that always set dogs off.

He was placing the cup on a drainboard when he heard a cat howl and hiss, noises which inspired more than one neighborhood dog to go into a frenzy of barking. Damned cats prowled at night along with other confounded varmints.

He padded to the back pantry, opened the door as the cat squawled again, and stooped down searching for a stone to pitch in the animal's direction.

Something hard and round pressed gently into the area of his kidneys. For two seconds Pete Donner stopped breathing, then straightened up very slowly with the gun-muzzle pressure increasing.

He turned his head to the left. The stranger was smiling so broadly that even in weak light Donner noticed that a tooth was missing from his lower jaw.

Behind the first man a second man was not grinning. He was simply pointing a cocked Colt. This one seemed to need assurance there would be no trouble before he said, "Sam'l, you got a real gift. It would've fooled me too."

The gap-toothed, grinning man jerked his head a little and pushed with the gun barrel. "Inside, Mr. Banker."

It was somewhat darker in the house than it had been on the rear porch, but even Donner's vision had adjusted. He stopped and turned, but the gap-toothed man gestured. "Into the parlor. Don't make no noise."

Donner tried a feeble ploy. "My wife's upstairs and—"

"You don't have a wife, Mr. Banker, an' ain't no one else here with you."

Donner walked awkwardly back to the chair he'd occupied while drinking coffee, sat down, and looked up at them. Both were beard-stubbled. Both had cocked guns in their fists. The one with a missing front tooth was wearing an old derby hat along with a coat that did not match his britches. His six-gun had an ivory handle. Neither of them seemed to be very old, but in the gloom, with whiskers, Donner could not be sure of that. But he was by now sure of something else. If his original guess about Fogarty's prisoners being broken out of jail by their friends was accurate, then whatever those charging horsemen he'd heard leave town earlier were chasing, it was not these two. It crossed his mind that perhaps these two were different, had nothing to do with the others, but the gap-toothed man settled that when he helped himself to a cigar from Donner's glass humidor, and after biting off the tip, spoke softly and calmly.

"You bein' a businessman, Mr. Banker, you'll understand us businessmen dassn't let opportunities slip past. An' we got to plan things, don't we? Like gettin' the town mad enough to chase us all over hell, an' us slippin' back an' talkin' to folks around town about your bank, and you being a single man an' all. We hit it lucky, Mr. Banker. We come on to an old peddler standin' around in his underwear fixin' to set up camp for the day. This here little hat belonged to him, like these britches and coat. We let our horses loose and come back to Sheridan in the wagon. Now then, Mr. Banker, we just got one more thing to do before we leave town for good an' meet up with the lads who took those fellers on a wild goose chase northward. You know what that thing is we got to do?"

Pete Donner's throat was tight. He did not answer the question. He said, "You can't do it."

"You mean we can't get away with it? Mr. Banker, we been outsmartin' folks a long time. Half the menfolk are worn out from tryin' to catch us, an' the other half is somewhere up north lookin' for us. Sure we can do it.''

"I didn't mean that," Donner croaked. "I meant you can't blow open the safe.''

The man called Sam'l lighted his cigar, trickled smoke, and savored the biting taste and the fragrance. He removed the stogie to admire it and said, "We never had much luck with blastin' powder, friend. Mostly, it makes too much noise, but it also does somethin' else, it makes so damned much smoke and all it's hard to see inside a safe.''

His companion finally smiled. "And one time we blew six thousand greenbacks all over hell and never got any of it.''

Sam'l clamped down on the cigar, leaned forward with the barrel of his six-gun barely touching Pete Donner's forehead, looked the banker steadily in the eye without blinking and said, "You got ten seconds, partner.''

Donner moved his head back a fraction and said, "If you shoot me, you won't get anything.''

Sam'l must have heard this before. He leaned and pushed the gun until it touched Donner again as he said, "All right. We never figured to win 'em all, Mr. Banker, so we'll ride away an' try another place. But your gawddamned brains'll be splattered all over the wall, won't they? We'll still win. We'll still be alive, but you won't.''

The other man looked steadily at Donner. Of the two, he seemed less inclined to conversation. "Ten seconds is up,'' he murmured and raised his cocked Colt.

Pete could hear his heart thundering in its dark place. "I got to get dressed," he said, and did not recognize his own voice.

Sam'l straightened up a little but did not take the gun out of Donner's face. "Naw. Ain't nobody goin' to see you in your robe. Ain't nobody goin' to see any of us. Josh's already scouted up the way to get over there. Stand up, Mr. Banker. . . . Just one thing for you to remember: Make any kind of a noise, any kind of a loud cough even . . ." Sam'l moved his bent finger inside the trigger guard. "Now get up!"

CHAPTER TWELVE

Toward Midnight

Lately James McGregor'd had his faith in Marshal Fogarty's judgment put to the acid test. First, when Joe'd set up that ambush that had backfired when a big wagon cut off his view of the jailhouse. Then the marshal had collared James and Hugh in the harness works about dusk when he should have been down in his jailhouse with a shotgun in his lap loaded for bear.

But now, squatting between Hugh and Fogarty in pitch-darkness inside a dilapidated carriage shed that smelled of animals, he thought how silly the three of them were going to look if it turned out the dozing horses tethered nearby hadn't been hidden here by the outlaws. Joe had talked like a Dutch uncle convincing James and Hugh he knew that was the case.

Hugh, who was less cynical, must have been thinking along similar lines, because he whispered to Fogarty that his assumptions still had loopholes. Fogarty's whispered reply had a sound of conviction to it.

"She saw it happen. She was coming back from Dexter's place, was crossing the alley at the lower end, and two of them ran straight at her, then whirled and raced back up the alley and out of town. She ducked into a doorway because she thought they'd run her down. From there she saw the four of them wave as the riders went hell-for-leather, kept going, and the other two led a pair of saddled animals into this shed and left them here.''

McGregor spoke dourly. "A female woman. An' it's dark in the damned alley. An' even if she didn't just see some cowboys havin' a horse race—"

"Horse race," snorted Fogarty. "In the dark? James, those two sure as hell were the lads from the jailhouse. They raised a ruckus to draw riders in pursuit."

"Well, they'll get caught, Joe."

Even Hugh could not accept that. "He just told you—in the damned dark, James."

McGregor would not give up, but he took a different tack. "It still would have been better for the three of us to set inside the jailhouse in the dark, an' when they come sneakin' around, blow them to Kingdom Come."

Fogarty's retort was sharp. "Like I told you in Hugh's shop—and suppose they didn't try to bust Matt and Billy out? Suppose when they snuck back into town they had something else in mind? Or suppose there was a lot of gunfire in the dark and we didn't get them? James, I had to do it this way; I had to trade off the two in the jailhouse for the pair I want for murder. I'd have to turn Matt and Billy loose anyway."

McGregor squinted in the darkness. "Those stolen horses was all you needed to—"

"James, damn it, I told you: That old mossback told Rusty he wasn't going to wait around. He took his horses out of the public corrals and left."

"You could have gone after him. How far could he get drivin' horses ahead of him?"

Fogarty's reply was delayed until a flash of temper had passed, then he said, "Far enough so's if I caught up with him, unless I used a gun, he wouldn't have come back, and meanwhile I'd have had nothing to bring Matt and Billy before a judge with."

McGregor was quiet for a while. It wasn't comfortable in the old shed, and when one of the horses peed, there was enough ammonia scent in the air to make a man's eyes water. Eventually he shifted position a little and resumed his garrulousness. "Suppose they didn't have in mind raidin' the damned bank."

"Why else would they risk hanging around after they busted Matt and Billy out? They'd already robbed the general store. Common sense tells you there's only one source of money left, Donner's bank."

McGregor did not dispute this, but he said, "There's no guarantee they'll come for these particular horses."

That was even too specious for Pepperdine, who rolled his eyes in the darkness before saying, "James, you're doin' it again. You're bein' pigheaded so's you won't have to admit you could be wrong. Like Joe told us earlier, the older ones, Sam'l and Josh, are murderers. Those two kids are just tools the older fellers use. An' I'll tell you what I think. Sam'l and Josh wouldn't have busted the lads out unless they'd already hatched a scheme to use them again—to draw men after them while Sam'l and Josh hung back to rob the bank."

McGregor said no more. He lifted out his six-gun, hefted it with professional concern, leathered it and leaned a little so he could see past the dozing horses into the alley. It was much lighter in the alley, even without moonlight, than it was inside the shed.

Joe, who had originally considered hiding inside the bank with his companions, had abandoned that idea because in order to get inside, he'd have to rouse Donner and get him to hand over the key. And Fogarty knew, as surely as he knew his own name, Pete would not do so.

A frenzy of dog barking erupted behind the shed somewhere, over in the direction of the most distant residences, over where Pete Donner lived. It continued until Pepperdine said, "Damned raccoons in someone's trash bin again." Eventually the barking stopped, silence returned, and the waiting became more difficult, but not even McGregor complained.

Fogarty was leaning against a low manger, arms crossed,

gazing out into the alley, thinking of his meeting with Mary Ellen Randolph. She had come up through a dogtrot looking slightly disheveled and breathless. He was surprised to see her emerge from between two buildings hatless and obviously upset. He hadn't said anything until she pulled him into the recessed doorway of Dennis's store and poured out the details of her experience in the alley on her way back to the hotel from Andy Dexter's place.

She'd looked particularly appealing, and because she clung to his arm, he'd been of two minds while listening to her; interested in what she said, and equally as interested, even a little more than equally as interested, in her. Even on a star-bright but moonless night she was extremely attractive.

He had walked her up as far as the harness shop, which was only a short distance south of the hotel, and had left her to continue on alone because he'd seen Pepperdine and McGregor leaning comfortably on Hugh's counter, talking.

She had squeezed his hand before leaving him and he had squeezed back.

Pepperdine spoiled Fogarty's thoughts with a hiss. He raised a long arm in the direction of the alley. Both Fogarty and McGregor straightened up to look. Hugh continued to point but remained silent even after all three men heard something.

It was a sound of whispery movement coming down from the north. Fogarty stepped forward with an outstretched arm to warn his companions to remain where they were.

The shuffling noise stopped and was followed by the rattle of metal. Joe eased up into the shed opening, leaned with a hand on his six-gun, and peeked out.

A mother skunk with four very small exact copies of her were sniffing around a trash barrel. Fogarty straightened back, gestured, then pointed when McGregor and Pepperdine crept up to look.

Eventually the mother skunk gave it up. The barrel was too full and therefore too heavy for her to tip over. She waddled on her way, with the smaller skunks lined out single file behind her.

The men settled back again. Only Pepperdine made a comment. "Just as well she didn't tip it over. That's Dagget's trash barrel. She'd have got ptomaine poisoning."

There were two twenty-one-strand horsehair cinches on the manger near McGregor, and for lack of anything else to do, he examined them. They had been removed from the saddles of the dozing horses only moments after the three men had entered the shed.

Without any preliminaries, Pepperdine said, "Joe, the more I think on it, the more it seems to me them bastards are pretty good at their trade. They didn't know that old peddler'd come along."

McGregor said, "Wouldn't have made much difference, if they'd already figured out to come back."

"Sure it made a difference," the harness maker said with spirit. "It give 'em one hell of a good way to drive right up Main Street without anyone payin' attention to them."

Silence returned and lingered until Hugh asked if the marshal had a watch. Joe flicked open the case but could not make out the hands in the dark, so he moved closer to the front entrance before he said, "A little past midnight," snapped the case closed, and was starting to move back when he stopped stone still.

McGregor and Pepperdine could see him near the entrance. Both older men slowly straightened up as Fogarty put a finger to his lips, leaned slightly but did not expose himself as he cocked his head for a moment before stepping soundlessly back in the direction of the manger. With the faces of his companions pale but visible, he raised a finger again to his lips.

It was a very long wait. What Fogarty had heard was the faintly discernible sound of a heavy door being opened and closed. The bank's door was thick oak with steel strapping. There was only one other such door in Sheridan; down at

Dennis's store. Fogarty discarded that possibility almost as quickly as it occurred to him.

One of the horses awakened, looked around, stamped a hind foot, and slumped back into a doze.

When enough time had passed, Joe whispered to his friends. "They should have been here by now. Unless what I heard was them going into the bank, not coming out of it."

McGregor whispered back. "Either way, they'll be coming along directly."

Pepperdine looked down his nose at his old friend but said nothing. McGregor's statement was proof that the cantankerous old haggis eater had believed all along the carriage shed was the best place to ambush the renegades.

The night was turning chilly, which none of them noticed because one of the horses threw up its head and tried to swing sideways so it could look out into the alley. The saddle fell to the ground, which spooked both animals. Only Fogarty's quick action prevented one or perhaps both of the horses "setting back" and breaking their reins, which would have allowed them to spring out of the shed and go racing in panic up or down the alley.

Fogarty slapped the saddleless horse on the rump with his hat. The animal came up on its reins as Joe moved to strike the saddled horse, but it evidently wasn't a "halter puller" because, although it had set back, it had not done it with much force.

Pepperdine turned the air blue with whispered profanity as he retrieved the saddle, put it back atop the horse from which it had fallen, and took a position close enough to the animal's head to be able to grab the cheekpiece if the animal did anything like that again.

Fogarty eased up to the opening to listen. If anyone out there had heard the brief commotion, they were not moving. He waited long enough to feel reassured, then moved back to the manger.

McGregor shuffled to the opening to listen, remained over there until he heard the same solid sound in the middle distance Fogarty had heard a half hour earlier. James moved to one side of the opening in darkness to hiss at the other two. "Bank door opened and closed. Hard to hear from that far off, but I know that door."

Pepperdine, who'd argued with the gunsmith over the years about which one was losing his hearing, had to forego this splendid opportunity. At least for now.

Joe swung his arms, flexed his fingers, twisted his body from side to side and blew out a sigh. It had been a long wait. Long enough to doubt his own convictions about this ambush. Relief made him feel much better.

Now the wait was accomplished in total silence without anyone moving except Hugh, who occasionally squinted at the horse he was holding. If Pepperdine's hearing was not all it had been once, the horse would pick up any sound in the alley.

What all three men eventually heard was not hastening footsteps. It was the slightly nasal, patronizing voice of someone speaking aloud but quietly, who said, "Now then, Mr. Banker, see how painless that was?"

There was no answer. Not even when another voice said, "You still got your damned silver. Stuff weighs a ton."

The three men in the shed slowly lifted out their belt guns. Their eyes were fixed on the shed opening and they scarcely breathed as the bantering voice sounded a little closer.

"You don't never want to underestimate folks, Mr. Banker. Fellers like you think all the brains in the world is inside your own heads. But tonight you learnt different, didn't you?"

This time there was a response. The men inside the old shed recognized Donner's voice at once when he said, "It'll ruin my bank." Donner hadn't sounded like he was whining, he sounded as though he were having difficulty believing the robbery had happened.

The bantering voice sounded amused now. "Naw. All them storekeepers an' cattlemen'll commence savin' again. Hell, by next year you'll be in good shape. Mr. Banker, you hadn't ought to begrudge a couple of hard-workin' fellers makin' a decent living.''

This time Donner sounded as though he were having trouble speaking. ''The bank'll never recover. It takes years to get folks to put their money in a bank. It's happened before. Folks'll lose their faith in the bank. It'll have to close.''

This time the men were close enough to the shed entrance for the ambushers to hear one of them laugh before he said, ''Tell you what, Mr. Banker. You come along with us. We'll get you this much money an' more. All you got to do is ride hard now an' then, maybe shoot folks a little.'' The speaker broke off to laugh again, but his companion, who had demonstrated no humor on Donner's back porch, did not demonstrate it now when he said, ''Sam'l, quit it. We're wastin' time.''

Nothing more was said. By now the men in the shed could distinctly hear steps in the alley. The horses also heard and raised their heads. Pepperdine was ready to stop either of them from moving. They could turn their heads but that was all.

The footsteps halted. For a moment there was total silence, then the listeners heard what sounded like a stick breaking followed by something falling.

Fogarty's jaw muscles rippled. Donner was now out of it. Whatever happened next he would not know.

The man called Josh spoke in his crisp, quick tone of voice. ''You sure these sacks'll hold? Once we're movin' there's goin' to be a lot of bouncin' around an' that gold's heavy.''

The only answer was a snarling sound as Sam'l approached the shed.

The men inside were poised, guns gripped in sweaty fists.

Sam'l stopped just short of the opening to turn back when Josh said, ''We'd do a lot better not goin' north to meet Billy and Matt. Them townsmen'll be all over the country out there.''

This time when Sam'l spoke the bantering sound was gone.

"We're going south. Due south until we're as far south as those horses'll pack us, then we're goin' to get fresh ones and head for Mexico through the mountains. Billy and Matt are used up as far I'm concerned."

Fogarty had a straight view of the opening. Hugh and James were to one side. They would be unable to see the outlaws until they stepped into the opening.

Sam'l was almost in Fogarty's view. In fact he could see an arm and part of a shoulder when Josh spoke again. "I thought we agreed to head for California. To the Barbary Coast out there where the livin' is good."

Sam'l's bantering tone returned as he said, "Sure, that's what we agreed on, but Mexico's closer an' they can't come over the line to get us down there. Wait a month or so, then we'll up stakes and go out yonder. Josh, give me one of them sacks. By golly they are heavy. If I'd known we'd end up with a lot of gold, I'd have got us saddlebags."

"It's not too late. Sure as hell this here old bullion sack is goin' to come loose. You could lead the horse down the alley while I go across the road, bust open that old man's harness shop door, and get us a pair of saddlebags."

Sam'l growled again. "That damned banker's not going to sleep forever. We wasted enough time. Look up, the sky's goin' to start gettin' light soon. Ride with the sack in your lap, that ought to keep it from bouncin' too much."

CHAPTER THIRTEEN

Before a Cold Dawn

In retrospect, Joe Fogarty would remember that nothing had happened fast.

The renegade who was incongruously attired in ill-fitting, soiled old clothing with a dented derby hat on the back of his head stepped into the shed doorway juggling a heavy sack with both hands. He did not look up even when the horses shifted slightly in an effort to see behind themselves.

His companion, the man called Josh, who had seemed less inclined to joke than his friend, was directly behind Sam'l, but as he'd already demonstrated, Josh was an alert, nervous individual. He saw Pepperdine holding the horse and stopped abruptly. As he made a gasping sound, his partner started to twist to look back. Then Josh screamed. "Ambush, Sam'l." He dropped his heavy sack, and instead of doing what the ambushers had expected—go for his gun—spun away and within seconds was fleeing southward down the alley, beyond sight of the men in the shed who were raising their weapons. Sam'l had only seconds to make a decision, and he was hampered by his two-handed grip on the heavy bullion sack.

Three handguns were cocked in the very short period of time when Sam'l had to make his decision. Each cocking sound underscored the futility of whatever Sam'l might ordinarily have attempted.

Fogarty did not raise his voice. "Don't move! Drop the sack! Put your hands atop your head!"

Sam'l obeyed each order with agonizing slowness, unable to quickly recover from shock, and perhaps also trying desperately to find some course that would help him in a hopeless situation.

McGregor stepped over and tossed the outlaw's gun aside. He groped for a belly gun or a boot knife and found neither. James was turning back when Fogarty passed him in a rush.

Pepperdine left the horses to approach his friend and the outlaw. His cocked six-gun dangled from one fist at his side as he gently wagged his head and spoke reproachfully. "Sam'l, you're a miserable son of a bitch." Pepperdine pushed past, stepped out into the alley, listened briefly to the sound of Joe Fogarty running southward, then strolled up to where Pete Donner was lying in the manured alley dust with a trickle of blood down one cheek.

Pepperdine rolled Donner onto his back, then leaned far down to examine the scalp wound where a gun barrel had struck. When Donner groaned, Pepperdine arose, making a little clucking sound as he said, "Out in your bedclothes this time of night. You ought to be ashamed." He turned back where McGregor was herding Sam'l toward a dogtrot and Main Street beyond.

There was no sign of the town marshal or the outlaw he'd pursued. By the time Hugh and James got their prisoner and the pouch of gold to the jailhouse, Pete Donner had recovered consciousness in the alley and was sitting with both hands to his head, gradually focusing on the bullion pouch which had been dropped in the alley by Josh.

When Pete could stand, he moved over beside the pouch and touched it with a foot to make sure it wasn't empty. The night was now silent, the cold was increasing, and Donner turned slowly as it occurred to him that he was alone. Something had happened about which he had not the slightest idea. But he picked up the pouch, gritted his teeth against the roaring pain in his head, and staggered through darkness until he reached the bank. There he opened the door, closed it after himself, put the pouch on his desk and fainted. Whatever else Pete Donner was, no one would ever question his dedication to the bank.

Down at the jailhouse, where the other pouch was sitting atop Fogarty's desk and the man who had dropped it was sitting dispiritedly on a wall bench, Pepperdine was building a fire for coffee. His friend the gunsmith was considering the man in the old derby hat with a stone-set face, still holding his cocked Colt.

McGregor was never loquacious. Hugh was, but for the moment he was having trouble with a smoking stove, until the gunsmith growled at him. "Open the damper."

McGregor then turned his attention back to the man in the incongruous getup. "If they don't hang you, I'm goin' to close up shop and leave this damned town."

Sam'l said nothing. He avoided looking directly at the dour gunsmith. When Hugh finally had the kindling blazing and slammed the little iron door, he straightened up, dusted his hands and looked at their prisoner. Pepperdine's disposition was very different from the demeanor of his friend. He went to a chair, dropped down, shoved his feet out, thumbed his old hat back and regarded Sam'l. Hugh sounded almost detached when he spoke.

"Y'know, when I was breakin' horses I used to think there never was a horse I couldn't find somethin' about him I liked. An' until tonight I about half felt the same way about people. But you, mister, you convinced me I been wrong about people. I can't think of a single damned thing about you I admire. Not a single damned thing. Why did you shoot that old man in the general store? He was as harmless as a baby. An' tellin' your friend in the alley you was goin' to abandon Matt and Billy . . . What's your full name?"

The prisoner answered quietly. "Sam'l Walsh."

"Mr. Walsh, if I never do anythin' else in this life, I want to lean on the rope when they break your neck."

For ten seconds there was silence inside the jailhouse and

out. Then two explosions occurred, one from a handgun, one from a shotgun. Their echoes ran up through town like cannon shots. Dogs began barking as Hugh shoved up to his feet and jerked his head.

He and James locked Sam'l Walsh into the same cell that had held Matt and Billy. There were no more gunshots, but the old men returned to the empty roadway where here and there a lamp could be seen brightening to life in the wake of those loud explosions.

The men turned southward in the direction of the livery barn. When they got down there no one was in sight, several stalled horses were nervously stamping, and the hanging lamp midway along the runway was gustily smoking. Visibility was limited, which wasn't very good even when the mantel was clean.

McGregor said, "I'll go down the south side." Hugh nodded and went over among the spidery shadows of corral stringers. The old peddler horse awakened long enough to watch him climb through, then went back to sleep as the lanky silhouette made its way toward the alley.

Northward, several hastily-dressed armed men met in front of Morton's saloon to stand in uncertain bewilderment. One of them was Rusty, and it would be recalled later that while the others still had shirttails half out of their britches, the saloon man was properly attired and had even taken time to put on a different brocaded vest from the one he'd worn during the day.

With nothing further to guide them, the men stood like statues looking down where those sounds had come from, until one of them said, "I sure don't favor goin' down there when I got no idea what's goin' on."

The others agreed even after one said, "Did you see someone slippin' through the public corral?" His companions looked stonily at him. They had seen nothing, and as dark as it was, they didn't believe he had either.

Another man, stocky, rumpled, with a nose like a strawberry, shivered and faced Morton. "Ain't no sense in standin' out here to freeze. Open up, Rusty, an' I'll stand a round while we ponder a little.''

Rusty was agreeable and had the door unlocked when they all distinctly heard someone either fall over or stumble against a loose corral stringer near Lee's barn.

They stopped, but when there was no further noise, the man with the puckery red nose shoved whoever was in front of him and said, ''Horse bumped something. Come on, I'm freezing.'' His companions followed Rusty into the saloon.

What had indeed sounded like a horse rattling around was Hugh Pepperdine climbing through and catching a boot heel on a stringer and sprawling flat in the darkness, stifling the curses that rose naturally in his throat. Otherwise there was not a sound as McGregor moved stealthily down the south side of Lee's barn, gun cocked and gripped as he approached the alley. When he could see the old peddler's wagon, which blocked his view of the corral beyond it, where loose stock was milling, he had to abandon shelter and go sideways out into the open.

The gunfire could have spooked those horses, and probably had, but even frightened horses did not have a very long memory. The gunshots had sounded at least fifteen minutes earlier.

McGregor only had a short distance to cover before he'd be able to see into the corral, but he'd be exposed. Darkness or not, McGregor had not achieved his present advanced age by being imprudent.

He did move a short distance away from the barn's protection, though not enough to see around behind the old wagon, and when Hugh made a racket falling over that stringer, McGregor went quickly back to cover.

Hugh did not try to arise after his mishap, and the darkness he'd cursed for having contributed to his fall he now hoped would conceal him as long as he didn't move.

There were milling horses south of him. He could see them without too much interference from the old wagon, and like the gunsmith, he did not believe they were still spooked by the earlier gunfire.

But for a long time he saw nothing but moving livestock. When a fluidlike silhouette moved into his view very briefly, then passed from sight behind the wagon, Pepperdine pushed warily up off the ground and slipped to cover near the northeast corner of the barn, where he would not be seen. He could no longer see into the corral very well, and waited for his lungs to recover and his heart to settle a little before he began edging around toward the barn's darkly weathered and badly warped rear wall.

He was poised to whip around the corner when someone inside the barn fired off one shotgun barrel, driving Hugh back flat against the north wall again.

There was no return fire, but something else happened. The wooden slide bar that held the corral gate closed shattered into a hundred pieces and the gate swung violently inward from impact. The already nervous animals inside needed nothing further; they streamed out the opening behind a big jug-headed grulla gelding and thundered northward up the alley. Two-thirds of the town would be wide awake, bewildered, and for the most part unwilling to rush forth, even though it had been common knowledge outlaws might raid the town this night and most of the townsmen had been making grisly predictions about what they would do to any renegades who dared enter Sheridan this particular night.

McGregor, baffled by that shotgun blast, hugged the opposite side of the barn, wondering where Pepperdine was. A scratchy voice yelled from the dark barn runway. "You ain't goin' nowhere, mister, so you might as well pitch your gun into the alley and walk out of the corral."

Instead of an answer, someone's red muzzle blast made a brilliant flash for a fraction of a second from the corral, and was answered immediately by another blast from the west side of the poles.

Silence settled behind diminishing echoes.

Eventually a voice both the harness maker and the gunsmith recognized called out toward the barn. "You can ease up the hammer on the shotgun."

The response was both swift and full of relief. "You got him?"

As he was climbing inside the corral, Fogarty acknowledged he did. "Yeah."

Again silence settled. It was broken from the south side of the barn. "That you, Joe?"

"James? Yeah, it's me. Where's Hugh?"

Pepperdine answered as he boldly walked around into sight. "Here."

Fogarty called back. "Go get Henry."

Pepperdine turned dutifully up the alley as McGregor emerged from the side of the barn, walked into the corral and halted where Marshal Fogarty was down on one knee beside the man called Josh. James said, "Dead?"

"No, but he's hit hard, the damned fool."

Josh groaned and tried to grasp a bloody upper leg with both hands. Fogarty yanked loose his britches belt and snugged it up tight, held it that way and looked unsympathetically at the man he'd shot as the livery-barn hostler arrived with his shotgun.

They did what they could to make the wounded man comfortable, which wasn't a hell of a lot, until Reg Lee's scarecrow of a hostler returned with an armload of dirty old tan army blankets. They covered Josh, fashioned a pillow, and the hostler stood sucking his teeth, a noise in the silent night that annoyed Hugh, who reached over and rapped the hostler in the ribs to make him stop.

Fogarty asked Pepperdine about the other one, and was told he'd been locked into a cell after Hugh and James heard the gunfire at the lower end of town.

Dr. Pohl arrived, hair askew, shirttail partially out, looking as harassed as he felt after being routed out twice the same night. The others stood aside. Henry made a professional tourniquet, handed Fogarty back his belt and, sounding a little cross, said, "Make a sling out of the blankets and bring him along."

The little cavalcade made its way up the alley to the rear of Henry's cottage. This time he hadn't been able to leave the house without awakening Eleanor, who met them at the back door fully dressed and with both hands to her mouth as they lugged the groaning, bloody outlaw through her kitchen.

Henry ordered everyone out of his examination room except Joe Fogarty. After the others had departed, Henry looked up from the broken leg which was beginning to swell, turning purple, and said, "Where's the other one?"

"Locked up."

The wounded man was grinding his teeth, an audible sound that sent Henry quickly and efficiently to work. The only noise for a while was made when Henry told Joe to pull until the bone ends meshed. The outlaw tried not to cry out, but probably because Henry wasn't satisfied and Joe stretched harder the second time, the man finally tried to muffle the scream but was not altogether successful.

Joe said, "Why don't you give him some laudanum, Henry?"

Pohl went on working as though he had not heard, and when he eventually looked up at Marshal Fogarty, his gaze was sulfurous. "Because it's only a busted leg with some flesh damage. Who shot him?"

"I did. In the corral across the alley from Reg's barn. He was trying to catch a horse to escape."

"You couldn't have called on him to stand before you fired?"

"Henry, he fired first, and yellin' would only have helped him find me in the dark."

The door opened and both men looked up. Mary Ellen Randolph stood in the opening with Eleanor behind her. Pohl looked down again, ignoring them both. Mary Ellen approached the opposite side of the bed, considered the bandaging process, and smiled at Fogarty. "I told you. He's very talented."

That brought Henry's head up. "Thank you. This is the second call tonight. The first one the man was already dead, so why they had to awaken me I'll never know. Dead men don't get on a horse and ride away."

There was a commotion on the front porch. Eleanor turned in that direction as Henry addressed Mary Ellen. "Put your thumb there. Don't let it slip."

She obeyed, leaned, then said, "Doctor, there's a lot of swelling."

Henry's voice recovered its waspishness. "You noticed, did you?" The sarcasm dripped.

Joe caught the handsome woman's eye and shook his head. She did not say another word until the bandaging was completed, and even then she did not have much of an opportunity to speak because McGregor and Pepperdine came pushing inside, supporting Pete Donner.

Fogarty and Henry Pohl stared at the banker from different perspectives. Fogarty had not taken time to examine the banker in the alley and was surprised to see how swollen his head and face were. Henry Pohl looked at Donner as another casualty in a night the like of which he had never experienced before. He pointed to a chair. Hugh and James got Donner settled and told Joe they'd been passing the bank and noticed the door was ajar. They had looked in and there he was, pouch of gold on his desk and Donner unconscious on the floor in front of it.

Joe passed Mary Ellen Randolph on his way out behind McGregor and Pepperdine. They exchanged a smile. He winked and she winked back.

There was now a distinct chill to the night, and while starshine was still about the only source of illumination, it too was fading. Dawn was not far off.

Hugh and James were tired. So was Marshal Fogarty, but he was a good twenty-five years younger than they were. McGregor, who was not exactly glad that they hadn't killed the two outlaws, was not entirely disappointed both were alive either. He said, "It wouldn't be seemly to hang a man with a busted leg, would it?"

Joe considered the craggy, lined face in porch gloom. "By the time a circuit rider gets to town, he ought to be able to get around a little. Hanging's up to the judge."

Pepperdine nudged the gunsmith. "Let's go. Joe, it ought to be over, hadn't it?"

Fogarty shrugged. "There's still a couple of loose ones."

Pepperdine had already made a judgment about that. "With that old stockman gone, what's the sense of ridin' your tail off after someone you can't stand up before a judge?"

Fogarty nodded, watched the older men troop to the little gate and beyond, down toward their places of business, where each man lived in a lean-to out back, and he smiled to himself. He was preparing to also depart when the door opened behind him and the handsome woman came out.

She did not seem aware of his presence; she looked at the cold, fading sky with its feeble starlight, looked northward, where a distant faint whisper of sound indicated that a number of horsemen were approaching town at a slow walk. She finally turned and smiled. "Eleanor came up to the hotel. I don't believe Dr. Pohl liked having me walk in like that."

Joe leaned on a porch upright. "He liked it. When I shook my head for you not to say anymore, it was because Henry doesn't like conversation under those circumstances. I know that from experience. He can get pretty sharp sometimes."

Mary Ellen's response also came from experience. "They all can, Marshal."

"Joe."

She smiled but looked away. "Joe. That man lost quite a bit of blood."

"Too much?"

"I don't think so. Usually if they die of that kind of injury, it's because of infection. Where did it happen, Joe?"

"In the corral across the alley behind the livery barn."

"Dirty corral?"

"Well, yes'm."

Her smiled faded and she changed the subject. "What happened to the other one? As I told you, I saw two in the alley."

"He's locked up."

"After the banker came to, he said they forced him to open the safe."

"Didn't do 'em any good, Mary Ellen."

She changed the subject again. "That box my uncle left with Mr. Dexter—he promised to find someone to carry it up to my room at the hotel in the morning." Her eyes ironically twinkled in the predawn cold. "My uncle was a wealthy man, did you know that?"

Joe hadn't, and in fact he had trouble believing it. She laughed softly. "Two hundred thousand dollars in the box, along with a number of other, personal things."

Joe stared at her.

"Two hundred thousand dollars engraved 'Treasury of the Confederate States of America.' " She moved toward the porch steps as she said, "I'm going to miss Sheridan, Joe. I packed this evening to be ready to leave in the morning. Good night."

He watched her pass through the little gate and turn in the direction of the hotel. When he could no longer see her, Joe reset his hat and also left Henry Pohl's porch. By this time the sky was steadily brightening toward morning and the cold had reached its peak. The temperature would remain until the sun arrived over false fronts and rooftops to the east of town, but even then the chill would not leave entirely until the sun was climbing.

Joe entered his cold, dark jailhouse office, fired up the little iron stove, tossed his hat aside, and placed the speckleware coffeepot atop the stove. He was fiddling with the stove damper when the first of the impromptu town riders walked in out of the cold.

It was the blacksmith's apprentice, probably the youngest and toughest of the riders who had tried to run down the pair of fleeing escapees. He went to stand with his back to the stove as he said, "Too damned dark, Marshal, and although we scouted in all directions up yonder, we never found 'em. Tell you what I think; we couldn't have been too far behind 'em, but every time we stopped to listen, there wasn't a sound. I think those lads been through this before. They sure as hell stopped so's we couldn't hear anything. They may be young, but they sure as hell aren't green."

Joe thanked the burly man, saw him out, and returned to his desk until the coffee was hot. Then he went down into the cell room.

He could have put this off for a few hours, but he didn't.

CHAPTER FOURTEEN

Ambush!

Sam'l Walsh rubbed sleep out of his eyes even after he'd been brought to the office, told where to sit, and had been given a cup of hot coffee.

Joe explained what had happened to his friend Josh and asked what the wounded man's full name was. Sam'l answered without hesitation. "Joshua Hobart. Got hit hard, did he?"

"Hard enough. He won't be walking much for a while. Sam'l, who shot the store clerk?"

Again the renegade did not hesitate before answering. "Josh did. I walked out front to see if there was anyone around. I untied the horses. He was almost to the door when he turned and shot the old man."

"Why?"

Sam'l tasted the coffee before answering. "He could identify us."

"There were two men in the store," Joe stated.

Sam'l lowered the cup. "Yeah. I didn't ask why he didn't shoot the other one too, an' we was too busy afterwards to talk about it."

"Who shot the old peddler?"

This time Sam'l hung fire and made a gesture of sipping more coffee. When he finally lowered the cup he did not look at Fogarty. "The old fool heard us an' was reachin' inside the wagon for a big old hawleg pistol. I shot him in self-defense."

Fogarty hadn't touched his coffee cup until now. He half emptied it and leaned on the littered table, had to push the bullion sack aside to get more room, and said, "There wasn't a gun. At least not where anyone could have reached it without climbin' in."

"He was reachin' for somethin' an' it was goin' to be a gun," Sam'l retorted defensively, still without meeting Fogarty's gaze.

Joe did not pursue this. "Where were you an' Josh supposed to meet Matt and Billy?"

"North. Up in the hills somewhere. They'd be watchin' for us to come along." As the outlaw spoke, he rose to refill his cup at the stove. He returned to the bench and said, "Didn't find them, did they?"

"No," replied the marshal, "an' no one's going to try real hard to. They're riding a pair of stolen horses. You and Josh got them from the corral across the alley from the livery barn. What did you do with that pair of H.E. horses you left town on after the raid?"

"Turned 'em loose when we had the peddler's outfit. Wouldn't be real wise to trail them back here behind the wagon, would it? Folks seen us on them. You saw us too. Turned 'em loose where some rancher or his riders'll come on to them."

Sam'l got comfortable on his bench. The room was warm, finally, and beyond the barred window dawn was breaking. Joe finished his coffee but did not refill the cup.

Sam'l said, "Liveryman get back them two horses in the carriage shed?"

"He will this morning. They're still tied over there."

Sam'l gazed at the cloth pouch with little sacks of gold in it. "How'd you happen to be in that shed, Marshal?"

"Someone saw the four of you in the alley, saw two leave

town and two tie the horses in there. . . . Sam'l, you're up to your neck in trouble. You an' Josh both.''

The outlaw made a death's-head smile. The gap in his lower jaw was visible. "We never been in anything else, Marshal. We're not the only ones. Anywhere you go between Montana an' Messico, California to Missouri, you'll find fellers who got no other way to exist except with a gun. If you been at the marshaling trade for long, you got to know that.''

The ring of keys in his hand, Fogarty got up to his feet as he replied to the renegade. "You're right, I've met my share of 'em. But not too many back-shooters. Finish the coffee and I'll lock you up.''

The outlaw rose and looked Joe squarely in the eye. ''When's the judge coming?''

Joe had no idea. As he herded Walsh back into the cell room he said, "When he gets here. They have schedules, but I've yet to know one to arrive when he was supposed to.''

As Joe locked the door, Sam'l turned with a little smile. "I'll tell you somethin', Marshal. My folks didn't raise no son to be hanged.''

Fogarty returned to the office, closed the stove damper, locked the door from the outside and walked northward in the direction of the roominghouse hotel. On the opposite side of Main Street the only building showing signs of life was Dagget's cafe. The window was fogged from the heat inside, where the cafeman was firing things up for the break-fast trade.

He was passing Pepperdine's harness shop when the morn-ing stage emerged from the corral yard. It made a big, wide sweeping turn before it could line out southward with burly Jack Carpenter on the high seat. Mary Ellen looked out at the marshal.

Joe stopped as she raised a hand in a little wave. He waved back but without any enthusiasm. The driver got his outfit heading south and whistled the hitch up into a fast walk.

She did not lean out to look back, and Fogarty did not move until the coach was nearing the lower end of town. Then, as he turned, Silas Browning beneath his huge old hat made a sniffing sound. To add to the incongruity of Silas's appearance, he had a thick woolen muffler wrapped around his throat. The old man wagged his head and spoke while also gazing after the stagecoach.

"Yonder goes the nicest thing that's come into Sheridan since I can remember. Didn't know she was a nurse, did you?"

"Yes, I knew."

Silas glared. "How'd you know?"

Fogarty considered the older man with a hard stare. "Because Henry told me, and I met her up at his place last night where Henry was patching up the outlaw who got shot out behind the livery barn."

As Joe continued on past, Silas's venomous glare followed him all the way to the hotel. Only when the marshal passed from sight beyond the front door did the old man step to the edge of the plankwalk, lustily expectorate, and return to his corral yard. The first person he encountered was a thick stubby Mexican yardman named Galindo. Silas stared at him. "What'n'ell you standin' around for?"

The Mexican did not respond, and then walked away, leaving Silas glaring after him too.

When the sunshine finally arrived, it brightened the entire town without noticeably warming it. Rusty Morton swept out his place of business wearing a flour-sack apron. For the first time since the death of his clerk, Hank Dennis opened the general store.

Elsewhere, tired men who had ridden with the morning posse, and the later one in the night, were sleeping the rest of the just, exactly as Joe Fogarty was doing. The marshal continued to do so right up until someone started banging on his door with a fist, making such a racket that the rooming-house proprietor came charging from his kitchen. He yelled something about folks trying to sleep and what in the hell did old Pepperdine want that wouldn't wait another hour or so.

Pepperdine ignored the angry man and continued beating on the door until Joe opened it. Pepperdine said, "You better get your britches on an' come down to the corral yard."

Fogarty scratched, eyed the lanky older man, and without a word turned back to get dressed. The proprietor looked in and said, "Now what? I got to tell you, I lived in this town dang near as many years as you are old, an' for a damned fact there's never been as much hoorawhing goin' on as has been goin' on around here the last few days."

Fogarty stamped into his boots, buckled the shell belt around his middle, and reached for his hat before the old man went back to his kitchen. The mush he had been cooking had boiled down to about the size and consistency of a rubber ball.

There was a small crowd in the corral yard, with Silas rushing around like an anxious mother hen trying to shoo them out the gates. A stagecoach was standing in the center of the yard with its pole on the ground, both doors open and everyone talking at once. Fogarty had to shoulder his way through to where Pepperdine and McGregor were standing with Rusty Morton. McGregor eyed him disconsolately and pointed to blood on the ground beneath the near-side door. "Got waylaid five, six miles below town," was all he said, but Hugh went over beside the coach with Marshal Fogarty to add a little more.

As Joe regarded the bloody interior of the stagecoach, his heart sank. He knew this coach, had watched it leave town dozens of times. It was the same rig Mary Ellen Randolph had departed on. He was turning when Hugh spoke to him. "It was them boys. They bracketed the coach from each side from out'n some rocks. Jack seen a horse half hid in the underbrush and was haulin' back when they jumped out. He shot one, an' the other one took to his heels, but Jack knew who he was. He loaded the one he'd shot inside for the lady passenger to look after, turned around and came back. Just before you got here the lady got some fellers to carry the lad up to Henry's place."

Fogarty asked if the passenger had been injured, and when Hugh shook his head, Joe looked around the yard for Jack Carpenter. Hugh said, "If you want to talk to Jack, he helped pack the lad up yonder."

Fogarty was leaving the noisy, crowded yard when Silas caught up with him, red-faced angry, with his huge old hat askew. "Wouldn't have happened if you'd chained them devils in their cells," he exclaimed. Fogarty did not even look around.

Up at the doctor's place three men, including the whip, were milling around in the waiting room. When Joe walked in Carpenter said, "Damned fools. I been waylaid ten, fifteen times in my life, an' those two didn't have the sense to find a good place to do it."

Joe brushed explanations aside. "How bad was he hit, Jack?"

"Bad enough. He bled like a stuck hawg. The lady did her damndest, and by golly she was good at it, otherwise he'd have been dead by the time I got back here."

Joe left them and rapped softly on the closed examination-room door. Eleanor admitted him, white-faced and tense. Across the table from the bloody, inert figure, Henry only spared a moment to look up. Mary Ellen, sleeves pushed to her elbows, raised her eyes, nodded, and went back to work as Joe edged close for a look.

It was the lad known as Matt, the tall one. He was stripped to the waist. Mary Ellen had washed him, and a nearby bucket full of blood-soaked cloth indicated that Carpenter hadn't exaggerated. The youth had been hit hard and had bled a lot.

Fogarty watched Henry expertly tying off torn flesh, considered Matt's waxen face and moved back where Eleanor was standing. "Any chance?" he whispered.

She was watching her husband and the nurse when she

replied, also in a whisper. "I don't know. The bullet did a lot of damage."

Henry abruptly said, "Speak out. No need to be quiet. He can't hear you, an' no, I don't think he's got the chance of a snowball in hell. The bullet went clean through him on a downward angle. Mary Ellen! Keep swabbing!"

Joe returned to the parlor. The other men had departed, but Jack Carpenter was still there, standing in front of a side-wall window, looking out. He heard Fogarty behind him and said, "Just a kid, Joe. I didn't have much time. He looked tall as a man."

Fogarty's reply was quietly spoken. "Where did it happen?"

"Below town, down where there's some old lava boulders on both sides of the road. Hell, if they'd known anything, they'd have gone on south, where I had to pass through a thick stand of jack pines. I been stopped down there twice. Them pock-marked boulders could hide a man, but it's open country all around 'em. Poor place to try'n stop a coach . . . I saw a horse's rump on the west side off in a spindly stand of brush."

Carpenter turned. "Like I said, Joe, I been stopped before; a hidden horse to one side of the road means trouble to me. I was haulin' 'em down to a walk from a trot and reachin' for my Colt when those two idiots came out onto the road about a hundred feet ahead. They didn't even have carbines, they had pistols. When they was runnin' for the center of the road, I shot three times. The tall one went down an' the littler one ran like a scairt rabbit. Didn't even look back." Carpenter raised thick shoulders and let them slump. "That's the whole story. Except I didn't know that lady was a nurse, an' the kid can thank God she was. . . . How did he look in there?"

Fogarty avoided an answer that would add to the distraught driver's worries. "They're doing everything that can be done. It wasn't your fault, Jack."

"Yeah. But hell, Joe, he hadn't even begun to shave yet."

Fogarty thought of something McGregor had said one time. When they start using guns, it didn't matter how old they were. Joe then asked, "Were you carryin' bullion or anything valuable?"

Carpenter's voice was raised in protest. "Hell no. Just some light freight in the boot and the good-lookin' lady. That was a crazy thing to do, Joe."

"Sounds like it, but how many highwaymen did you ever hear of that used their heads?"

Eleanor came out to the parlor, blue eyes very dark, chalky features softly set. "Henry doesn't think he can make it through the night, but Mary Ellen and I'll stay with him, do everything that can be done. Mr. Carpenter?"

"Yes'm."

"You don't have to wait."

"Yes'm," Carpenter said, dropped his hat on and left.

Eleanor looked at Marshal Fogarty. "I'm so sick of this, Joe. And I owe you an apology. That youngest one fooled me completely. Henry told me about that, and he was right, wasn't he? Billy was a little scoundrel. But so young, and an orphan . . ."

Fogarty softly smiled. "Nothing to apologize about, Eleanor. He's a professional hypocrite. Hugh said he'd never change. I think he was right. About Matt . . . that's a real heart-wrencher. I got to know him a little at the jailhouse. My feeling was that he really wasn't bad, he just didn't know what else to do, how else to survive. I wish Jack had shot the other one."

Eleanor approached a chair, sank down upon the edge of it, and gazed out the same side-wall window Carpenter had been looking out of. "Just lately," she said, "there's been so much, Joe. More lately than we usually have all year."

He stood watching her profile. Eleanor was a beautiful, robust woman. He'd thought so the first time he'd seen her. She did not belong in range country, but she'd persevered for a number of years, had helped the community, and had been her husband's right hand many times.

She swung her head to meet his gaze. "I'm sick of it, Joe."

He groped for something to say, could come up with nothing, and wisely kept quiet.

"Sometimes they are so young," she went on. "Like that one in there. He hasn't even started to shave yet. Joe . . . ?"

"Yes, Eleanor."

"This won't make sense to you because you're single, but someday I want children. Maybe a girl and a boy. But not out here, not where they shoot young boys."

Joe found some words this time. "Eleanor, you're not balancing things. There are dozens of young boys around town. They'll grow up to own stores and what not. For every one like Jim and Billy, there are hundreds who never even carry a gun."

She arose to move in the direction of the closed door and turned to show him a wan smile as she reached for the knob. "I agree with Henry. He says you're the most level-headed man in Sheridan. And, of course, you're right. It's just that . . ." She smiled, twisted the knob and closed the door after herself.

Fogarty left the house, returned to the corral yard, where old Silas was scolding two men he had cleaning the old coach. Silas peered from beneath his hat brim when Marshal Fogarty walked in looking for Jack Carpenter.

Silas raised a scrawny arm to point rigidly in the direction of the saloon. "Over there. I saw him go in not fifteen minutes ago." The arm dropped as Silas glared. "Always got to go dunk his head in a bottle, don't he? Well, let me tell you, Marshal, when a man does that an' gets down to the bottom, what does he see?"

Fogarty answered quietly. "In Jack's case, he sees the face of the lad he shot lookin' up at him."

Silas still had his mouth open as Fogarty walked out of the yard on his way across to the saloon. Silas saw the pair of hostlers watching him. They'd listened to what had been said and were not even smiling, they were just looking at him.

Silas returned their stares and surprised them both. "There's a good man, boys. There's a man's got heart an' still carries a gun."

As Silas walked away, the hostlers looked at one another big-eyed. Both had worked at the corral yard for a long time, and that was the first time either of them had ever heard old Silas Browning say anything good about another living soul.

CHAPTER FIFTEEN

"Joe!"

When Fogarty had returned the bullion pouch to the bank, Pete Donner had a bandage under his hat, some swelling still in his face, and a pony of brandy on his desk. He shared the bottle with the marshal as he gruffly thanked him for saving the bank's assets. He had also said he'd heard from Silas Browning that his southbound coach had passed a circuit rider up near Bluestem heading south.

Bluestem was about eighty miles north of Sheridan, so Fogarty didn't bother writing up his charges against Sam'l Walsh until the day before he thought the judge would arrive. Instead he hovered between the jailhouse and Henry Pohl's cottage. Mary Ellen had met him on the hotel porch, where she'd got her room back, to say that despite everyone's gloomy predictions, including her own, Matt Hampstead was still desperately hanging on.

She also told him she'd written her fiancé back east that she wouldn't be able to return until an injured boy she was helping the local doctor care for was sufficiently recovered not to need her.

That morning Joe began writing his charges against Sam'l Walsh not only because it had to be done, but also because it kept him busy. Mary Ellen had never before mentioned having a fiancé, but of course that hadn't been obligatory.

She and Joe had become friends. The difficulty for Joe Fogarty was that a woman like Mary Ellen Randolph could never have remained simply a friend.

He cared for his prisoner dutifully, though with very little conversation. When he told Sam'l the judge would be arriving within the next day or so, Sam'l had gazed steadily at him from within his cell without saying a word.

The routine was broken the next day by a scarcely readable letter from the man who had reclaimed two of his H.E. horses and had tired of waiting around for the other two animals to appear. It was authorization for Marshal Fogarty to auction off the other pair of his horses, if they were ever recovered, keep ten percent for his trouble, and mail the balance to an address Joe had to reread three times to understand. Even then he was not sure he'd interpreted it correctly.

When Reg Lee came in to ask about the wounded lad, Joe showed him the letter. Reg handed it back. "Can you read that? It looks like turkey tracks." He sat down to also say, "I was glad he give up and rode home. He was stirrin' up trouble."

Fogarty hadn't worried when he'd been told this before and he didn't worry now. "Cranky old cuss is all, Reg. He couldn't just ride into town, him a stranger, and talk up a lynching. Not in Sheridan."

"How's the lad?"

"Still alive. God knows why, Henry don't. According to Mary Ellen the way that slug—"

"Who is Mary Ellen?"

"That nurse lady. You remember, the one who came to town looking for old Caulfield Randolph."

"Oh. Her. She's helpin' Henry?"

"Yes. She came back on the stage after it was stopped."

"I heard about that," Lee said, and made a wintry smile. "Them damned fools. They'd have done better to stop one of Jack's stages if they'd stood up a bottle of rye whiskey in the middle of the road."

Fogarty let that pass. Jack Carpenter's employer wasn't

the only person in the countryside who'd drawn inferences after seeing Carpenter hike directly over to the saloon after coming in off a run.

Joe said, "They'd have done better to try another coach. Jack's an old hand."

Lee shrugged. "You still got the other one locked up?"

"Yes. I think the judge might get to town maybe tomorrow. I was writing up charges when you came in. Horse stealing, murder, robbery."

Reg smiled. "He'll hang."

Fogarty thought so, but as the liveryman arose to depart, he simply said, "If you hear about those two H.E. horses, let me know," and went back to work after Lee had departed.

An annoying thought kept interrupting his concentration. Mary Ellen had mentioned her fiancé so offhandedly, as though she had been talking to someone whose interest in her had been nothing more than a casual friendship.

He had winked at her and she had winked back. He had squeezed her fingers and she had squeezed back. There wasn't a law that said those things had to mean something, but in a man-woman relationship . . .

"Marshal." Joe looked up. Henry Pohl was standing in the doorway. "Are you busy?"

Joe tossed aside the pencil as he shook his head. "Nothing that won't keep. Come on in, Henry."

Dr. Pohl sat on the edge of a chair, cradling a small black satchel in his lap. "A while back I delivered a baby out yonder a few miles. A ranch family named Buell. Well, it was a tough delivery. The baby was good-sized and the mother was a little slip of a thing. Joe, I have to go back out there. I'll be lucky if I get back before dark. Mary Ellen is staying with the Hampstead youngster. Eleanor's been sitting up with him too. I was wondering if you'd look in on them a time or two before I can get back."

Fogarty nodded. "Sure, but what can I do?"

"Just look in on them, let them know you're around. They both set a lot of store by you, and I'd feel a lot easier." Henry arose and went to the open doorway before also saying, "As far as I can see, there isn't a single medical reason why that boy is still alive. Between you and me, man to man, he's not going to make it and he's prolonging the agony of those two woman by still being here. . . . I'll get back as soon as I can."

Fogarty continued to lean, gazing out into the roadway after Henry had left. Finally he hunched forward, forced himself to complete the list of charges, and finished with the sun high and Sheridan bustling around him. He reread the paper, folded it, then arose, reaching for his hat.

He crossed to the emporium, where Hank greeted him with an unsmiling nod. Hank finished waiting on a pair of women over at the bolt-goods counter and said, "There's talk going around about that lady nurse. Those women I just waited on told me they'd heard she singlehandedly brought that young outlaw back to life."

Joe gazed at the older man without saying a word for a long time, not until he'd leaned on the counter. Then he wagged his head. "Did you ever wonder why people do that, Hank? Start those impossible stories? She worked with Henry and Eleanor and she's a very good nurse, but she's no more a miracle worker than you are. Or than I am."

"The lad, Matt, still alive?"

"As far as I know, he is," Fogarty said, and checked the impulse to repeat what Henry had told him at the jailhouse not half an hour earlier. He straightened up off the counter. "According to my prisoner, it was the one called Josh who shot Arthur Jackson. I guess it'd be safe to say that, wouldn't it, with Josh dead? He died during the night. Gangrene worked fast."

Hank's reply was curt. "Was Josh the one with the broken tooth in his lower jaw?"

"No. That's the one I got locked up."

"Well, the one with the broken tooth walked outside. It was the other one that shot Arthur."

Joe had no difficulty believing that. Even though he'd been

skeptical of Sam'l, he had believed him about that. "You'll need a replacement for Arthur?"

"Yes. The sooner the better. Every time I look around, he's not there. After so many years when I get more customers than one man can handle, I just naturally look around for him to lend a hand. But Joe, it seems indecent to hire another person before Arthur's cold in his grave."

Joe nodded about that and returned to the roadway. Replacing his long-time clerk was something Hank would have to handle by himself. There wasn't a damned thing an outsider could say that wouldn't sound banal.

Pepperdine was making a long-legged crossing from the direction of the gun shop toward his harness works, where two saddled horses were standing hipshot. Old Hugh had seen two possible customers enter his shop while he and James had been discussing the lad in Henry Pohl's sickroom.

The entire town was discussing the youth's fight for life. Even McGregor, to whom outlaws were anathema, had admitted to Hugh that while he was not a praying man, he was mightily tempted if he thought it would help the boy any.

As Hugh was leaving the gun shop he'd said, "Might be better for the lad if you didn't, James."

Fogarty crossed to the west plankwalk and looked in as he passed the harness shop. Two rough, weathered men were hovering around the completed bronc saddle which had been on display in the window but was now on a saddlemaker's horse, without the ratchet strap holding it there.

When he reached Pohl's cottage and turned in where Eleanor was sitting on the porch swing, she smiled as he approached. She leaned to arise, until he pulled off his hat and sank down next to her.

"Still among us?" he asked.

"Yes. Mary Ellen's with him. She's so good with him, Joe. Like a mother. They talk a little, she holds his hand, and once when he cried, she kissed him on the cheek. My heart's ached so much the last few days, there's nothing left but hurt."

They read each other's eyes. Joe sat forward, turning the hat in his hands. He did not say what was in his mind. He instead said, "Henry asked me to stop by in case you needed anything."

She had glistening eyes when she said, "Can you provide a miracle, Joe?"

He did not straighten up nor stop turning the hat. "No. . . . I'd like to see him, though, if you don't think having a lawman walk in on him would upset him."

Eleanor sat awhile with a tiny balled-up lace handkerchief in her fist before abruptly standing up. "I don't know. I have no idea whether it would upset him him or not. We could ask Mary Ellen."

When Eleanor rapped gently on the sickroom door, Mary Ellen opened it and looked quickly from one to the other as Eleanor asked if Marshal Fogarty could see Matt. Without answering, the handsome woman moved aside for them to enter.

Joe, who had seen a lot of ill people, was shocked at the wasted look of the wounded youth. But when Fogarty smiled from the bedside, he noticed the clear-eyed look Matt gave him and said, "I'm glad you're on the mend."

Mary Ellen and Eleanor remained over by the door as Matt spoke in a weak voice. "I reckon you want to know what happened."

Joe shook his head. "No. The stage driver told me."

"When I'm better you'll put me back in a cell."

Joe balanced one of two replies to that and took a chance. "I don't know, Matt. It didn't come off; that'd make a difference, I think."

The youth's alert eyes clung to Fogarty's face and his voice got a little stronger when he said, "He run off, Marshal. He tucked his tail and left me out there."

Joe swung a chair around, straddled it, and leaned on the back. "Matt, I heard Sam'l and Josh talking in the alley. They weren't going north to meet you and Billy, they were going to take the bank loot and head south to Mexico."

Matt did not show any surprise. After a long silence he said, "Yeah. I believe it. It come to me the last year or so that Paul, me'n Billy did the work. Sam'l an' Josh scouted up the places, told us how to do it, then they'd be settin' in the shade when we got back. Marshal, Billy said we had to get some money and some saddleguns. That's why we tried to stop the stage. We had to get fitted out before we left the country."

"Where were you going?"

"Back to New Messico," the youth said. Then, looking Marshal Fogarty straight in the eye, he added, "But that's not where I'm goin', is it?"

Joe smiled while groping for words. "What's wrong with stayin' right here, Matt?"

"Sure, Marshal. That's what I meant. Stayin' here out yonder with Paul."

Joe looked at the women, found no help there, and looked back at the youth. "Matt, you'll win. Partner, anyone who can fight back like you're doing will win." Joe stood up and pushed the chair away. "Want to know something? The whole town's pulling for you. And you've got the best helpers a man could get. Dr. Pohl and Miss Randolph. Matt—"

"Sure, Marshal. Even them two old men who was goin' to burn our feet."

Joe shook his head. "They weren't going to and they didn't have to. Those two old gents could bluff a mountain lion with a den full of pups." Joe leaned and softly touched the youth's shoulder. "You owe me, Matt. Tell you what I'll take to even the score."

"What?"

"Don't give up no matter what. Don't quit. Tell you what . . . the day you walk out of here, I'll give you a horse. For once in your life you won't have to straddle one that don't belong to you. . . . Matt?"

The boy's eyes were wet but he did not look away. "It'll cost you if I get to pick him out, Marshal."

Joe said no more; he had a lump in his throat half the size

of an apple. He winked and Matt wetly winked back. Fogarty passed the two women without looking at them, left the room, and returned to the front porch to put on his hat and blow out a ragged big breath.

Mary Ellen spoke from the doorway. "What you did I've been trying to do."

He turned to face her, expressionless and drained dry.

"He said the town hated him; they'd lynch him if they could." She stepped out onto the porch, said, "Joe," and felt for his hand, squeezed hard and did not let go.

He needed to sit down. He'd never considered himself an emotional individual, at least not one whose emotions could undermine his strength. He glanced at the porch swing without making a move toward it because if he did, he'd have to free his hand. The next thing she said caught his attention.

"Henry said when you came up, if Matt wasn't sleeping, it might help if Eleanor and I let you talk to him."

Fogarty gazed steadily at the handsome woman. Henry . . . doggone him anyway, he'd known Mary Ellen would be waiting. "Yes, well, he said that maybe you and Eleanor would need a little help or something."

"He was right," the handsome woman said, releasing her grip on his fingers. She smiled, moved to the swing, sat down, and continued to smile up at him.

He did not smile back. "Mary Ellen, bein' casual acquaintances isn't easy for me."

Her smile faded but she did not avert her eyes.

He leaned on a porch upright. "I didn't know you were goin' back east to get married. I know it wasn't any of my business, but it was a hell of a jolt."

She had both hands in her lap as she continued to look straight at him. "Joe—"

"It's all right. But that day we went buggy riding out to your uncle's grave, and other times . . . I guess I was a fool. I know I'll be one again, maybe lots of times, but this time . . ."

"Joe—!"

". . . This time it's painful." He straightened up, tugged his hat forward, nodded, and started down the steps as she arose from the swing to call to him.

"*Joe!* Don't walk away from me!"

He turned.

She remained on the porch. "I can't go back. This probably won't make any sense to you. Back there I have my job. I'm one among thousands. Another woman, another nurse in a huge hospital, another person among thousands of other people. Here, people are interested in me, one of them needs me. I mean something to him. I was awake all last night while Matt slept. I wrote a letter to the hospital back there. I wrote another letter to my fiancé. It doesn't make much sense, does it?"

He stood looking at her. "It makes sense, Mary Ellen. But sitting in there with Matt, with your heart bleeding for him, isn't the same as maybe walking out under some trees in broad daylight when you're not upset. If you want to stay, I can tell you the town'll be pleased as punch and so will I. . . . Tell you what. If the circuit rider don't come to town tomorrow, maybe we could go for another buggy ride. Maybe take some sandwiches from the cafe and drive out a ways. Get you out where the air's clear and the sun's warm. Where you can lie back an' watch clouds pass. Relax and rethink things. It's worked for me all my life."

She smiled softly at him. "If I'm not here, I'll be at my room at the hotel. What time, Joe?"

"Be late afternoon if the judge arrives, otherwise maybe about noon."

"Whenever you arrive, I'll be ready," she told him. She quickly returned to the house, closed the door, and stood with her back to it until Eleanor came out and saw her there.

Eleanor stopped stone still, looked anxiously into the handsome woman's face, then said, "Come along. You need something to eat. I ought to be ashamed of myself, not thinking of that before."

Out in the roadway Reg Lee, wearing the black frock coat

he hadn't been able to button in years, was slow-pacing his matched pair of blacks hooked to the elegant hearse with the glass sides. He was driving through town to the distant little knoll where his passenger, old Arthur Jackson, would be buried. Behind him, on foot in the hot sun, getting redder by the minute and carrying his hat instead of wearing it, Hank Dennis led a solemn procession of townsfolk.

Fogarty stood hatless in front of the harness shop as the procession passed. Hugh Pepperdine and James McGregor saw him there from amidst the mourners, muttered something to one another, and neither smiled nor nodded to Fogarty.

The town was nearly empty, afternoon heat was on the way. Horace Dagget was emerging from the jailhouse, where he had provided pails of coffee and stew to the prisoner, when Fogarty came along.

The cafeman looked up to where the funeral procession was beginning to angle northeasterly after clearing town and said, "A man won't really ever know how many folks'll miss him, will he?"

Fogarty thought that was probably true. "Most likely not."

The cafeman said, "I fed your prisoner," and shouldered past on his way back to his place of business.

Joe walked in, hung his hat on the floor, cocked his chair back, planted both booted feet atop the untidy table that served as a desk and half closed his eyes.

Fortunately, old Pepperdine and McGregor would be unable to visit the jailhouse for the next hour or two. Otherwise, if they had walked in, they would certainly have made one of their remarks about how it wasn't often folks saw a grown man wearing an expression identical to one found on the face of a sick calf.

CHAPTER SIXTEEN

The Law

Fogarty reread his document of charges, tossed it aside, and crossed to the cafe for either an early dinner or a late breakfast. On his way back he saw a scarecrow of a gaunt, tall man dressed entirely in black beating dust off himself out front of Lee's barn.

Up until this morning he'd wanted the judge to arrive so Sam'l Walsh could be tried. But now, hovering out front of the jailhouse like an indecisive vulture, Joe envisioned a long day which might eventually overlap the afternoon buggy ride. Might even preclude it altogether.

He went down into the cell room to look in on his prisoner and was turning away when Sam'l spoke from the middle of the cell. "No judge yet, eh?"

Fogarty answered brusquely. "Yeah. He's here," and resumed his hike back to the office. He was locking the cell room door when the gaunt, tall, older man with salt-and-pepper beard stubble walked in and nodded. " 'Morning, Marshal. It's been a while."

The judge crossed to the little stove, shook the pot, took down a thick mug, filled it, and returned to a chair. "Gent that runs the tradin' barn told me you got a good one this time. Murderer an' horse thief." The judge tasted his coffee, and the fact that it was strong enough to float horseshoes in did not faze him.

Fogarty sat at his table. This particular circuit rider was a tediously tiresome man, a stickler on points of law. He carried two thick little books in his saddlebags and would halt a trial at any juncture where he thought it appropriate to sonorously read passages from his law books.

His name was Josiah Featherstone. He was unkindly called "Fuss and Feathers." Fogarty'd brought prisoners up before him many times and still could not predict the sentencing. He handed the judge his written charges, leaned back in silence while His Honor drank coffee and read the charges. When the judge folded them to tuck inside a coat pocket, he said, "Well, if you'll set up the benches, put the flag in its stand at the firehouse, I'll get somethin' to eat an' meet you an' the prisoner up there in an hour."

Featherstone turned back in the doorway. "I understand there was a gang of them. Five or something like that."

Fogarty was arising as he replied. "Two are dead, one's in my cell, one is shot up bad at the doctor's place, and one escaped."

His Honor struck out for the cafe. Fogarty watched him go, then put on his hat, locked up from outside, and went up to the firehouse. There was a Masonic Lodge upstairs, but trials were held downstairs, where Joe lined up benches that ordinarily stood against walls. He inserted the flagstaff into the steel pipe used solely for that purpose, and dusted the scarred old table utilized by judges for trials in Sheridan.

He was still at it when Hugh Pepperdine peeked in, watched briefly, then came forward to help with the table as he said, "Saw the old scarecrow goin' into the cafe."

Joe grunted, made sure the table was facing properly, and shoved back his hat. He would have liked things better if gorilla-built, cigar-chomping Judge Bullard had arrived instead of Featherstone. Bullard worked swiftly and unerringly. His sentences were unvaryingly predictable.

Pepperdine gazed at the only window in the firehouse. It

was slightly to one side and behind the hand pumper against the east wall. There was an array of leather buckets hanging on both walls beside the window. He turned and eyed the town marshal.

"How's the lad doing?"

"He was hanging on when I was up there a while back."

"Rusty said someone told him Henry said he'd never make it."

Fogarty bit back a sharp retort as several local idlers ambled in to select seats up front. When Fogarty said, "I'll fetch the prisoner, Hugh," the idlers' interest quickened.

Fogarty hadn't been gone ten minutes when James McGregor arrived with other townsfolk, but did not look for a seat. He went up where the harness maker was leaning on the firecart and said, "It won't happen, Hugh."

Pepperdine looked down his nose while replying. "All right. But suppose it does an' you're settin' in here listenin' to that old windbag?"

McGregor's poker-faced expression did not alter one iota as he bucked his way through the incoming traffic to go back outside.

When Fogarty removed the wrist irons from his shoulder before opening Walsh's cell door, he pitched them through and told Sam'l to put them on. The marshal waited until this had been accomplished before opening the door and gesturing for the prisoner to precede him.

Sam'l stopped in the office, manacled arms low in front. He said nothing as Fogarty went over to the gun rack to slip the chain loose and take down a shotgun. The marshal went to his desk to load both barrels, snap the thing closed and jerk his head. "Out the door, walk slow, cross the road and walk up to the firehouse. Sam'l, you got a chance with the judge, but if you do something rash, you won't have a chance in hell."

The prisoner gazed at Fogarty as though he would speak, but in the end he went as far as the door, looked northward across Main Street, where people were filing into the fire-house, and wagged his head.

He said nothing until he was being herded from behind up past the saloon, then he turned his head a little. "You know this judge, Marshal?"

"Yes."

"What kind of a reputation's he got?"

Fogarty replied truthfully. "You never know with him whether he's going to give a lecture or pass judgment."

"That's not exactly comforting, is it?"

They were close, people had seen them approaching and were standing aside, staring. Joe gave Sam'l Walsh a brusque order. "Don't stop or talk to anyone. Walk on in and go up front." Joe brushed Walsh's back with the shotgun barrels.

Old Silas Browning was in the forefront of the solemn spectators. Fogarty heard him sniff but ignored it until the old man said, "I donated the rope, mister."

Joe glared. "Shut up! Sam'l, keep walking!"

Inside there were people on every bench and standing along the walls. There was a sprinkling of women but the majority of onlookers were men. Even Horace Dagget was there. Fogarty did not notice that McGregor was not in the crowd as he guided the prisoner to a chair near the judge's table and pushed him down.

His Honor was sucking his teeth over by the water pumper, ignoring the quiet crowd. He did not move until someone closed and barred the roadway door from the inside, then His Honor approached the table while studying Sam'l Walsh. When the judge was seated, he rapped the tabletop for silence in a room where there had not been even any whispering, and cleared his throat. He put his little books one atop the other and groped for a tin case that held his spectacles, then hooked the glasses into place without haste and scowled as he read the charges.

He raised his head, removed the glasses, and stared at the prisoner. "How do you plead, guilty or not guilty. You'd ought to bear in mind pleadin' not guilty complicates things and can be construed to annoy the court, which operates on a regular schedule. I got to be down in Bordenton by tomorrow evening. . . . Walsh, is it? Yes. How do you plead, Mr. Walsh?''

The prisoner had his gaze fixed on the ceiling above the distant doorway when he replied. ''Your Honor, I stole a horse from the livery barn.''

His Honor waited, but evidently that was all the prisoner was going to say. Judge Featherstone hooked the glasses back into place, bent his head and reread the charges. The room was totally without noise when His Honor looked up again. ''You shot a peddler in the back, Mr. Walsh.''

''No sir, Your Honor. I stole a horse.''

Featherstone looked at Marshal Fogarty. ''Witnesses that he shot the peddler, Marshal?''

''The only witness died of blood poisoning, Your Honor. But this one was wearing the peddler's clothes and driving his wagon—with blood on it—when he came into town.''

Featherstone pushed the glasses up onto his forehead, considered the expressionless prisoner, then opened one of his books, and Fogarty groaned to himself.

As he flipped through pages he addressed Fogarty again. ''There was another killing. A store clerk, wasn't it?''

''Yes sir.''

''Marshal, was the prisoner on hand during that killing?''

''Yes sir. It was his partner, the man who died, that shot the old man while they both were robbing the general store. The old man wasn't armed.''

His Honor stopped turning pages, lowered his glasses and sat hunched like a rumpled stork for so long, people were fidgeting before he reared back, shoved the spectacles up again, and addressed the prisoner.

''Mr. Walsh, I'm going to read you a passage from a copy of *Texas Territorial Law*. It says, 'Whereas one person is in the company of another person who commits a crime, shall under these statutes be held equally as responsible and subject to the same sentence.' You understand that, Mr. Walsh?''

Sam'l turned slowly to face the judge. "This ain't Texas," he said, and someone, probably old Silas, snickered among the spectators.

His Honor did not look toward the spectators, but Fogarty saw his thin fingers tap irritably on the table before he addressed the prisoner again. "Yes sir, Mr. Walsh, you're plumb right. But let me explain something to you. This here is a territory, not a state. Not yet anyway, although there's talk about that, along with somethin' else that's a whole lot sillier: voting rights for women. That won't go anywhere, but we don't have to expound on that. What I'm saying, Mr. Walsh, is that territorial law is founded on statehood law. This other little book is on points of law for the State of Massachusetts." His Honor turned toward the spectators, clasped bony hands atop the table, and assumed a benign expression as he continued speaking.

"Statehood law bein' the basis for territorial law, an' because territorial law is copied verbatim—which is a legal term from latin meanin' taken word for word—why then, you see, territorial law an' statehood law say the same thing most of the time.

"In this case they say the same thing. Anyone who commits a crime in the company of an accomplice, which is like a partner, the partner is equally as subject to the same punishment. In other words, if this gent's partner killed an old man in cold blood while this feller was standin' there, why then, this man's equally as responsible for the murder. You folks want to bear that in mind. Now then, Marshal Fogarty, about the old man's murder—you got a witness to that one?"

Hank Dennis arose before Joe could reply to the judge. He introduced himself to the court, then told exactly what he had seen the day his clerk was shot to death.

Hank sat down. The room was deathly still as His Honor removed his spectacles, carefully folded them into their tin case, pocketed them, and turned back toward the prisoner.

"Mr. Walsh," His Honor said in his finest presentencing voice, "horse stealin' is a capital crime. Most places they don't hang 'em anymore, but the penalty if a man's caught is danged stiff. But it's within the purview of the court to dismiss this charge against you. That's called magnanimity. Anyway, it's not goin' to make any difference. . . . You got anythin' to say before the court imposes sentence?''

Sam'l Walsh had not removed his eyes from the judge throughout His Honor's harangue, nor did he remove them now. His conviction had been that he could not be sentenced for killing the peddler because there were no witnesses. He was still expressionless, but he was also a little grayer in the face as he said, ''I wasn't even in the store when Josh shot that old man. I was out front untyin' the horses.''

His Honor slowly inclined his head. ''Untying the horses for what reason, Mr. Walsh?''

''Well hell, so we could leave town.''

''Yes indeed. So you and your partner could flee after robbin' the store and shooting down a defenseless old man in cold blood.''

Sam'l's forehead began to bead with sweat, and it was not all that warm in the room. Stuffy, but not too warm. ''I told you, I wasn't even in the damned store.''

''Mind your language, Mr. Walsh, there's ladies out yonder. But you were freein' the horses for the getaway. Now then, that's accomplicing if I ever heard of it.'' His Honor paused but did not take his eyes off the prisoner as he resumed speaking. ''Mr. Walsh, ladies and gents, it's my sworn duty to pass judgment based on the codes of territorial law. Mr. Walsh, it's the decision of this court that you be hauled out of here, incarcerated—that means be locked into a cell— and kept there until it's practical for you to be hanged by the neck until dead. Marshal, you got a scaffold in Sheridan?''

''No sir.''

His Honor turned, closed his law books, looked out at the spectators, and said, ''Well, Marshal, you better set about building one.'' He winked jovially at the spectators, arose with both law books under one arm and regarded the prisoner.

Sam'l was perspiring profusely. He stared up at the tall judge with his jaws locked hard together. There was no color in his face.

"Mr. Walsh," His Honor said, "I been readin' a book by an English lady about folks not goin' to heaven so much when they pass on, but sort of slipping over into another—I think she called it a 'spectrum'—where they can't talk to us here on earth but can pass us signs. I'd take it kindly if when you get into that—spectrum—you'd sort of pass me a sign. Maybe rattle a window or make a lamp turn on by itself, somethin' so's I'd know for a fact she's right."

No one said a word. Fogarty was staring at Judge Featherstone. His Honor turned, nodded around, and strode toward the closed doors where someone lifted the bar and His Honor passed out into the sunlight.

People arose in silence to make their way out of the firehouse. Fogarty tapped Walsh on the shoulder. The prisoner was staring after the judge and ignored the prodding to get him to his feet. He finally turned, looked at Fogarty and croaked. "Send him a sign? I'll strangle him with my bare hands. He's as crazy as a pet 'coon."

Fogarty prodded Walsh with the shotgun, said nothing until they were nearing the door, where a crowd was milling around out front, as bewildered and in some cases as outraged as the prisoner also was. Joe said, "Slow, now. Walk right through them. Be careful, Sam'l. Don't open your mouth."

The sun was high, the day was turning hot, Horace Dagget was hurrying southward to fire up his stove for the diners he expected. Hugh Pepperdine was watching the prisoner like a hawk as the man and Marshal Fogarty started through the crowd.

Pepperdine saw Walsh begin to list to one side before Joe noticed it. Joe was calling for the crowd to give way when his prisoner suddenly bowled over a large, heavy woman and two totally astonished men as he plunged into the crowd and broke free on the north side. He was running harder, even with manacled arms, than he'd probably run before in his life.

Pepperdine raised his handgun, but spectators were yelling and bumping into one another as they fought to get clear of the confusion.

Fogarty charged into the people, raising his shotgun as Sam'l Walsh swung toward a dogtrot. Pepperdine reached out with a long arm to knock the shotgun upward. Joe turned on him in a fury. Hugh yelled over the screaming and confusion. "He won't make it."

Ten seconds later a solitary gunshot sounded out in the vicinity of the east-side alley. That inspired the wild-eyed spectators to scatter in all directions, to duck into stores, press against buildings, and renew their screaming.

Pepperdine holstered his six-gun and started walking northward. At the entrance to the narrow space between buildings, he poked his head in and yelled. "James?"

The answering yell came back up from the alley. "Hurry up. He's still wiggling."

Fogarty followed the harness maker down through and out into the alley, where James McGregor was leaning on a long-barreled rifle, solemnly considering the writhing man at his feet whose wrist irons prevented him from flailing his arm.

Fogarty knelt, leaning on the shotgun, looked up, and said, "Get Henry."

McGregor did not move nor even act as though he'd heard, but Hugh went back up through the dogtrot. Joe eased the writhing man onto his back; the spasms diminished for a long moment then ceased altogether. Fogarty watched as the bleeding trickled down to a stop, and rocked back on his heels looking up.

McGregor said, "Did he tell you his folks didn't raise him to be hanged?"

Fogarty did not reply.

McGregor continued to regard the dead man. "He told Horace that when Horace took some grub over to him, and seems he was right."

Joe stood up, dusted his knee and hooked the shotgun in the bend of one arm as he stared stonily at the gunsmith. "James . . . ?"

"It was Hugh's idea. He said if the judge sentenced him to hang, he wouldn't have a damned thing to lose if he tried to make a run for it. So I agreed to wait out back here, even though I thought Hugh was crazy. A man wearin' irons wouldn't be that foolish. Well, he was that foolish, wasn't he?" McGregor raised pale eyes to the marshal's face. Fogarty returned the gaze for a moment, until the noise of someone rushing down the dogtrot distracted him. When Henry burst into the alley with Pepperdine behind him, Fogarty did not say a word. Neither did either of the older men until Dr. Pohl had made his brief examination and arose scowling.

"Who shot him?"

McGregor answered. "I did, why?"

Before Henry could respond, another long, lanky figure emerged from the dogtrot. Judge Featherstone saw the dead man, fished out a blue bandana to mop sweat off his face and neck with, then stuffed it back into a pocket with half the bandana hanging out. He said, "Well, I expect he didn't fancy waitin' while you folks built the damned scaffold. Can't say as I blame him." His Honor wagged his head. "That's too bad."

The lawman and the pair of merchants nodded in agreement.

His Honor then said, "Now how'm I goin' to know if that English lady knew what she was talkin' about or not?"

His Honor turned and went back up through the dogtrot to Main Street. McGregor considered his companions from a puzzled set of pale eyes. Neither of them enlightened him. Not then, but later that evening when he and Hugh Pepperdine were sitting out front of the gun shop during a balmy evening, Hugh explained about His Honor wanting Sam'l Walsh to give him a sign from beyond the grave.

CHAPTER SEVENTEEN

Calling Henry Pohl

Henry was over across the alley when they brought the corpse to his shed. He regarded the manacles as the men who had carried the body silently filed back out into the sunshine. He said a violent word before starting to work. He was still smoldering when Fogarty walked in, unlocked the irons, and slung them over his shoulder.

Henry spoke waspishly. "Was it necessary? Couldn't McGregor have just challenged him?"

The marshal's answer was slow arriving. "I wasn't back there. You'd have to ask James. Henry, everyone reacts differently, and when they've only got a few moments to decide . . ."

The doctor sighed. "Well, it was a dead-center shot. No powder burns, so maybe McGregor didn't do it point-blank."

Eleanor appeared in the doorway. She loathed the shed. For one thing, its odor of embalming fluid was unpleasant. "Mary Ellen's at the house if you need her," she told her husband, who barely acknowledged the message.

"Don't need anyone, tell her thanks."

Joe followed Eleanor outside. He did not believe Mary Ellen felt like buggy riding now, and neither did he.

Inside the kitchen Mary Ellen was sitting at a table with a cup of coffee. When Fogarty walked in behind Eleanor, Mary

Ellen's gaze did not leave his face as Eleanor went after two more cups of coffee.

Joe made a wan smile at the handsome woman. "I know what you're thinking, but it really isn't like this."

Eleanor handed him a cup and backed him up. "Since Henry and I've been here, there's never been trouble like this. Never." She looked at Mary Ellen with widening eyes. "Matt . . . ?"

Mary Ellen switched her gaze to the other woman. "He's sleeping, but he's losing ground."

Eleanor left the room. Joe sat down, still gripping the cup from which he did not drink, and did not meet Mary Ellen's gaze until she spoke.

"How long have you been at it? Being a lawman, I mean."

"About ten years. Mary Ellen, it's really not like this. In ten years I've collared a fair share of outlaws, and rarely has there been gunfire. Fights, sure, rangemen come into town on Saturday night and drink enough to feel ten feet tall and unbeatable, but you more'n likely have the same thing back east."

"Joe," she said evenly. "If Matt dies, that will be six gunshot deaths since I've been here, about a week."

He searched for something to say and was saved by the arrival of Henry, smelling slightly of embalming fluid even though he'd scrubbed out back. He got a cup of coffee, sat down at the table, and looked from one of them to the other, raised his cup, half drained it, and said, "That accounts for the band of young marauders." He suddenly raised his eyes to Fogarty. "No. One got away. Correct?"

"Correct," Fogarty replied without taking his eyes off old Caulfield's niece. "We could ride out in the morning, after breakfast, when everything is cool and quiet."

She regarded him almost dispassionately, but finally smiled. As she arose she said, "I'll be waiting on the hotel porch," and left the kitchen.

Dr. Pohl stepped to a cupboard, fished far back, brought forth a bottle of malt whiskey, and tipped a dram into both their cups, then topped it up with more coffee. As he resumed his seat he studied Fogarty from the side of his vision before speaking. "She's never seen a cowtown before."

"I know that, but I don't think that's it, Henry. She said six killings since she's been here. Well, it'll be six if Matt dies."

Henry threw up his arms. "How many are killed every week where she comes from? In any big city? Dozens, sometimes more'n that every blessed week." Henry stopped waving his arms to lean like a conspirator on the table and speak in a subdued tone of voice. "Take her up where trout are jumping in the creeks and pine sap perfumes the air. Show her the mountains and the critters. Keep her out all day."

Joe's spirit rallied, in part from the "medicine" in his coffee. As he arose he said, "I'll do my damndest." Then he also said, "I'll tell Reg to rig out the hearse again."

Day was waning when Fogarty got back to Main Street. It was difficult now to realize that only a few hours earlier the town had been full of terrified, screaming people. Even over in front of Morton's saloon a pair of range cattlemen, lined and brown as berries, were leaning in relaxed conversation at the hitch rack.

Halfway to the jailhouse Hugh Pepperdine popped out of his shop looking pleased with himself. Joe thought he would mention arranging that bushwhack out in the alley. Instead Hugh dug out a roll of greenbacks and flourished it. Without waiting for the crowing certain to come, Marshal Fogarty stepped past to halt in the doorway, looking around. The bronc saddle was nowhere in sight. As he turned, Hugh said, "Top dollar. They whittle the stick, you know, so I stuck it up to forty dollars, and you know what? They counted it out, handed it over without a word, and took the saddle."

"Must have been greenhorns, Hugh."

Pepperdine's face fell. "Range stockmen, Marshal, frazzled down to bone and sinew. I'd guess they was never greenhorns in their lives. They just recognized quality when they saw it. I haven't had time to tell McGregor yet."

Fogarty got down to the jailhouse before looking back. Old Hugh was just disappearing through the gun-shop door.

Later a familiar sound brought Fogarty back to the doorway. One of Silas's durable but rough-looking stages was moving southward on the Bordenton run. As it passed the livery barn, a gaunt scarecrow all in black riding a sixteen-hand bay horse turned out of town in the same direction. It seemed perfectly capable of carrying the beanpole of a judge on its back, but the large army-style saddlebags bulged.

Fogarty hung his wrist irons from a wall peg near the gun rack, closed the cell-room door, looked around, found nothing particularly pressing, and left the jailhouse without bothering to lock up from the outside.

Over at the cafe Horace had several diners, but it was too early for his regulars, and for once when he served the town marshal he came almost unbearably close to being civil. He said, "I been sayin' you sure outsmarted that son of a bitch, havin' McGregor out there in case he made a run for it. Good job, Marshal."

Fogarty nodded in silence and continued eating until the possum-bellied liveryman came in, dropped down at the counter, and nodded. Fogarty told him there'd be use for his hearse again, and Lee rolled his eyes. "At two dollars a hire, the way things been goin' lately I could sell off the barn and just keep the hearse. By the way, Joe, you on the town council this year?"

"No. Why?"

"Because they still owe for that young feller named Dagney. If that feller James shot belongs to the same bunch, they'll owe for him too, an' that one yet to be buried, the one called Josh."

The cafeman shuffled along to stare at Lee. The liveryman shrugged. "Whatever you're servin' today, Horace." The cafeman returned to his cooking area as a pair of lined, nut-brown stockmen walked in, looked around, saw a vacant place on Fogarty's left side and went over there.

Fogarty knew all the ranchers in his area, not always by

name, but certainly by sight. He nodded at the nearest one as the man spoke. "M'riders brought in a horse day before yestiddy. Been used hard. Damned shame the way some folks treat animals."

Joe nodded and spoke between mouthfuls. "What about him?"

"M'neighbor here found another one, same shape. Both branded H.E. We don't know any such mark so we come in to see if you did."

Fogarty finished eating, pushed the plate away, and snugged up the coffee cup before replying. "Yeah, I know about them. Some outlaws stole them down south and turned them loose when they got a buggy. Did you bring them to town?"

"No," the cowman said. "We got to thinkin' up in front of the saloon. It'll take the rest of the season to get 'em fed up and back in shape, which we're willin' to do, you understand, but grass is money, so if you know who owns 'em, he can come get 'em or he can—"

"He lost four H.E. horses," Fogarty said. "He got two back and gave up waiting around for the other pair to show up an' went home. Back down in New Mexico."

The cattlemen gazed at Fogarty. One of them said, "Well, I don't know as I'd come all the way back up here for a pair of bone racks with sore feet. But if he did that, by the time he got here, them horses would have ate up enough of our grass for us to have a feed bill against them."

Fogarty and Reg Lee exchanged a look. Lee had picked up on what the old ranchers were doing before Fogarty had, but Lee was himself a horse trader.

Joe spoke while gazing into his coffee cup. "What are they worth, gents?"

There was no hesitation before the answer arrived. "Bein' charitable, Marshal, eleven dollars each. At auction you'd maybe get six dollars from wolfers."

Fogarty nodded. "Pay up, gents. I'll write bills of sale when I get back across the road, and you can pick them up on your way out of town."

The leathery-hided man next to Joe fished forth a scrap of wrinkled brown paper and a stub of a pencil, pushed them in front of the marshal as he and his friend began digging in pockets for crumpled greenbacks. Joe wrote the bills of sale, accepted the money, and the stockmen departed. Reg Lee showed an impish grin. "They had that figured out before they came in here."

Fogarty drained his cup before commenting. "Most likely."

"Did you figure out the address that stockman left you down in New Messico?"

"Yep." Fogarty arose, spilled silver beside his plate, and said, "Reg, don't forget about the hearse. Henry can tell you when it'll be needed."

Lee twisted to look upward. "I got my horses back from that shed, but I'm still shy two, a cranky gray mare and a pretty fair bay those two young renegades made off on."

Fogarty answered candidly. "I think the one that buck-toothed little lyin' bastard escaped on you can kiss good-bye. The other will most likely turn up like those H.E. horses did."

"An' some connivin' cowman'll make me buy him back for the feed," Lee said.

Fogarty grinned, slapped the liveryman lightly on the back, and went out front, where a battered old springless light wagon was moving northward in the direction of Henry Pohl's place. It was driven by a sinewy, youngish stockman with sun-bleached brown hair, beside whom on the splintery seat was a small woman holding a bundled baby and looking a little frightened.

Joe watched the man jump down and tie up out front of Henry's place before helping the woman down. He grinned to himself, recalling something Henry had told him not very long ago about not having enough business to require a full-time nurse.

Reg Lee emerged from the cafe chewing a toothpick. Joe

collared him. "I'll need a top buggy in the morning, Reg, with a nice quiet buggy horse."

Lee gazed up and down Main Street while working on the toothpick as he said, "Pretty hard to catch outlaws in a buggy, ain' it?"

Fogarty gave a straight-faced reply. "I don't know. I never tried it." He stopped this from going any farther by leaving the liveryman standing in front of the cafe as he crossed to the jailhouse.

Two events occurred before dusk. The first one was that when Jack Carpenter arrived in Sheridan at a dead walk, he had a loose horse tied to the rear of his stage. Fogarty was at his desk when he heard Jack yell to someone at the lower end of town.

"Hey! Tell Reg I think this horse belongs to him. He can come up to the corral yard and get it."

Joe was in his doorway when the coach passed by. Carpenter threw him a wave but said nothing. Joe waited until the horse was in view out back. It was gray.

The second event occurred sometime later, when one of Silas's Mexican yardmen came breathlessly to the doorway to summon Marshal Fogarty up to the corral yard. That was all the man said before loping back the way he had come.

By the time Joe got up there, Reg Lee, Hugh Pepperdine—who had been attracted by the commotion—and two poker-faced corral-yard hostlers were standing behind Henry Pohl. Squirming on the ground, turning the air blue with profanity, was Silas. Throughout all his movement the big old hat remained firmly on his head.

Fogarty asked what had happened, and Reg responded in a sepulchral voice. "The gray mare kicked him."

Henry looked up. "Broken leg."

Reg spoke quickly and defensively. "She never offered to kick Jack when he found her out there tryin' to find water. He said she walked right up to him, let him tie her in back, and never pulled back on the way to town."

Silas's face was sweat-shiny. He glared at the liveryman.

"You knew she'd kick. You got no right keepin' mean animals. Suppose some little kid'd walked behind her? Marshal, I want Reg locked up!"

Fogarty asked on what charge, and the furious old man on the ground began jerking and twisting. Henry straightened back, looked bleakly at Silas, and said, "You've got a compound fracture, and if you want me to set it, you lie still. Someone sit on him and hold his damned arms."

A burly Mexican moved forward, but Silas screamed at him. "You touch me an' you'll never work in this town again as long as you live!"

Pepperdine, who had been watching Browning's antics since before Fogarty arrived, did not make a sound. He leaned to smile and swung a big bony fist. When it connected, Silas slid along the ground for a foot. When he stopping sliding, he was as inert as a rag and Pepperdine was grinning from ear to ear.

Every spectator was shocked. One of the Mexicans crossed himself, but Henry Pohl said, "Thanks, Hugh. Now get hold of his leg, and when I tell you to, pull. Keep pulling until I tell you to stop."

Setting the leg proceeded professionally without Silas even beginning to blink his eyes until two wagon spokes had been splinted on both sides of the broken leg and securely bandaged into place. By this time McGregor and Rusty Morton had arrived, and because Rusty was a confirmed believer in the medicinal values of certain mashes, he'd brought a pony of his best brandy with him.

Silas was making sputtery sounds as consciousness returned. Pepperdine took the bottle from Rusty, motioned for McGregor to hold Browning's head off the ground, and hunkered down, squeezed both the old man's cheeks so hard he had to open his mouth, and poured.

Instinctively Silas swallowed. Pepperdine continued to hunker with the bottle poised, maliciously grinning from ear to ear. Everyone in Sheridan knew of old Browning's fierce loathing of anything that had been distilled.

Silas's reaction was awesome. His eyes sprang wide, he gagged and flung out his arms, tears flowed, he struggled for breath and would have kicked, but Joe and Henry each had hold of a leg. The yardmen walked away until it was safe to double over in glee.

As Silas's furious struggling lessened, Henry said, "Listen to me. Keep your weight off that leg until I tell you not to. Stop the damned struggling. If you reinjure that leg, at your age it'll likely never heal, and if it does, it'll be as stiff as a ramrod. Silas . . . we're going to carry you inside. Hold still, you darned old fool. *Hold—still!*"

When they got him into the office and pulled up a chair for his stiff leg to rest upon, he had to continually wipe his eyes. But when he looked out at them, he seemed not entirely concerned with his leg. He had a lump alongside the jaw which he explored gingerly with stubby fingers.

"Where's that damned Reg Lee?" he snarled. No one had missed the liveryman until this moment. When nobody replied, Silas said, "That damned mare hit me in the jaw too. I guess I didn't feel that because of my leg." He eyed Joe Fogarty slyly. "You tell Reg I'll give him thirty dollars on the barrelhead for that gray mare."

In a country where spoiled horses ended up dead in deep canyons, no one misunderstood Browning's meaning. Fogarty offered a curt reply. "Tell him yourself. Why did you walk behind her?"

"I didn't, damn it. Do I look like a greenhorn? I never walk behind strange horses. That danged animal—I was comin' up beside to take her loose. She cow-kicked me. Never even saw it coming. That mare's dangerous, Joe. You'd ought to do something about her before she kills someone. Maybe a little kid."

Fogarty left the office. Southward, just turning in at the livery barn, Reg Lee was leading his recovered gray mare. Rusty and Pepperdine came out front too, but not in time to see Lee and his mare disappear down south. Rusty's vest was magnificently resplendent. It had some men in baggy britches with towels wrapped around their heads, serving something in an ornate pitcher to a near-naked woman who was reclining among a passel of pillows. Hugh Pepperdine broke the silence as he laughed until the tears came.

Rusty was reproachful. "That was some of my best imported brandy. Came overland all the way from Chicago. You didn't have to half empty the bottle in the old bastard."

Pepperdine checked his outburst long enough to say, "Sure I did. When they get that old, Rusty, a little dram don't even get their circulation fired up."

McGregor called from over in front of the saloon. He'd seen all he'd had to see, and with dusk coming, his interest turned to more important things.

Fogarty joined the harness maker and the saloonman on their hike across Main Street. They did not know until the following day that shortly after they'd left Silas in his office, he'd finally begun to absorb the brandy. When his corral yard boss went to the office in response to loud shouting and a noise that sounded like jackasses being savagely tortured, Silas had fallen off his chair, was lying on the floor singing at the top of his voice. He did not even see the astonished yard boss.

CHAPTER EIGHTEEN

The Day It Didn't Rain

Joe and the cafeman exchanged a long look when the marshal said he wanted some sandwiches, and some pie if there was any, put into the wicker basket he had handed over.

The cafeman looked from Fogarty to the basket and was on the verge of speaking when the lawman touched him in the middle of the chest with a rigid finger and gently shook his head.

Reg and his dayman were backing a big stud-necked sealbrown mare between the shafts of a light top buggy when Marshal Fogarty arrived. Greetings were exchanged, otherwise nothing was said until Joe drove north up Main Street with the pair of liverymen watching his progress from the front barn opening.

The hostler slapped his leg and burst out laughing. "You see the look on his face, Mr. Lee?"

Reg had indeed seen it. "Yep, and that's why I never opened my mouth. I've seen him look that way other times. It means don't start askin' questions."

The dayman nudged Lee with a bony elbow. "Look yonder. That pretty gal who come to town lookin' for old man Randolph just stepped off the porch and climbed into the buggy."

Reg had missed that, but his reply would have been the

176

same if he hadn't. "What did you expect he hired the rig for; to go huntin' for that measly little bastard who escaped on one of my horses?"

It was one of those warm, still mornings that delighted townfolk and that kept rangemen glancing up every now and then. Huge cloud galleons were moving with ponderous slowness down from the north and in from the east. The clouds contributed to the beauty of the day. To men in their saddles they also meant enormous reservoirs of wet air were approaching.

While Mary Ellen admired the huge fluffy clouds, her companion said, "This time of year when they open up, the result is too thick to drink and too thin to plow."

She laughed, changed her attention to the distant mountains and asked Joe what lay beyond. He launched into a fairly accurate description of the country for a hundred miles in all directions, and ended up by asking if the mountains were as high where she came from.

They weren't, and they were more gentle, not as ragged and untamed-looking. She thought these were breathtaking, even a little frightening.

Their conversation was desultory, relaxed, and easy until he turned off the road where the ride was more bumpy. Joe pointed to a rim of tall fir trees. "Used to be a *rancheria* down the far side." At her blank look he said, "In'ian camp."

"They're not still there, are they?"

"They're not supposed to be," he told her with a perfectly straight face, "but you never can tell."

She sat straight up. "Joe . . . ?"

He smiled at her. "No ma'm. I was just aggravating you. Hasn't been a bronco in this part of the country since the army made its final sweep years ago."

But as they neared the topout of the long, gentle swale, she continued to sit very straight, watching the country ahead.

To people from back east who'd matured reading penny dreadfuls of the skirmishes, battles, and massacres west of the Missouri River, it didn't help any that when they visited the far west the country was still wild in appearance. The electrifying news coming out of the west about Custer's fiasco on the Little Big Horn seemed not all that long ago, and from the appearance of the virgin countryside, could happen again.

When they topped out among the trees and could see down the far side where a river coursed through a wide meadow, Mary Ellen's obvious anxiety made Fogarty want to laugh. Instead he put an arm lightly around her shoulders, gave her a little hug, and eased the rig forward as he said, "There's nothing to worry about. Look yonder; see those circles near the river? That's where they had their hide houses. Look across to the far edge of the meadow over there. See those tumbledown old scaffolds? That's where they put their dead. Bundled them up and lashed them atop those things. Hardly anything left."

By the time they were down to level ground where grass and tiny violet flowers grew in profusion, she had seen enough evidence that the area was an old, long-abandoned *rancheria*. Mary Ellen was able to relax, to gaze with interest on the vestiges of what had once been a large Indian village.

She counted those slightly sunken places where tepees had stood, and as Joe was slackening near some tall old pines, she said, "Sixty-six of those circles next to the river. Back a ways on both sides, dozens more. It must have been a very large village." As he was helping her down after tying the horse in tree shade, she asked a question. "How long ago did they leave?"

He had to rely on casual stories he'd heard from old-timers. "Twelve, fifteen years ago."

"But why? Aren't there fish in the river? Surely there was game in the mountains."

He led her by the hand closer to the river as he replied. "Fish in the river and wapiti in the mountains—and soldiers everywhere else looking for the slightest excuse to avenge General Custer."

She seemed totally bemused as they strolled among the tepee rings. She found some arrow points which she put in a broken little trade pot, and eventually came upon a broken redstone pipe. After examining it carefully and noting the glass-smooth exterior, she held it out for Joe to see. "Is there a mountain somewhere up here where they have this kind of rock?"

There wasn't. He'd seen several of those old redstone pipes, and the first one he'd ever seen had belonged to an old man who had died five, six years ago. The old man had told Fogarty that redstone was very valuable among Plains Indians, that it came from Minnesota and nowhere else.

When he explained this to Mary Ellen, her interest heightened. She pulled him along by the hand in search of other lost, discarded, or abandoned items. She missed a find that Joe had noticed out here before, little copper bells, very small and crudely manufactured. He picked up half a dozen for her, and as they too went into the little cooking pot, he said, "Hudson Bay trade goods." When she frowned slightly over the small bells, he also said, "The women'd tie those things to their sleeve fringe, and when they walked they made a pretty little sound."

She laughed. "Did it work?"

"Work?"

She looked swiftly at him and away. "Did it get them husbands? Why else do women do things like that, any woman, except to attract attention?"

He reset his hat, glanced across the river, and shrugged. "I don't know." Then he turned back. "You don't wear fringe, so we can't experiment."

For three seconds something awkward lingered between them before she pulled him along again. When they came to the bank of the river she looked across where the village extended. He said he knew a place where they could cross on rocks so she could see the tumbledown old burial racks, but she declined.

"That's pathetic, Joe. It's terribly sad. What's left is on

the ground or about to collapse. Why didn't they bury people in the ground?''

He had no idea, had never thought about it, in fact, so he lamely said, ''Maybe part of their religion or something. A few years ago when I was buck hunting back in the mountains, I came onto a place where there was no village, just a lot of those old scaffolds. I guess it was a special burial ground. Nearly all the bundles had been torn apart.''

She looked round-eyed. ''People had plundered them?''

''Well, maybe, but seemed more likely to me it was buzzards and varmints. I'll take you up there someday, but we'll have to go horseback.''

She smiled politely. ''That would be very kind of you.''

The way she said it made him smile. He recognized reticence when he heard it, and as a matter of fact he hadn't felt at all comfortable when he'd ridden into that secret place, nor had he lingered.

An hour later, with her little iron pot full of odds and ends they'd found, he herded her back to the shade of the buggy, where the horse was dozing between the shafts. Joe retrieved the picnic hamper and spread everything on an old blanket in fragrant pine shadows.

As she ate she alternated between carrying on a desultory conversation with Fogarty and selecting things from the iron pot to reexamine. He talked about the high country and she listened politely. When he mentioned Henry and Eleanor, she smiled and nodded. He purposely did not bring Matt Hampstead into their discussions, but being aware of her curiosity concerning Indians, rummaged his memory for all he'd learned about them, and a lot that he'd been told. Many of these stories he'd been skeptical about, but at no time did he say anything that might dampen her enthusiasm, not even when she asked him about the Little Big Horn.

All he could say on that subject was that he'd probably heard the same stories she had heard back east. If one discarded most of that, it had always seemed to him that Custer should have done a better job of reconnoitering than he obviously had, because if he had, there might not have been any battle. He might have discovered what became common knowledge years later: that was the largest concentration of fighting Indians anyone had ever seen.

The cafeman had done a masterful job in filling the picnic hamper. Even the pie was fresh, and the coffee in its burlap-wrapped jug was still warm enough to be palatable.

During one of Mary Ellen's periods of concentration, as she placed the contents of the iron pot in neat rows to study them, Fogarty wondered at the way Dagget had filled the hamper. Everything had been done with obvious forethought and consideration, things Fogarty had never associated with the surly cafeman.

Later, after Mary Ellen had replaced everything in the iron pot and ate a piece of apple pie, she gazed over at Joe with an expression of mild surprise. "Who made this pie?"

"The cafeman in town."

Her surprised expression lingered. "That's hard to believe, isn't it? He impressed me as rather disagreeable and not particularly talented."

Joe dryly said, "Yeah. Me too. And everyone else in town, for that matter. But he always has fresh coffee, and cooks steaks that melt in your mouth. But this other stuff, pie and knowing how to keep the coffee hot . . ." Joe leaned against a tree and smiled. "I got to ask him about that."

"Don't," she said quickly.

He looked quizzically at her.

"Well, he obviously wanted our picnic to be a success," she explained. She drew both legs up and encircled her knees with both arms as she ranged a slow look out and around where total stillness was background for miles of flawless wild magnificence. "He's not married, is he?"

"No ma'm."

"But sometime, somewhere, he cared about someone."

Fogarty had no reason to believe this and had no intention of trying to find out.

"He put everything together with care, Joe, with feeling.

With understanding.'' She looked back toward him. ''You saw that, didn't you?''

He'd noticed that Dagget had put the picnic together with untypical thoughtfulness and care, so he nodded, but said nothing.

She smiled slightly at him. ''It's odd. At home I've eaten in a hundred cafes and can't remember a single thing about the people who cooked my meals or served them. Here— what's the cafeman's name?''

''Horace Dagget.''

''Here, Horace Dagget is a puzzle. He's something individual and noticeable. Like you, Joe, and Henry and Eleanor, and that strange old man who wears the huge hat. And those two old men, one tall, the other one not tall, who always seem to be arguing.''

Joe settled his hat forward to shade his eyes. ''Pepperdine the harness maker and McGregor the gunsmith.''

''And the others. That man who wears those outrageous vests, and Mr. Dennis at the store.''

Joe said, ''Where there aren't a lot of people, everyone shows up as being unique, I guess. Sheridan sure as hell has its share of unique folks, and out over the range there are more. Someday I'll take you buggy riding out among the cow outfits.'' He peered steadily at her from beneath the lowered hat brim, but if she noticed the way he'd said that, she gave no visible sign of it.

Then she jarred him wide awake. ''And Matt.''

He pushed up a little straighter against the tree, met her soft gaze, and waited for whatever she would say next. It was a short wait.

''We've talked. Joe, I've been a nurse for almost seven years, so I've seen a lot of suffering, but Matt is . . . different. He's so young and so brave. I've had to fight hard to keep from crying. Eleanor told me she's had so much heartache since they brought him in that she just can't ache any more. I know exactly what she meant. He told me about his childhood, about meeting the others, especially about the one that escaped.''

''Billy Smith.''

''Yes. He told me that his name wasn't really Smith but that's the name he used, and Matt along with the others accepted that because it didn't make any difference, any more than their lives made any difference.''

Fogarty pushed back his hat and leaned off the tree. This was exactly what he'd brought her out here to escape from. He thought he saw tears forming, but before he could steer her away from this topic, she said, ''He told me last night that he knows he's going to die.''

''Maybe he won't, Mary Ellen. He's hung on this long . . .''

''Joe, even if he didn't die, he'd never recover. He'd never be able to sit a horse again nor walk without crutches, and some of his bodily functions have been destroyed.''

Fogarty sat staring at her. In his conversations with Henry, none of this had been mentioned.

She smiled through unshed tears as Fogarty got to his feet and held out a hand to pull her up. He led her down toward the river by the hand, and when he squeezed her fingers, she squeezed back the way she had done at other times. Where they stopped and their shadows fell across the water, dozens of trout panicked in all directions.

He'd deluded himself. Matt would have come up regardless of what Joe tried to do to help her regain some serenity. So he didn't try to change things. He simply said, ''Sometimes it's a hell of a life, Mary Ellen.''

She squeezed his fingers again without speaking.

''Well, I expect we'd better drive back.'' He wondered whether he should tell her how much it had meant to him being out here with her, and decided not to.

She turned a little to look up into his face. ''I think I know why you arranged this, Joe, and it was a nice thing to do.''

''But the country's wrong for you?''

''No. I don't think so. I don't remember what I expected,

but it certainly wasn't quite what happened.'' She freed her hand. "I think it's just so different, it will take me a long time to become accustomed. There is no indifference out here, is there? No passing people on the sidewalk and not seeing them, no caring for the injured without suffering with them . . . Joe?''

"Yes'm.''

She paused, put her head slightly to one side, and looked steadily up at him. "Not 'yes'm.' ''

"Yes, Mary Ellen.''

"Henry asked me to stay and work with him.''

He smiled. He'd suspected lately that Henry's business was increasing quite a bit. "Will you do it?''

"Do you think I should?''

"You hadn't ought to ask me. My answer would be real unreliable.''

She laughed softly and bumped him with her shoulder. "That's why I asked you. Right now I need an unreliable answer.''

"I think you should. I saw a rancher with a spindly little wife drive up to Henry's place with their baby. And I know for a fact there are other folks who need Henry, and I also know he's been crankier'n a bitch wolf lately from running all over the place and getting rousted out of bed in the middle of the night.''

She turned him by the arm and slow-paced with him back where the dozing horse heard their approach and nickered. Joe said, "If you'll shove everything back into the hamper, I'll water the horse. That's what it was whinnying about. It's thirsty.''

She had the hamper in the back of the rig before Joe got back from watering the horse, so she leaned on the buggy watching him—and softly smiled.

He had to push the rig away from the tree where the horse had been tied before backing the animal between the shafts and buckling it in. Mary Ellen stood slightly to one said to watch, and when he threw her a grin, she asked, "Have you been around horses all your life?"

He answered without thinking, "Yes'm."

"Yes—what?"

"Yes, Mary Ellen, all my life, one way or another."

He handed her up, went around, climbed in, and evened up the lines before talking the horse into moving. The way back to the stage road was as bumpy as it had been when they'd left the road, but Joe didn't notice and Mary Ellen did not appear to.

Just shy of the stage road Joe hauled back, stopped the rig and jutted his jaw. "Stage coming."

It swept up out of a swale, trailing a dust banner, and rocketed past. The whip saw the rig, recognized Marshal Fogarty, threw him a high salute, then turned to stare back. He hadn't recognized the woman, but by the time he faced forward, what he had seen he would not soon forget. If he had been Jack Carpenter, he would have grinned like a bear and hollered something at them.

Joe was in no hurry, so they did not reach town until dusk. He handed her down up at the hotel then continued on southward to Reg's barn. Reg was having supper at the cafe, the hostler said, and hovered like a hawk dying to ask questions which he did not ask. As the big lawman strode toward Main Street the hostler leaned on the horse's thick neck, rolled his eyes, and let go with a loud sigh, which proved the fallacy of the commonplace statement that men who looked at the rear end of horses all the time developed an unfavorable philosophy about life.

CHAPTER NINETEEN

The Storm

Henry Pohl broke the strap on his little satchel, and while waiting for Pepperdine to make the repair, rolled his eyes and unburdened himself.

He only had two spare rooms for the ill at his house, and one of them was occupied by that wounded youth, and now the other one was occupied by a cowman's smidgin of a wife who had, among other things, milk fever.

And if that weren't bad enough, old Silas kept Henry running down to the corral-yard bunkhouse where Browning would insist the swelling and the itching were a sure sign he had gangrene, and if not that, it was blood poisoning.

Hugh looked up from his sewing horse. "Does he have anything?"

Henry snorted. "No! And the fool keeps his yardmen jumping and fetching. He acts worse'n a woman with a new baby."

Old Silas's yard boss told Rusty over a tepid beer that if folks thought Browning was a cranky old gaffer when he was up and around, they'd ought to have to be around him when he had a busted leg.

Henry watched Hugh work for a moment, leaned on the counter, and said, "Did you know Joe's been sparking old Caulfield's niece?"

Pepperdine replied without looking up from his work. "Pretty hard not to notice things when you got a front window, Henry."

"I don't think he's making much progress."

"Why not? They make a fine-lookin' couple."

"I think she wants to go back home. Back east somewhere. I offered her a job, but she said it didn't seem to her Sheridan could afford two medical people. Hell, she's up there now with Eleanor, looking after one after another, and that's not counting the people who walk in with mumps or horse kicks or kids that fell out of trees. There is work enough here, Hugh. Didn't used to be, so I used Eleanor, but she never liked it. And Mary Ellen's a trained nurse."

"I saw them go buggy ridin' yesterday," said Hugh, not really listening to all the doctor's complaints. He climbed off the sewing horse, tossed the satchel on the counter, and said, "Two bits."

Henry paid, hefted the satchel by its repaired handle, and nodded. "Good job."

"How's the lad doing, Henry?"

Dr. Pohl fidgeted. When he replied, he avoided Pepperdine's gaze. "Tough kid. Thanks, Hugh."

Pepperdine leaned on the counter watching the doctor depart, groped for his cut plug, got a cud tongued into his cheek. He continued to lean, looking out into the roadway, until he saw the marshal walking southward across Main Street, then he went back to work.

The evening after he had gone buggy riding, Joe Fogarty stopped out front of the Pohls' cottage to wave to Eleanor, who was rocking on the porch swing. She called to ask him to come up to the porch, and without raising her voice told him Matt was losing ground fast now. Mary Ellen was with him, and he had unintelligible moments and was running a slight fever.

Possibly because she anticipated his reaction, she said it would be better if he did not go inside right now. Then she asked if Joe had seen Reg Lee take the man McGregor had shot out to the graveyard. Since Fogarty had been out buggy riding yesterday when that event occurred, he shook his head.

She looked straight at him. "There were no mourners, Joe."

He could understand that, but Eleanor's expression warned him against a practical retort.

He asked about the rancher's wife, and Eleanor's face brightened a little. "She's doing very well. Isn't it odd that some women just can't bring themselves to discuss personal ailments with their own husbands?"

He nodded without quite understanding, and Eleanor gave him no chance to make inquiries, which he wouldn't have made anyway. She told him about the baby, what a lovely little girl it was, and the longer she talked, the more it occurred to Marshal Fogarty that the change in Eleanor from gloom to an expression of almost beatific wistfulness might be the key, or at least one of the keys, to her dissatisfaction and restlessness. But he did not pursue this subject either.

His mind was pulled abruptly away from it when James McGregor came up from the roadway looking solemn. He nodded to Joe, turned toward Eleanor and said, "Henry around, ma'm?" and when she said he wasn't and probably wouldn't be back for an hour or so, McGregor looked at Marshal Fogarty. "It's Hugh. I went over there a while ago an' he wasn't out front. He was lyin' on his bed in the lean-to out back, sick."

Fogarty's eyes widened. He'd never known Pepperdine to be ill in all the years they'd known each other. "How sick?" he asked, and the dour gunsmith's reply was curt. "Sick enough. He wants to see Henry."

Eleanor arose from the swing. "He had three calls to make, James. I'm not sure where he'll be, but when he returns, I'll send him down to the harness shop. Maybe, if you stayed with Hugh until Henry arrives . . . ?"

After the gunsmith's departure, Eleanor looked at Joe and

rolled her eyes. "Another one. Joe, Henry's health is going to suffer."

Fogarty was soothing. "I'll go look in on Hugh. He's tougher'n rawhide. When Henry gets around to it . . . Tell Mary Ellen . . ."

"Yes?"

Fogarty shrugged mighty shoulders. "I don't know."

Eleanor understood, and patted his arm as he was turning away. "She'll be glad you came by."

McGregor wasn't the only person in Pepperdine's dingy living quarters behind the harness works when Marshal Fogarty got down there. Reg Lee, who'd ambled in with some torn halters, was also back there, along with big, always-smiling Jim Young. Jim was recalling an incident from years back when his uncle Josiah had been alive; he'd had the identical symptoms Pepperdine had. Old Hugh was flat out on his bed, listening closely. When Joe Fogarty walked in, Hugh sank back with a groan and half closed his eyes.

McGregor spoke to Marshal Fogarty in a half whisper. "He's no better. If Henry don't hurry up, maybe we'd ought to dose him with molasses an' coal oil. Sounds to me like he's got the summer complaint."

The big, grinning tanner, whose fearsome aroma easily overwhelmed every other odor, departed to take care of a load of green hides which were attracting blue-tailed flies by the hundreds. McGregor rolled his eyes but said nothing as the tanner left. He filled and lighted his foul little pipe in self-defense as Joe went to stand at bedside, where Hugh's color was noticeably high even in the gloom of the little room.

Joe explained the doctor's absence and Hugh feebly nodded. James had already told him about that. He said, "Joe, maybe that nurse lady could look in on me."

Fogarty gently shook his head. "She's with Matt right now."

"How is he?"

"Not doing too well, Hugh."

Both the old men looked steadily at the marshal. Fogarty went to sit on an upended horseshoe keg before saying, "He's losing ground."

Pepperdine repeated his earlier statement. "Maybe if the nurse'd come down—just until Henry shows up . . ."

"She can't, Hugh, not right now, but if Henry don't show up soon, I'll go talk to her. Where does it hurt?"

"Here," Pepperdine replied, touching his middle. "An' here," he moved his hand upward to his chest, then gently massaged his throat. "An' right there."

McGregor nodded. "Same symptoms Jim Young's uncle had. Joe, he's got summer complaint. He needs a dose of molasses and coal oil to thin down his blood. When I was a lad they gave us that every springtime as regular as clockwork."

Fogarty nodded helplessly. All he knew about diagnosing illnesses could have been put on the head of a horseshoe nail without causing any crowding. He arose. "Keep an eye on him," he told the gunsmith and headed for the door. "I'll be back directly."

He went down to the jailhouse to open his mail, and was still sitting there, hatless and frowning over some wanted dodgers he'd received, when Henry came bustling in on his way back home. Fogarty told him about the harness maker and Henry rolled his eyes, groaned, and departed wagging his head.

Fogarty considered the untidy mess atop his table, which now included several wanted dodgers, and picked up his hat on the way out.

Over at the cafe Horace Dagget was nursing a tumbler of well water and rye whiskey. His counter was empty as Joe sat down and exchanged a look with the cafeman before Dagget took his glass with him and disappeared behind the old drapery that closed off his cooking area. Neither of them had said a word.

The sun was slanting away, puny shadows were creeping out front of buildings on the west side of town, there were very few people abroad, when the first raindrop fell. It was the size of a spur rowell, and where it landed, roadway dust exploded upward.

When Fogarty's meal arrived, Horace stood back with his head cocked before saying, "It's raining."

Joe didn't have to look out into the dusty roadway because he could hear rain on the cafe's roof. He did not comment. As the noise increased, though, he became more interested, and by the time he was down to pie and coffee, he walked over to the door and looked out.

The mountains had vanished behind an advancing screen of water. He estimated its arrival in town at maybe fifteen or twenty minutes, went back to finish eating, and Horace Dagget padded over to also look outside. When he returned he said, "Gully washer. I hope those damned ranchers'll be satisfied." He'd had to raise his voice to be heard above the increasing tumult.

Fogarty went out to stand under the warped, leaky wooden overhang and watch the water arrive. It appeared to be advancing in close ranks, one sheet of it directly behind the other. Within ten minutes Main Street had rivulets, within half an hour the town was being battered, trees writhed, there was not a two-legged nor a four-legged creature in sight. When Joe crossed toward his office, muddy water running at storm depth compelled him to take careful steps to avoid erosion holes.

One hour after the storm struck it was difficult for Marshal Fogarty, standing in the doorway of his jailhouse, to make out storefronts upon the opposite side of Main Street. Those awesomely magnificent cloud galleons Mary Ellen had admired yesterday had opened up directly overhead.

The noise was nearly deafening. About the time Fogarty was being thankful there was no wind with the downpour, a high gust tore loose a length of metal from the roof of Dennis's store and carried it southward out of sight, as though it had been a feather.

Experience and folklore indicated that these cloudbursts

did not last long. As the wind increased, Fogarty wondered how long this one would last and speculated that if it continued, there would be major damage to the town.

Dampness appeared in his log-walled, old building, so he fired up the wood stove. Premature darkness made him light an overhead lamp, and even with the door closed, the lamp swayed as though it were suspended from the ceiling of the master's quarters on a sailing ship.

There was one blinding flash of blue lightning somewhere near the upper end of town, followed by a roll of thunder that made every structure in town quiver on its foundation. Immediately afterward the sounds seemed to be dwindling. Joe went to stand in his doorway again.

It was true, the storm was spending its power on a westerly course, leaving Sheridan battered and breathless. Water still came down, but with diminishing force, and the wind departed.

By the time the rainfall was a steady drizzle, people appeared again. Hank Dennis, wearing a hat, went to the very edge of the plankwalk looking for the cause of water seeping into his store from overhead. Down at the blacksmith's forge opposite Lee's barn, the smith and his apprentice were shoveling like mad to keep water from running into their earthen-floored place of business.

Fogarty was turning back when he saw a hurrying figure, completely encased in something dark like a huge cloak, coming toward the jailhouse and leaning forward as it progressed.

There was a sense of urgency in the hurrying person's bearing. He could make out nothing of the face because the upper part of the cloak covered the head. He watched, wondering who it was and where they were going in such a hurry.

He had his answers when the billowing figure turned abruptly toward him in the doorway, reached with strong, cold hands to grab him, and fell against him sobbing.

He pushed back the hood and recognized Mary Ellen Randolph. Joe kicked the door closed at his back, positioned her near the stove, and unwound the cloak which was soaked through.

She remained with her back to the popping little stove even when he would have led her to a chair. When she looked up at him, most of the moisture on her face was not from the rain, and his heart sank.

The noise was down to a steady whisper which, inside the log building, was even fainter when he reached for both her clammy hands. He held them as she said, "He died, Joe. When that lightning flashed, the whole room was as brilliant as sunlight. Before the thunder came he sat up in bed, looked straight at me and said, 'I'll miss you, ma'm,' and when I opened my arms, he went back down very slowly . . . and died."

Fogarty held her while the silent sobs shook her entire body. He was still holding her when the last of the downpour died away, replaced by a silence that was intermittently disturbed by bumbling little winds running at cross purposes, and was still holding her when the winds too departed.

He took her to a bench, got a cup of hot coffee, fortified it a little from a bottle in his nearest drawer, then sat down beside her as she held the hot cup in both cold hands and sipped from it.

There was nothing to be said. She sipped, he sat back with his legs thrust out and crossed at the ankles, gazing steadily into the middle distance. Every vestige of the cloudburst vanished, leaving in its wake a battered town inhabited by stunned people.

She emptied the cup and shook her head when he would have refilled it. She was warm—inside as well as outside—and with most of her initial anguish spent, she felt terribly tired.

When she finally spoke she looked at him from dry eyes and a white face. "It just . . . hit me. I've seen it before, but this time . . . it wasn't like any other time. It was frightening, and at the same time it was . . . very painful, genuinely

physically painful, as though Matt's pain had been trans-
ferred to me just for a few moments. I had to run, Joe.''

He poured himself a cup of laced black java and returned
to his seat at her side. There still was nothing for him to say.

Somewhere up north a man shouted and another man
shouted back. Evidently people were venturing forth to consider the damage, which, though not devastating, was still
extensive, especially the depth of the gashes in the roadway
and the number of ruined roofs.

Joe went to lean in the doorway, looking out. Behind him
the handsome woman arose, a trifle unsteadily at first, and
came over to stand with him, damp, chilly fresh air in their
faces.

She said, ''Are you superstitious, Joe?''

He wasn't. ''No.''

Her reply was neither forceful nor convincing. ''Neither
am I. But I'll never forget it. First that blinding flash of raw
brilliance, then Matt sitting up, looking at me as he must
have looked when he hadn't been hurt, perfectly calm and
rational, then speaking, and one moment later the thunder
. . . and he was dead.''

Men increasingly appeared, most of them dressed against
bad weather. Sheridan's momentous not-to-be-forgotten
cloudburst had come and gone. In its wake there was nothing
that wouldn't be repaired before much time had passed,
although for a time it must have appeared to some residents
that the town would be flattened and washed away along with
the people in it.

The sun broke through a veil-thin moving overcast and
steam rose. People noisily called back and forth about the
damage, some profanely, some with more relief than indignation in their voices.

Joe saw Henry Pohl emerge from the harness shop heading
for his residence. Mary Ellen saw that too, and went to retrieve the sodden cloak, fold it over an arm, and return to the
doorway.

''Joe?''

He turned.

"Thank you for being here."

He nodded with a little smile.

"I'd better get back. There are patients to look after. . . . Joe? Can he be buried tomorrow?"

Fogarty glanced at the devastated roadway. "I guess so, but not up through town. Around on the east side, and it'll be soggy getting out there."

"We should wait?"

He lifted a tumbled dark length of hair from her forehead, put it up where it belonged, and continued to softly smile. "Maybe. The road won't be filled in and leveled for a week, but the ground should be able to hold up Lee's hearse in a day or two, if the sun continues to shine. I'll talk to Reg, he'd know if anyone would, and the town carpenter. He's likely to be pretty busy for a day or two. I'll let you know."

She put her fingers on his arm, squeezed, and stepped out to walk away. He watched her with solemn eyes. If this experience didn't cap all the others since she'd arrived in Sheridan, to reinforce her earlier feeling of alienation, he could not imagine what would.

Some things, he was fully aware, just simply were not meant to be.

He got his hat, closed the door, and walked up to the harness works.

CHAPTER TWENTY

In the Wake of the Storm

James McGregor was sitting with Pepperdine when Fogarty walked in. At the lawman's quizzical gaze, McGregor said, "There won't be any business today. Maybe not tomorrow either, an' I got little else to do. How's he look to you, Joe?"

Fogarty studied the lanky man on the bed whose gaze was fixed on his face, and deftly sidestepped a direct reply. "What'd Henry say?"

"Not much," the gunsmith replied. "Examined him, stood beside the bed without opening his mouth for a spell, then handed me that little bottle on the table an' said to dose him with that this evening an' Henry'd come back in the morning."

Fogarty looked at the small bottle, couldn't make out what had been scribbled on the label, put it aside and asked Hugh how he felt. The answer was given in a quavery tone of voice. "To tell you the truth, Marshal, I got to feel a lot better just to be sick enough to die."

The windowless little room smelled like a boar's nest. Fogarty would have opened the alleyway door but McGregor growled at him. "You want to give him the croup along with everything else?"

Fogarty lingered a little longer then returned to the roadway, where men were laying planks atop the mud so that people could cross from one side of Main Street to the other. The town carpenter was atop Dennis's store replacing the piece of tin that had been ripped off by wind.

He called up, asking the carpenter to come to the jailhouse when he was finished, and went down to Lee's barn, where floodwater had flowed through from the front to the back, making the runway slippery but not muddy. Too many years of horses moving or standing on that ground had compacted it to a depth of four or five inches.

Reg and his dayman resembled a pair of drowned storks. They'd battled the storm trying desperately to create a raised place out front to divert the water. It had washed their mound away about as fast as they could build it up.

Fogarty went to the harness room with them, where both exhausted men stood near the popping little iron stove as Fogarty asked about the hearse and Reg's eyes steadily widened as the marshal talked. He said, "The lad died?"

Joe nodded. "At the height of the storm. If the sun keeps shining, can you maybe make the trip out yonder tomorrow by going around town?"

Reg did not think so. "Day after tomorrow, if the sun keeps shining, but it'd be too muddy tomorrow, Joe. The rig is heavy even without nobody inside. It'd bog down to the hubs. I'm sorry about the lad."

Fogarty returned to the roadway, saw Henry Pohl carrying his little satchel, hurrying along upon the opposite side of the road. Joe made a shrewd guess that someone had either slipped and hurt themselves or been hit by a flying object at the height of the storm.

He was wrong. The initial difficulties arising from the storm were not physical injuries, they were pulmonary. People, particularly the elderly ones around town who'd had breathing problems before the storm, needed Henry now more than before.

He encountered the carpenter up near the center of town, explained about the lad dying, and the man dumbly nodded as he agreed to go up and measure Jim for a coffin as soon as he finished the store roof.

He was watching the carpenter walk away when the cafeman called from across Main Street. Fogarty utilized one of the treacherous plank crossings to get over there. Dagget offered him a free cup of java. There was no one in the cafe as they both had a cup. The surly man offered Joe some crumpled greenbacks and would not meet his gaze as he said, "For the lad's box, an' maybe for a decent marker."

Fogarty slowly pocketed the money. "That's mighty decent, Horace."

Dagget darkly scowled. "This here is between you'n me."

Fogarty nodded. "By the way, that grub you fixed up for the picnic was real good. You outdid yourself."

"She liked it, did she?"

Joe lied like a trooper. "She said you're a wonderful cook. She thinks the world of you."

Daggett noisily finished his coffee, asked if Joe wanted a refill, went over to get one for himself, and with his back to the town marshal, he said, "Joe, for crissake, don't never do anythin' to hurt her."

Fogarty considered the man's broad back. "Horace . . . ?"

"I got work to do, Marshal, an' so've you," the cafeman growled, and went marching out of sight behind his cooking-area curtain.

Out front the sun was hot, the sky was flawless blue, and sweating men were already at work with fresnos and teams scraping, leveling and tamping. It was hard work. Every loaded scraperful had to be pulled through mud by horses up to their hocks in mud and straining into their collars.

Fogarty wondered why the teamsters hadn't waited another day or two, when the surface would have been dry enough to avoid all the straining. The reason, which he did not know until later, was local merchants, with Hank Dennis at the top, had offered double wages to have the road repaired in one day.

Pete Donner, still wearing his bandage although all the swelling was gone, teetered on the duckboards in front of the bank, feeling immensely pleased with himself for having built a gunnysack barricade outside the front door of his bank. Inside there wasn't a drop of water. When Marshal Fogarty waved to him from in front of the saloon, Pete called out. "If folks don't plan ahead . . ." Donner gave one of his rare broad smiles.

Behind Joe, in the doorway of his saloon, Rusty Morton growled. "His damned front door's four feet wide, the narrowest damned door in town. It took him and his clerk fifteen minutes to lay them sacks. Look at the old fool; you'd think he saved Carthage single-handed."

Fogarty turned to enter the saloon. "Carthage?"

Rusty answered as he was moving behind the bar. "A city in a book I been reading. Somewhere on the other side of the world. Joe, I got a fresh delivery of Missouri peach brandy. Guaranteed to make a ramrod out of your backbone."

"No thanks. A beer."

Rusty had his head down and his apron up to protect his handsome vest as he said, "The lad died, eh?"

"Yes. At the height of the storm."

Morton set the glass in front of Fogarty and turned to his cash drawer, counted out some greenbacks, placed them beside the glass and said, "For a decent send-off. Maybe you could find someone who could put up a decent stone with the lad's name on it instead of one of them wooden ones that every time a dog hoists his leg the damned things lean a little more."

Fogarty took the money, pocketed it, and raised his glass in a silent toast. He had to wait until Rusty had drawn off a glassful and returned the silent salute.

When Rusty dried his lips on a sleeve, he said, "Henry's runnin' around like a chicken with its head off."

Fogarty nodded about that.

"And that pretty lady too. Joe, she's the best thing that's

happened to this town since I been here. We sure need some-one like her.''

Fogarty nodded again while gazing pensively into his glass. ''Yeah. That's what I've been telling her.''

Morton's expression smoothed out. ''You think she might not stay?''

''I don't know.''

''She's got to stay,'' the saloonman said, making a gesture with outflung arms. ''Sheridan needs her, for crissake.''

Fogarty smiled as he placed a coin beside the empty glass. ''You don't have to convince me, Rusty.''

After Fogarty returned to the roadway, Morton shed his apron and crossed to the harness shop, using one of the duck-boards in the muddy roadway to get over there.

When he walked into Pepperdine's back room, Hugh and James were having a drink. Hugh was sitting up, but at the sound of approaching footfalls he handed James his little glass and sank back flat out on the bed.

Rusty burst in and without preliminaries told the old men what Fogarty had just said. He then waved his arms as he'd done before as he said, ''I'll pitch in twenty dollars to make a purse to get her to stay here. How about you gents?''

McGregor regarded the excited saloonman calmly. ''Keep your money. Folks are gettin' sick all over town. She can't leave with some kind of plague all over the place.'' James nodded at his old friend on the bed. ''Hugh's got a bad case of the summer complaint. Look at him. You ever see anyone look so measly before? Can't hardly get off the bed to go into the alley to pee. An' gettin' worse every day. Rusty, right this minute I'm comin' down with a scratchy throat, havin' trouble breathing. Listen to this.''

McGregor's breath wheezed in and out.

Morton gazed from one of them to the other without say-ing a word. He eyed the whiskey bottle with two glasses on a little rickety stand and pursed his lips in thought.

Without another word he left the shop, navigated the duck-boards again, got back to the saloon—where there was not a single customer along his bar—and went on through to his storeroom, where he dug among several dog-eared books until he found one he wanted. Its title was *Doctor Ambrose's Guide to Homeopathic Illnesses—Symptoms and Diagnoses*. He read and reread a particular chapter and did not put the book aside until he heard muddy-booted teamsters stamping in from the roadway.

The trails of Henry Pohl and Marshal Fogarty crossed just short of suppertime in front of the abstract office, which was adjacent to Pepperdine's leather works to the south.

Henry was on his way home and looked like he'd been yanked through a knothole. When Joe asked about the lad's passing, Henry leaned against the front of the abstract office, acting as though his little satchel weighed as much as he did.

"I told you, Joe, there wasn't a chance in the world. At first I had hope, even though I knew the internal damage was not repairable. Not even if I'd been a surgeon. What I can tell you is that I never saw anyone who wanted to live as much as that lad did after he and Mary Ellen became close." Henry sighed. "For him it's over. Hopefully he went to a better place. In fact, when I think about it, I think it's got to be better no matter how bad it might be.

"For Mary Ellen . . . and you know, that's strange. She's a professional. She knows better'n to wear her heart on her sleeve around sick folks."

Joe took a chance by saying, "Maybe back east it was a row of faces lying on pillows, too many too often. Here, it was just the lad. Just the lad and Mary Ellen."

Dr. Pohl agreed. "Yes, of course. But it tore her apart."

Joe already knew this. "Is she at her room up at the hotel?"

Pohl's eyebrows shot up. "Mary Ellen? No, she's working herself to a nubbin just like I am. She's got a rancher's wife to look after, and two cases of something that sounds like pneumonia, not to mention folks who keep coming to the house with everything from broken toes to bellyaches while I'm running from one place to another."

In the face of the exhausted physician's agitation Marshal Fogarty's calm formed a very noticable contrast as he said, "Any more talk about her leaving, Henry?"

"Leaving? How can she? It's like a plague. Hugh's flat down, McGregor's having difficulty breathing—I told him to throw that horrible little pipe away and he swore at me—and now I'm on my way to see Rusty at the saloon."

"What's wrong with him? I just talked to him this—"

"Chest pains that come and go. He feels weak and one arm throbs," Pohl announced and fixed Fogarty with a keen look. "Sound familiar?"

"No."

"Heart, Joe. His heart. Wonder to me there isn't more of it, what with men who haven't done any physical labor in years shoveling dirt and bailing like mad during that confounded storm. Joe—take care."

Fogarty turned to watch the physician walk away. He ranged a quiet gaze northward upon the opposite side of the roadway. Hell, Morton's saloon was one of the few buildings in Sheridan that a man had to walk up two steps from the hitch rack to enter. Rusty hadn't had to bail water or shovel dirt.

And McGregor. He'd looked and acted normal when Joe had last seen him over in Pepperdine's lean-to. And Pepperdine . . .

Fogarty went to his jailhouse office, fired up the little stove for coffee, sat at his table with both feet propped up, and concentrated on rolling a smoke. After lighting up and disposing of the smoky lucifer, he wasted half an hour perfecting an idea before he crossed to the general store, got three small bottles of medicine, pocketed them, and went down to the cafe for supper.

The counter was full, talk of storm damage was loud and in most cases wildly exaggerated. Horace exchanged a blank look with the lawman and eventually brought his meal, still looking blank and without a word passing between them. They would have had to shout to be heard anyway.

Scarcely did one place at the counter become empty than someone else came in tracking mud to take it. Horace's initial irritation about the tracked-in mud had long since been compelled to yield to the demands of impatient and hungry diners.

The town blacksmith, with his good-natured Hercules of an apprentice, sat beside Marshal Fogarty, shoveling in food and swilling it down with black coffee. When the edge had been taken off the blacksmith's hunger, he turned and said, "Reg's got an infected toe. He can hardly get around."

Fogarty chewed, swallowed, considered this bit of trivia, thought back to his recent visit to the barn when Reg and his hostler had neither complained of injuries nor acted as though they had any, and neglected to raise his voice above the noise farther along the counter as he said, "Something is going on."

The blacksmith went back to his meal as though he had heard, but gave no evidence that he actually had.

When Fogarty returned to the roadway there were lamps hanging from wires along the outer edge of wooden overhangs in the central part of town so that people who had to cross the still treacherous roadway could at least see where they were stepping.

Those who occasionally misjudged and sank to their knees in the deceptively smooth roadway surface turned the air blue.

Fogarty ambled up to the saloon. Rusty was not behind his bar. When Joe asked the bearlike big man who was back there where Morton was, the big man jerked his head. "In bed out back. Sick."

Fogarty went back there, heard someone behind the closed door slam a book at the sound of his approach, and when he walked in, Rusty's most elegant brocaded vest was carefully draped across the back of a chair and Morton, looking as though he were at death's door, weakly motioned Marshal Fogarty toward a chair as he spoke in a wavery, low voice.

"It's m'heart."

"Must have come on sudden, Rusty."

"It did. That's how it happens. One minute a man's fine, the next minute he commences to sweat, his right arm gets to aching, he gets breathless and puny. There's a fierce pain in the middle of the chest . . . How do you feel, Joe?"

"Fine," Fogarty replied, gazing at the edge of Morton's pillow where the spine of an old book showed. The full title was not visible. All Joe could make out was . . . *Symptoms and Diagnoses*.

Fogarty said, "Mind if I smoke?"

"No. Go right ahead. I'd like to pass on smelling tobacco smoke, Joe."

Fogarty got his quirley fired up, shoved back his hat, and studied Morton for a long time. He then brought forth one of the little bottles he'd bought at the emporium as he told a barefaced lie. "Henry asked me to give you this. He said one tablespoon tonight and no more until he comes around in the morning."

Morton accepted the little bottle, shook it, eyed its contents, then nodded weakly. "Thanks, Joe. I'll take it. Let's shake hands. You been a good friend."

Fogarty paused outside the sickroom to consider the end of his smoke, then returned to the barroom, walked on past, and returned to the roadway.

There was a light at the harness shop. He crossed over, went through to the lean-to, and when old Hugh showed a feeble smile and gesture of welcome, Fogarty sat down. He saw the bottle and little jolt glass across the room where the helpless old man would have to go to get a drink, despite what McGregor had said about Hugh being too weak to leave the bed, and gravely handed Pepperdine another of those little bottles as he said, "Henry sent me down to give you this. One tablespoon tonight before you go to sleep and no more until Henry returns."

Hugh let his arm fall back listlessly with the bottle in his hand. "I'm obliged, Joe. I'll be up and around. Summer complaint can be real bad but I don't recollect ever hearin' of folks dyin' from it. But I could be the exception, eh? Thanks again, Joe. A man don't know who his real friends are until he's flat on his back.''

Fogarty returned to the roadway. The gun shop was dark, but he went over there anyway, rattled the door until a gasping, wheezy voice called irritably that it wasn't locked, then he entered.

McGregor was sitting on one chair with his feet on another chair, and while there was no sign of his pipe, the room reeked as he called from the darkness. ''Over here by the window, Joe . . . I saw you come out of Hugh's shop. He dead yet?''

Fortunately the darkness was nearly total as Marshal Fogarty straddled a chair beside the gunsmith. ''Not yet.''

''Well, Hugh's tough, Marshal. Old but tough.''

''Yep. By the way, James, Henry gave me this little bottle to give you.''

The bottle changed hands in darkness as McGregor said, ''What is it?''

''I didn't ask. Something for your breathing, I guess. You're to take one tablespoon full before you go to bed an' no more until Henry comes around tomorrow.''

McGregor pulled in a painful, noisy breath before speaking. ''I'm obliged, Joe. It was decent of you to bring it. I heard Rusty was sick.''

Fogarty's reply was succinct as he arose to depart. ''Heart, I guess. He never seemed like someone who'd have heart trouble, did he?''

McGregor's wheezing breath was suspended long enough for him to reply. ''Oh yes. It's bothered him over the years. He just managed to hide it from folks.''

Fogarty gave the gunsmith a light slap on the shoulder and returned to the roadway, where a cobalt sky studded with diamond chips reached from one far curve of the earth to the other.

CHAPTER TWENTY - ONE

The Ambush

Mary Ellen was sitting in darkness on the porch swing when Fogarty reached the Pohl cottage. He could not make her out very well until he was at the foot of the steps and she wanly smiled.

He told her it would be day after tomorrow before Reg could drive out to the graveyard, and she nodded because she'd already heard that from Henry, who'd gone down to look at the liveryman's toe.

Fogarty, harboring a suspicion, asked about the toe and learned that the injury was genuine; a horse had stepped on Reg's foot.

She also told him the town carpenter had measured Matt, and caught her breath in mid-sentence. He felt for one of her hands and held it.

He told her the saloonman, the gunsmith, and the harness maker were ill, and she surprised him. "Yes, so I heard. Henry examined Mr. Pepperdine and couldn't find a thing wrong with him. In fact he told me he'd thank God if his heart was just half as strong when he was Mr. Pepperdine's age."

Joe settled back on the swing. "That makes me feel relieved, for a fact. I visited Hugh too and come to pretty much the same conclusion. But I'm real glad Henry confirmed it."

"Yes," she said softly. "He's a close friend of yours, isn't he?"

Fogarty had to ponder that before replying. "Well, he has been, Mary Ellen, but I don't know whether he still will be tomorrow."

She turned in the gloom, looking quizzically at him, but he moved to another topic before she could speak. "Awful lot of ill people in town, aren't there? I met Henry this evening on his way home and he looked pretty tucked up."

"It's been hectic," she acknowledged. "I take the ones that come here, and Henry makes the house calls. If I run into anything I can't handle, I send them home and give him their names when he gets back."

"How's Eleanor taking it?" Joe asked.

Finally, Mary Ellen was on a topic she could enthuse about. "She is one in a million. We have a cowman's wife, Mrs. Buell, and her baby. Mrs. Buell is having trouble with her milk, and Eleanor is the most gentle person I ever saw with a breast pump."

Joe looked straight ahead and changed the subject. "Good thing we went buggy riding when we did. It'll be a week before anyone can go out there again."

"Joe, I showed Eleanor those things I brought back in the pot. She couldn't identify most of them, and neither could I, but she said that man who kept my uncle's chest used to be an army scout and Indian trader. She thought I should show him those things."

He agreed with Eleanor, although he hadn't known Andy Dexter'd been involved in the Indian troubles. But he and Dexter were no more than acquaintances.

He arose, finally, to depart. She arose with him. In the gloom she looked very young, the way he thought she'd probably looked at maybe seventeen or eighteen. He asked a practical question. "You'll help until things are back to normal, won't you?"

She said "Yes" without elaborating.

"Folks think the world of you, Mary Ellen. The saddle

maker particularly wanted you to look in on him. You've made quite an impression.''

Her even white teeth shone in the shadows. ''Sheridan's made quite an impression on me too. I'll look in on Mr. Pepperdine in the morning. Good night, Joe.''

He teetered for a moment, turning over in his mind whether or not to tell her not to look in on Hugh in the morning, gave it up and said, ''Good night, Mary Ellen . . . Maybe after the funeral, day after tomorrow, we could ride west of town where the wildflowers are thickest.''

She reached, put a palm against his chest and nodded. ''I'd like that . . . Joe.''

She kissed him on the cheek, and as he was walking away he was very conscious of having not done much of a job of shaving that morning.

Sheridan was turning in. There had been too much agitation and anxiety, not to mention manual labor, for folks not to be tired.

The road looked like there had been no erosion. Its surface was as smooth as flapjack batter. The duckboards were still in place to indicate that looks could be very deceiving.

A few townsmen were still at Morton's saloon, but even their ranks had thinned out considerably since suppertime.

Reg had his two carriage lanterns alight out front of the livery barn. Up at the roominghouse, where the proprietor hadn't been threatened with flooding, the old man was puffing a pipe on the front porch, with the biting scent of shag mingling with the nearly overpowering fragrance of that big, flourishing bush of blue flowers that cut off all the view to the west.

When Fogarty stepped up onto the porch, the old man removed his pipe, lustily expectorated, and cocked his head. ''I went down to visit Silas before supper. You seen him since he's been laid up?''

Joe remained standing as he replied. ''No. How's he doing?''

The old man mimicked Silas's sniffing sound and grinned. "You ever had a busted leg, Marshal?"

"No."

"I have, three times. As long as it's splinted right an' a man don't move it, there ain't no pain at all."

Fogarty abandoned his notion of going to bed and sank down on an old bench. "Is that a fact?"

"Yes sir, it's a blessed fact. You want to know what I think?"

"Yep."

The old man puffed hard for a moment, removed the pipe and again sprayed the big bush on his right. "Silas is a danged fraud. He lies there makin' his yardmen an' everyone else who comes close run errands for him, fetch this, fetch that, don't touch m'leg, it's sore as a boil, and goes on about Reg Lee keepin' mean horses an' he thinks he's catchin' the lockjaw an' all."

Fogarty grinned in the darkness. "He don't get much attention, as a rule. Maybe he needs that."

"Needs hell," snapped the old man. "He needs someone to haul him onto his feet and kick his butt up between his shoulder blades."

Fogarty leaned to arise, but the old man wasn't finished. "He wanted me to fetch that pretty nurse lady down to look at his leg. Said to keep the swellin' down she could maybe massage it." This time the old man leaned to knock dottal from his pipe before speaking again. "That dirty, connivin' old scalawag."

"Did you tell the nurse lady?"

The old man put a gimlet stare on Marshal Fogarty. "No I didn't, an' I ain't goin' to. Silas is an evil-minded old screwt, an' I told him so."

"I thought you two were pretty good friends."

"We are. We been friends since he come to town. But that don't mean I can't see through him, and it don't mean there's things I don't like about the old bastard. Marshal, if he don't stop doin' them things, I'm going to curb him once and for all.''

"How?"

"I'll fix his dadblasted wagon for him; I'll tank him up on croton oil until he won't be able to lie down or set down for a week.''

As Marshal Fogarty arose he said, "Do you think that'll work?'' and looked steadily at the old man, awaiting his reply.

"It'll work, Marshal, take m'word for it. I've seen malingerers like him lyin' in bed and whining jump up and run like scairt deer. Even with splinted legs.''

Fogarty went inside to his room, did not bother with the lamp, bedded down, and gazed at the black ceiling until he fell asleep without knowing when that happened. He awakened just short of sunrise and was the first hotel inhabitant out to the wash house. This time he shaved with more care.

Instead of unlocking the jailhouse first off, as he usually did, Fogarty went over to the cafe for an early breakfast and ran into a crowd that had entertained the same idea in order to avoid the usual morning rush.

As Joe sat down, Reg Lee hobbled in, eased down very gingerly, and said, "Don't move your right boot, Marshal. I got a sore toe down there,'' and before Fogarty could acknowledge the warning, the liveryman looked around and also said, "Where's Hugh an' James an' Rusty? They're usually in the first rank.''

Joe went on eating as though he hadn't heard, so the liveryman put a scowl on him and repeated the question. This time Joe shook his head. "Haven't seen 'em this morning.''

"Sick,'' pronounced the liveryman. "Hell, everyone's sick. Doc Pohl looked like somebody'd been beatin' him with a tired stick when he worked on my foot yestiddy. He's goin' to quit an' go to some town where he don't have to be up all day an' all night.''

No one heeded Lee's garrulousness, which ended when the cafeman put a platter in front of him.

Fogarty crossed to the jailhouse, opened up for business, and was firing up the little potbellied stove to take the chill off when Dr. Pohl walked in. He looked fresh for a change as he watched the lawman tinkering with the stove. "It's tapering off," he announced. "The chronic ones are the same as before the storm, but what seemed like an irrational run of other ailments has tapered off."

Joe murmured something about being glad of that and sat down behind his table. "You look rested, Henry," he said.

The physician smiled. "I am. Last night Mary Ellen and Eleanor formed a skirmish line and ambushed folks so I could get a full night's rest."

"Mary Ellen," murmured Joe, and got no further.

"Joe, she's a regular Miss Nightingale." At the lawman's blank look, Henry explained about the famous English nurse and added a little more. "Tough, Joe, never loses her poise, never gets cranky with patients, never lets on when she's dead on her feet."

"Then keep her," Fogarty said.

"I'm going to. That's why I stopped in this morning. I have reason to believe you can persuade her to stay better'n I can."

"I've been trying, Henry."

Dr. Pohl smoothed his coat without meeting the lawman's gaze when he said, "My wife's the best person I ever knew to size womenfolk up." Henry stopped smoothing the coat but still did not raise his face. "She can talk to a female for five minutes and tell me exactly what I got to know as a doctor. I never knew anyone like her."

Fogarty slowly bobbed his head. He'd never had to tell either of the Pohls of his admiration for Eleanor, and he did not do it now. He simply said, "Mary Ellen thinks Eleanor can dang near walk on water."

Henry finally looked up. "Yes indeed. Would you like to hear what Eleanor said about Mary Ellen?"

"Yes."

"She said Mary Ellen's sweet on you, and that's why I

said you can come closer to talking her into staying here than I can. Now I got to go down and change the bandage on Reg's toe.''

Fogarty neither spoke nor moved as the physician bolted from the jailhouse office. He eventually rolled and lit a smoke.

That large, burly man who had minded the bar last night for Rusty appeared in the doorway, expressionless and curt. ''There's somethin' goin' on up at the harness shop, marshal.'' He made his announcement and left, did not go very far, so that when Fogarty started up the plankwalk, the big burly man watched his progress from a recessed doorway, still expressionless, except up around the eyes. There his look was of mild malevolence.

Hugh was not behind his counter but James was in front of it, and Rusty Morton, for the first time since Joe could remember, was without one of his resplendent vests, standing near the rear door.

Fogarty walked in, nodded, missed Pepperdine and asked where he was. McGregor replied in a flat voice. ''Across the alley. He waited as long as he dared.''

Joe forced a broad smile. ''Glad to see you boys up and around.''

Morton started to speak, put his head slightly to one side as though listening to a voice no one else could hear. Then he spun and ran through Hugh's lean-to out into the alley, where he passed Pepperdine on his way back to his shop.

They did not exchange a word.

McGregor heard Pepperdine coming and addressed Marshal Fogarty. ''You know what was in that medicine you give us last night? An' don't tell me Henry give it to you to give to us, because I talked to Hank Dennis this morning an' he told me you bought those three little bottles from him.''

Fogarty approached the counter to lean, saw Pepperdine appear in the doorway where Morton had been, and said, ''I'll tell you something. First off, Henry and Mary Ellen didn't need any more sick folks. They still don't. Secondly,

I know why you did that, an' being fond of all three of you, I appreciate what you tried to do. But—''

Hugh abruptly reversed himself and disappeared in haste back toward the alley. Before Joe resumed speaking, Rusty returned to the doorway.

''. . . But all you were going to do was strain the hell out of Henry and Mary Ellen, who used every blessed minute looking after genuinely sick people.''

McGregor started to speak, stood erect for a moment, then he too fled out through the lean-to in the direction of the alleyway.

Fogarty flapped his arms and looked at Morton. ''Rusty—''

''That was a dirty trick, Joe.''

Fogarty did not dispute the charge. Before he could have, Morton whirled and also vanished in the direction of the back alley. Pepperdine took his place in the doorway and rolled his eyes. Of the three, only McGregor was really angry. Hugh regarded the big, younger man from soulful eyes. ''You notice a hollow echo when I talk, Joe? You could have said take half a spoonful.'' Before the marshal could respond, the harness maker also said, ''And one of us should have smelled the stuff before taking it. That's what I told James when he came over here this morning. He said he never figured you bein' a friend an' all that you'd ambush us, an' I told him it was our own damned fault. He should have known every blessed time we get to helpin' you comes out bad. You know why we did it?''

Fogarty smiled as he nodded. ''Sure. An' I appreciate it, Hugh, but you couldn't keep it up and I'm not sure any of you could have fooled her, or Henry, for long. But the point is, I appreciate what you wanted to do, only it's got to be done some other—''

''Excuse me,'' croaked the harness maker and fled.

No one appeared in the lean-to doorway for a moment, so Joe Fogarty returned to the roadway. Hank Dennis collared him, looking upset. Joe told him he already knew who had told the old men and Rusty it had been croton oil in those little bottles, but Hank, who was a very prudent individual, was not entirely mollified. "They were mad as hell, Marshal."

Joe acknowledged that too before he replied. "Pretty hard to stay mad when every few minutes you got to run like a scairt rabbit and the rest of the time you dassen't even cinch up your belt. Give 'em a little time, Hank."

Fogarty returned to the jailhouse, where someone had brought his mail over from the general store and put it atop his littered table.

Reg's dayman arrived to say his boss had tested the road out front, had decided it wouldn't be able to hold up the hearse for another three, maybe four days, but going around town on the east side where the land was rootbound, he'd be able to make the trip to the cemetery tomorrow.

The real surprise of the day was when Pete Donner walked in. He was no longer wearing his bandage. Since neither Fogarty nor Donner were particularly fond of the other, they exchanged a nod, an unsmiling greeting, and the banker got straight to the point.

He'd heard around town that folks wanted to donate so's that lad who had died would have a respectable send-off. He handed Joe a sealed envelope. "I know. He was one of *them*, an' most likely if he'd had the chance, he'd have been in on trying to rob the bank. But there are a few of us around town who came up about like he did, no parents, no trade, not real bad but pretty hungry at times. It seems to me he probably tried."

Fogarty nodded because he also believed that.

"I guess the difference is the rest of us made it and the lad just couldn't."

Joe arose and extended a hand. Donner gripped it, nodded, and walked back out into the sunshine. There was a small fortune in the envelope. In fact Joe now had enough for the best pine box money could buy in Sheridan, with enough left over to hire the stonemason down in Bordenton to make a fine headstone.

It was late afternoon when Joe was out front watching some rangemen riding in from the south. Reg's hostler ran out to wave them down to a stop and explain that despite the look of Main Street, it was unfit for traffic. The rangemen halted, gazed from the hostler to the invitingly level roadway, and one man urged his horse forward.

He got about twenty feet before the horse began sinking. Fogarty strolled down and watched as the man's companions unslung lariats to yank the horse out. Reg hobbled to his doorway and berated the exasperated range rider. The man ignored Reg until he and his horse were back on solid ground, then he swung off, tugged at his gloves, and started walking.

Fogarty stopped the angry cowboy just short of the barn's front opening. "Mister, you were told it wouldn't hold you up."

The cowboy turned, still snugging up his gloves. "Why'n't somebody put up a sign?"

Fogarty acknowledged that that wasn't a bad idea, but he also said, "Maybe a rider wouldn't pay any more attention to the sign than you paid to the verbal warning."

The cowboy stopped pulling at his gloves and stood in expressionless silence regarding Joe Fogarty. From behind him one of the mounted men called. "Come on, Ace. What the hell; we can go up an' around. Saloon's at the upper end anyway."

Reg and his dayman were like statues in the barn opening. Across the road the blacksmith and his apprentice appeared in their open-fronted big shed to also stand and watch.

The stone-faced rangeman turned back toward his friends, swung up, and without another glance in Fogarty's direction led off toward the east side of town.

Reg shook his head. "Like a damned banty rooster, Joe."

Fogarty turned back toward the jailhouse. He hadn't finished reading his mail. There wouldn't be much of interest in it, because there seldom was. Maybe some more of those dodger posters mailed from as far off as Missouri and Montana to file in his storeroom. They made good starting paper for kindling during the winter.

CHAPTER TWENTY-TWO

"I'd Love to, Joe."

For the second day in a row, as the day of the funeral arrived, Fogarty shaved very carefully. He also brushed his hat, used his spare pair of britches, which were spotless, and even wore his white shirt under his coat.

There wasn't a cloud in the sky, the sun was climbing. It was still chilly after Joe had breakfast and went over to unlock the jailhouse, but it was going to be a magnificent day.

Sheridan came to life as it usually did, very gradually, but this particular day there were more brushed hats and white shirts than usual. The duckboards were still in place, but the roadbed was almost firm enough for people to make the crossing without them. By tomorrow it would be.

Reg was hobbling around down at the livery barn, dusting the rather elegant but forbidding black hearse while his day-man had the pair of blacks out back, cuffing them until their coats shone. He'd washed them the day before, then turned them into a corral to roll. For some unknown reason, dark horses with dust in their hair could be cuffed to a higher sheen than horses that had been washed but had not rolled.

When Joe returned to the jailhouse after an amble around town, Mary Ellen, all in black, was waiting. She looked stunning, even though she greeted him quietly and without smiling.

He knew that this was not really a good day for them to go buggy riding after the funeral, but he kept this to himself as he offered her coffee, which she declined. He waited until she was seated before sitting down at his table.

She said, "Henry and Eleanor asked me to ride out to the graveyard with them."

He nodded about that. The alternative was to walk, like most of the other people would, and it would be hot out there, not to mention the length of the walk. Joe would walk, as he'd done on similar occasions.

She said, "I looked in on Mr. Pepperdine this morning."

Joe scarcely breathed while waiting for the rest of it.

"He looked a little peaked, but he said he'd walk to the cemetery with Mr. McGregor and the man who runs the saloon."

"Did he say anything else?"

"Not much. Just that the gunsmith and the man who owns the saloon feel much better. A little weak, but no longer ill. Henry was mystified by the saloonman's recovery from what seemed to be an impending heart attack, but he told me he thought the harness maker was for some reason making out he was ill. And his friend from across the road probably only had a slight but not serious attack of asthma. I'm glad they recovered, Joe. We just don't have the time to care for more ill people."

Fogarty professed relief that his friends had recovered. He asked about other ill people around town, and Mary Ellen told him they'd be able to send the cowman's wife and baby home soon. Otherwise she thought the routine illnesses would remain exactly that.

She then said, "At breakfast this morning we were wondering what could be done about the one that escaped, the one called Billy."

Fogarty's reply to that was forthright and factual. "Nothing. By now he's to hell and gone from here. I could make up some wanted posters and mail them around, but I can tell you from experience they aren't much good. That one got away. That's the end of it unless he returns, which he'd be foolish to do." Joe smiled a little. "In my business a person figures averages, Mary Ellen. You can't catch them all, but even if you could, there'd be another crop next summer. As far as Billy's concerned, somewhere down the line someone is waiting." Joe arose, looked at his watch, and stepped to the door to look for Lee's hearse. There was no sign of it. He thought it was probably hidden on the east side of town by buildings. He was wrong. It had already gone up the back alley to Dr. Pohl's embalming shed, where the body was being loaded. Fogarty turned when Mary Ellen came up to the doorway beside him.

She looked up Main Street. People were beginning to appear, moving without haste toward the upper end of town. She eased past Joe to the plankwalk, looked back and smiled, then walked away.

Fogarty locked the jailhouse, reset his hat, and also walked northward. When he was abreast of Pepperdine's shop, James McGregor glared at him from the doorway, deliberately turned his back, and growled at Hugh and Rusty that the procession was moving out.

Fogarty finally saw Reg turn eastward from the west side of town, figured out what the liveryman had done—gone up the back alley—and gradually merged with the other mourners.

So far there was no great amount of heat, which was fortunate because very few mourners were dressed for it. This was a solemn occasion. For centuries people had dressed in their best attire, a lot of which—such as too-tight vests and corsets with whalebone stays—seemed to have a basis in some kind of self-flagellation. They were not only supposed to be solemn, they were also supposed to be uncomfortable at burials.

Fogarty turned as an unsmiling Pete Donner came abreast. The banker neither returned the look nor spoke. His forehead was beaded with sweat, his jaw was set, his dark eyes were fixed on the slight rise out where the graveyard was located.

There were several buggies already atop the graveyard hill. There was also an old wagon with wooden sideboards, into which the pair of sweaty-looking tobacco-chewing gravediggers had flung the same damp earth they would fill the grave with as soon as the mob cleared out and they could back the wagon to the edge of the hole for easier unloading.

Someone had asked the unkempt pair of diggers to please stand on the far side of their wagon. Their appearance was not appropriate to the solemnity of the occasion.

Mary Ellen was up there with Henry and Eleanor, but the shiny top buggy with the fringe belonged to Hank Dennis and his wife, both of whom were properly long-faced and lugubrious.

The Baptist minister was beside Hank Dennis, at whose behest the preacher had made the trip up from Bordenton. It was a tiresome journey, but Dennis had him come, expenses paid, every time there was to be a respectable funeral. The honorarium for his appearance was usually five dollars in a sealed envelope, sufficient incentive to a holy man whose normal Sunday offering down in Bordenton, a town larger than Sheridan, rarely exceeded two dollars in small silver coins.

When Fogarty finally got out there, he was surprised at the size of the crowd. The last time he'd been out here for the burial of an outlaw, the crowd had not been this large nor had it been as solemn. But the Dagney boy's send-off had been accompanied by a feast back in town afterward, and at least one of the mourners, James McGregor, had marched out and back in order to qualify as a proper mourner entitled to be fed.

Fogarty watched Mary Ellen as the preacher began his exhortation. She held a tiny lace handkerchief to her face. The thought that came to him out of nowhere was that Mary Ellen had a strong maternal instinct, which was why she'd become so close and protective toward the youth the preacher was extolling.

A lanky silhouette in black eased up close and whispered. "Déjà vu."

Fogarty turned slowly, regarded old Pepperdine for a moment, then just as slowly faced forward again, still frowning. He did not say a word.

Hugh leaned closer. "I didn't figure you'd know what that meant. Rusty lent me a book that says sometimes folks get the feelin' they been somewhere before. Déjà vu—we been here before."

Fogarty grunted, ranged a slow look around and stopped where Mary Ellen was standing. She was no longer holding the handkerchief to her face. From the distance separating them she seemed to be dry-eyed. Her lips were pulled flat and her jaw was set.

The minister, conceivably conscious of Hank and his wife's close attention, made a very fine oration. He signaled the end of it by picking up a handful of earth, teetering upon the edge of the grave, and muttering something unintelligible as he allowed crumbled earth to trickle through his fingers.

The pair of grave diggers were seated with their backs to the proceedings, on the shady side of the old wagon. Beneath it they'd had a jug wrapped in sacking which they kept moist by trickling water from a canteen on the cloth.

When the minister's sermon ended, one grave digger rolled around until he could see beneath the running gear, got back into a sitting position and told his companion they had plenty of time. As large as the crowd was, they'd be another half hour straggling back toward town.

He was right. In fact, at the earlier funeral for Matt Hampstead's friend, Dagney, the moment the minister had finished the exodus had begun back toward town. This time people milled, talked quietly in small groups, and only belatedly began the hike back.

Fogarty avoided Mary Ellen. There was nothing he could say that hadn't already been said, nor did he believe she'd welcome companionship just yet. He watched her climb into the rig with Henry and Eleanor, and swung his attention in a different direction only when Horace Dagget spoke from one side.

"While the minister was goin' on an' on, I got to thinkin' that if everyone who walked out here today had put up just one silver dollar, it'd make a respectable pile, and if it'd been given to the lad to get a decent start with, we wouldn't be standin' out here right now."

Fogarty regarded the cafeman for a moment without speaking. He'd eaten Dagget's grub and tolerated the man's surliness for years. Only within the last couple of days had he acquired any inkling that behind the pulled-down lips and the bad temperament, there was a normal human being. He said nothing, but he slapped Dagget lightly on the shoulder as he was turning for the walk back.

From the slight eminence of the burial ground it looked like a serpentine of plodding humanity that reached almost half the distance from the graveyard to the town.

The pair of grave diggers backed their hitch to the edge of the hole, climbed up in back, and leaned on shovels as one of them said, "Must be close to the biggest turnout we've ever had. For a kid no one knew, a damned renegade to boot."

His companion made a remark that suggested he would not be a grave digger all his life. "We don't do this right, Elmer. Instead of two dollars for makin' the hole then fillin' it in, we ought to set the fee accordin' to the number of mourners there'll be."

The first man spat before saying, "An' how'n'ell would we know how many mourners there'd be?"

"Easy. By listenin' to the talk around town. This time, folks got so wrapped up in whether the lad'd live or not, sure as hell they'd feel somethin' personal when he died."

The first man spat again, but this time into his hands, as he then gripped his shovel. "Let's get this over with. It's hot out here."

It was also hot by the time Sheridan's mourners reached town and hastened to their residences to shed mourning attire and get back into everyday, infinitely more comfortable clothing.

Joe Fogarty did not change back. He hadn't worn anything he wasn't comfortable in, not even the white shirt, but he was a little conspicuous. By mid-afternoon he was about the only man in town attired in a white shirt.

He leaned in the jailhouse doorway trying to decide whether to go down yonder and get the top buggy or just forget about it.

He went down there because he'd told Mary Ellen he'd meet her, but as he watched Reg's dayman settle the stud-necked big seal-brown mare between the shafts, he had a feeling that this was not going to be a pleasant afternoon. Even a damned lizard couldn't change its feelings this fast.

He drove up the alley instead of the main thoroughfare, tied up beyond that overpoweringly fragrant bush and walked around it. She was sitting in a rocking chair looking south-ward down through town. She was wearing a loose blue blouse and a full dark skirt. When he came around the bush, she looked up quickly, then smiled. "How'd you get up here? Where's the buggy?"

She'd been watching for him to come up Main Street. He gestured. "Buggy's tied back yonder. I came up the alley."

They exchanged a look, then he shrugged. "Seemed better this way. Today anyway." He perched on the porch railing. She was a beautiful woman, and the fragrance of that big old bush enhanced her flawless features in shadows cast by the porch's overhang. He had to say something, he couldn't just perch there staring, so he wondered aloud if Henry might not need her this afternoon and evening.

She did not tell him that Eleanor had urged her to go buggy riding with him as an antidote for her feeling of depression after returning from the graveyard. Instead she said, "They'll make out. They did before I arrived, didn't they?"

"Not half as well."

She arose. "Will I need a coat or a sweater?"

"There's a buffler robe in the buggy. It won't get cold before we get back anyway."

He led her around to the west side of the building, where

the stud-necked big mare eyed them dispassionately. The horse turned obediently when they were in the rig, to plod westward from town with the sun above and an almost imperceptible breeze coming down-country, bringing with it a faint wildflower fragrance.

The big mare neither hurried nor slackened. She was smooth-mouthed, which meant she was old enough to have been on drives like this before and understood perfectly that there was no schedule nor destination, which suited her very well.

She had no check rein, so as she passed an occasional tall grass clump, she would lip it from the side of her mouth and walk along chewing. She also knew better than to do this too often or to make too big an effort about it. People who rode or drove horses did not ordinarily like the idea of their animal grazing as it went along.

In this instance she could have put her head all the way down to snatch an occasional mouthful; neither of her passengers were paying much attention to her. Fogarty had the lines sloppy slack in his hands, and the handsome woman was relaxed against the upholstery, watching the land forms change in shape and shadows.

Her silence was slightly inhibiting. Joe looked ahead, rummaged around for something to say and was saved from risking banality by a rabbit with legs nearly as long as a small dog springing clear of a grass clump directly in front of the mare. It raced in zigzag desperation when the mare threw up her head, missed a lead as she faltered, then loudly snorted.

It happened very fast. The next moment the mare resumed her normal plodding. Once, she yanked enough slack in the lines to look over her shoulder, and Mary Ellen laughed. "She's embarrassed, Joe."

"She ought to be. She's bigger than a ton of rabbits."

"You can't blame her. I was startled too."

"I don't blame her, Mary Ellen. It's her nature. Horses are natural cowards."

Mary Ellen gazed at the powerful big animal. "Cowards?"

Fogarty settled back. He was now on safe ground. Not exactly appropriate to buggy riding with a handsome woman, but safe. "Did you ever notice how a cow eats?"

"No."

"A cow eats until one of her stomachs is full, then she goes somewhere to lie down and rechew the grass and swallow it into her second stomach. She isn't built to run from enemies. Cows aren't fast on their feet. Not like a horse anyway. But cattle got horns. Some of those razorback Texas cattle that were around when I was a kid got a six-foot span of horns."

"Now, a horse always eats. You've noticed that. They graze along, don't lie down to digest food. A horse is always hungry. He's got a small stomach, and nature made him fast. He's not likely to be slowed down by a gutful of food. An' he don't have horns. Nature made him wary and mostly cowardly, with no big gut to keep him from running full tilt to escape enemies."

Joe turned, beaming. She was sitting there looking at him with a hint of a grin around her lips. "And the mare saw that rabbit as an enemy?"

"Not after she saw what it was, but when it first jumped out, she reacted naturally. It scairt her and she was gettin' ready to flee from it."

Mary Ellen waited until they had gone down the near side of a swale, across the grassy bottom, and up the far side before speaking again. "But the rabbit was running *away* from her, Joe."

He drove for a short distance in silence. The way things were going, they could spend the rest of the afternoon discussing something that by now both the mare and the damned rabbit had forgotten.

He raised an arm. "See that blue mountain up ahead? There's an In'ian *rancheria* on the top. Last time I was up there it didn't look anyone'd been there in years."

"How far is it?" She asked.

"To far to reach today. I'd guess it to be about forty, fifty miles."

"What's up there?"

"Odds and ends. Like you picked up at the other old camp. More beads and little trade bells."

She stared far ahead as Joe made a slight change in course so that they would come to a cottonwood grove in another mile or so. "It's fascinating," she murmured, and he looked doubtfully at the unkempt old cottonwoods, then saw the way she was sitting forward, staring at the blue-blurred distant topout. Her expression was alive with interest.

He got into cottonwood shade, climbed down to secure the mare, and when he turned to hand her down, she was already on the ground standing beside the buggy, looking far ahead.

When he walked back, she said, "Don't you wonder about them, Joe?"

He looked far back, then at her face again. No, he didn't wonder about them. They'd been here and they were gone. "Yes indeed, I wonder about them, Mary Ellen."

"Where I grew up we didn't have anything like that. The Indians live on reservations. We'd see one now and then, but not like this." Her eyes shone as she smiled at him. "When we went out to that camp by the river, I could feel something. . . . Couldn't you?"

He reset his hat before answering. He'd felt hungry. "Yep, I felt something." He took her hand and walked her in among the old trees. Where they emerged on the far side, she stopped dead still.

There was a wide, broad virgin plain covered with every imaginable variety of wildflower. Less than a half mile out a big bull wapiti was meandering among several cows, each one of which had a sassy-fat calf at her side. The cows were trying to eat while keeping a wary eye on the prowling bull.

Mary Ellen clasped her hands. "They're wild, Joe," she murmured, and he nodded because there was no other kind of upland elk. "Why doesn't he stop walking and eat like the others are doing?"

Fogarty told his biggest lie of the year. "Well, he's keeping guard. Sort of moving around, looking for an enemy."

"Does he think that one he's nipping is an enemy?"

Fogarty did not even look around. He took her by the hand and led her back through the trees and out the far side, where the stud-necked mare opened one eye, watched them briefly, then slowly closed it. They were not going to approach the buggy, which was her only concern.

There was a little step-across creek along the southeast boundary of the cottonwood grove. Joe was still holding her hand as he leaned cautiously to see if he could find a trout before it saw his shadow.

She stepped up to the edge of the watercourse and three huge Dolly Vardens fled from their cool place beside the creekbank with the speed of arrows.

Mary Ellen looked swiftly at Fogarty. He forced a smile but he also gently told her about casting shadows over trout streams. Then they went out into the sunshine among the wildflowers—and had a cock prairie chicken explode under their feet, making a racket probably calculated by some unknowable intelligence to cause heart attacks among hunters. Mary Ellen sprang into his arms with enough force to nearly bowl him over.

He held her as he dryly said, "In'ians."

She raised a white face, looked left and right, looked up at his broad smile, and pushed him away with surprising strength.

"Prairie chicken," he explained. "They'll do it every time. Maybe that's why they're still around, because otherwise you can kill them with a stick."

"Why do you kill them?"

"Do you like roast chicken, Mary Ellen? Prairie chickens are even better."

"Joe, I couldn't eat anything like that."

He continued to smile at her. "Well, someday, maybe

when we go a-horseback up yonder to that secret In'ian *rancheria*, and we got to shoot our supper for a while after we run out of town grub, you'll starve.''

She stood gazing up at him. "Someday, Joe?"

"Would you like to, Mary Ellen?"

"I'd love to."

CHAPTER TWENTY-THREE

"Joe . . . ?"

On the drive back, Fogarty was conscious of their occasional brushing at hip and shoulder until they reached the stage road, which was less bumpy. From the slight elevation of the northward distance, they had an excellent view of Sheridan, and he eyed it critically, wondering what she thought, certain it did not compare favorably with places she'd seen. But she surprised him.

"It's a beautiful setting, isn't it? So much wild distance on all sides, with the town's tall trees and buildings correctly aligned. It's like a picture postcard, Joe."

He had always liked the town, had in fact thought it actually was handsome, what with its brick buildings, its broad main road, and its older log structures.

It had an appearance of stability. Unlike many younger communities in the territory, Sheridan exuded a sense of permanence.

"I like it," he said simply, and drove along hunched forward with slack lines in his hands. "And it'll grow, Mary Ellen. There's talk a railroad spur will pass through one of these days."

Her expression changed slightly. "I wouldn't like that. It'd be too much of a change."

He quickly said, "Then again, maybe it's nothing but talk.

You know how small towns are. Always some tomfool notion floating around." He shot her a sidelong look.

"Joe, what's that log building inside the rickety fence on the east end of town?"

Fogarty groaned to himself. "Tanyard. Run by a feller named Jim Young. It used to be down near the center of town, but folks raised so much cain, the council made him move up where the smell and flies wouldn't bother them." He considered the distance before they would be abreast of the dilapidated fence, then said, "If you breathe through your mouth when we drive past, you won't smell anything."

Her interest moved along. She knew most of the stores and she also knew which was the saloon and the pool hall. She startled him with a question and a statement. She pointed toward the vacant space between Dennis's store and the smithy. "No one ever built there?"

As far as Fogarty knew, no one ever had. "Nope." He almost added that every summer the blacksmith killed rattlesnakes in the thickets of weeds that grew there, but caught himself in time.

Mary Ellen sat up a little straighter on the seat. "Wouldn't it be an ideal place for a church, Joe?"

He looked stonily ahead at the empty place and forgot to breathe through his mouth until it was too late. Mary Ellen did not appear to notice the powerful stench from the tanyard. "It would put a finishing touch to Sheridan, don't you think?"

"One time," he said, speaking slowly, "the feller who runs the bank offered to buy that piece of ground and give it to the town if the council would agree to build a church on it."

"What happened?"

They were past the tanyard and nearing the brick-fronted bank when he told her. "Mr. Dennis is a Baptist. He was on the council that year when Mr. Donner, who runs the bank, made the offer. Mr. Dennis asked Mr. Donner what kind of

a church, and when Mr. Donner said a Catholic church . . .
The lot is still empty.''

When they reached the hotel he cramped the wheels so
her skirt wouldn't get dirty, and after she'd alighted and turned
to thank him, he said, ''Folks are wondering, Mary Ellen.''

She looked him straight in the eye when she said, ''Do
you like Sheridan well enough to stay?''

He nodded.

She laughed up at his solemn look before replying. ''So
do I.''

He watched her until she was on the porch. When she
threw him a wave, he waved back and smiled. Joe clucked
up the mare and drove the full length of town to Lee's barn,
where he turned in, climbed down as Reg hobbled over to
take the rig, and gave the liveryman a resounding slap on the
back. Reg caught a handful of harness to keep from falling
and turned to put a bewildered look in the direction of the
big man walking jauntily toward Main Street.

When his hostler came up, Lee turned, still scowling.
''You see that? He liked to knocked me down.''

The hostler had seen, and laughed. ''He likes you, Mr.
Lee.''

''Well, it'd suit me fine if he liked me a little less. Take
care of the rig.''

When Marshal Fogarty made a round of the town, men
who had known him since he'd arrived in Sheridan eyed him
warily. McGregor told Hugh Pepperdine if he didn't know
better, he'd say Joe Fogarty had been drinking.

Pepperdine was straddling his sewing horse, working on
those torn halters Reg had brought up a week back, and
commented without missing a stitch. ''Him and old Caulfield's niece went buggy riding this afternoon. . . . James,
move away from the window, will you? You're cuttin' off my
light.''

McGregor moved. ''Want me to light the lamp? It's too
dark in here, you'll strain your eyes.''

Pepperdine ignored all that. "He's sweet on her, or hadn't you noticed?"

McGregor did not say whether he'd noticed or not, he said, "That's a two-way road."

"Ain't the first time they've gone buggy riding," replied Pepperdine as he kicked the ratchet loose that kept the jaws of his sewing horse closed.

McGregor moved along the counter. "I know that."

Hugh was leaning to feel for his under-the-counter bottle when he smiled at the gunsmith. "Maybe we didn't have to go through all that fakin' after all."

He put the bottle in front of McGregor, who eyed it closely. "This isn't a trick, is it?" he asked, and got a stare. "Because the last time someone shoved a bottle at me—"

"No, it's not a trick. That's malt whiskey from back east somewhere. I got it from Rusty."

Pepperdine tipped the bottle, blew out a flammable breath, and handed the bottle to the gunsmith. McGregor had two swallows and grimaced as he put the bottle down. "It'd be nice if they get married, wouldn't it?"

Pepperdine thought it would. "Make a fine-lookin' couple, and Joe's the right age to get hitched double."

McGregor was regarding the bottle without making any attempt to reach for it as he replied. "I don't know about that, but Sheridan sure needs her."

Dusk was settling and roadway traffic had been dwindling for an hour or so. Pepperdine finally fired up his lamp and was hanging it from its ceiling wire when someone came in from out front, making an odd sound as he progressed. Both old men turned. McGregor grabbed the bottle and was looking for a place to hide it when old Silas snorted shrilly and said, "I seen it, James. You can't hide old barley corn. When a man's been drinkin' the devil's brew, you can smell it on him a country mile. That's what you two old degenerates do in here evenings. Drink whiskey. Someday you'll get the dropsy and get bedridden. Your teeth'll fall out, your memory'll give out, and you won't be able to hold your water an' folks'll shun you.''

Hugh went back behind his counter to lean as McGregor addressed the corral-yard man. "Silas, I don't expect to live to a hundred, but if I did an' I thought the world would be full of gents like you, I'd drink twice as much."

Browning made his sniffing sound and faced Hugh. "I got some leather traces that need resewing."

Pepperdine nodded. "Where are they?"

"You didn't expect me to lug 'em down here on crutches, did you? They're up at the yard, an' I got to have them by tomorrow afternoon. That's when the special goes south."

"What special?"

"Special stage Pete Donner contracted for to haul some silver bars down to Bordenton."

For a moment both old men were silent as they regarded the older man beneath his huge hat, hunched over on crutches, looking uncomfortably like a male witch.

"Silver is heavy," McGregor said.

Silas glared, "Don't you expect I know that?"

"How many bars, Silas?"

"Four crates. That's why I want those traces in top shape. I'm putting my stoutest team on the rig."

"Why don't you use a freight wagon?"

"Because, confound it, the stage will be faster an' Pete's hired four armed guards to ride inside, that's why. Now then, about them traces . . ."

Pepperdine nodded. "I'll come up for them first thing in the morning."

"An' you'll guarantee to have them back to me tomorrow afternoon, maybe a short while after dinner?"

Hugh's response was as dry as corn husks. "I don't guarantee anything and never have—and you know it. I'll do my best. Silas, sewing two traces is a full day's job."

McGregor entered the conversation. "A man could likely do it in time, Silas, but he'd have to miss dinner an' get up before daylight, an' for that, seems to me the pay'd ought to be a little more.''

Silas glared. "You ain't the harness maker, James!"

Pepperdine smiled at Browning. "I was just going to say that, Silas. You're askin' me to put in a longer day than I'd put in for most folks.''

"You bandit!" shrilled the old man, sniffing loudly.

Hugh was unperturbed. "Get one of your yardmen to do it. I know for a fact one of those Messicans worked in a harness works years back. He told me that one time over at the bar.''

Silas had to shift position because the crutches were causing his armpits to ache. He shed one crutch and leaned heavily on the counter. "I know that," he told Pepperdine. "I've never seen his work, besides, we don't have the things up yonder a man'd need. Hugh, you're holdin' me up.''

Pepperdine nodded in the direction of the liveryman's torn halters. "First come, first served. I've always run the shop like that, Silas, an' you know it. Reg'll be needin' those halters in a day or two. In his business a man can't—" "How much?" old Browning asked in a raised voice. "I'll remember this, Hugh!''

"Dollar a trace.''

"That's your usual charge.''

"Be all right with you if I finish, Silas? Dollar for repairing the traces an' another two dollars for my extra time.''

Browning's eyes bulged. He started to speak but Hugh cut in with an upraised hand. "Silas, hunt around among your other sets of harness, find a stout pair of traces and put them on the pair you want fixed.''

Silas was red in the face. For a moment he simply glared, then he snatched the leaning crutch, hitched around to get it into place, and leaned as though he would spring at someone before he said, "Hugh Pepperdine, so help me Gawd you'll never ride another of my stages as long as you live! Come get them damned traces first thing in the morning!" He swiveled around and went bounding awkwardly to the door.

There, he turned and leveled a malevolent glare at Mc-Gregor.

"That goes for you too."

They listened to the echoes of his uneven stamping after the old man was no longer in sight, then Hugh reached for the bottle with a loud sigh. "Can you imagine a mother ever givin' milk to him?"

McGregor did not reply as he accepted the bottle from the harness maker and had it raised when Mary Ellen Randolph appeared in the doorway. McGregor lowered the bottle and held it behind his back as Hugh covered his friend's embarrassment with a loud and flowery greeting.

The handsome woman smiled at Hugh, giving the gunsmith enough time to back toward some piles of old harness and lose the bottle there.

She said it was a beautiful evening, to which Hugh hastily agreed and enlarged upon. "This time of year it's like this just about every evening, ma'm. In fact, if folks was to come right down to it, they'd have to say Sheridan's got more beautiful evenings in spring an' summer than just about any place they could think of."

McGregor came back up to the counter and offered the beautiful woman one of his rare smiles, and added his enthusiam to Pepperdine's by making a reckless remark. "It's a real nice town, ma'm. Solid and substantial, and healthy. Which means a lot . . ." He let it dwindle off as it struck him no one knew better than the handsome woman that Sheridan wasn't all *that* healthy a place. He struggled to recover by also saying, "Except for accidents an' storms an' such like."

Hugh interrupted as it became clear his friend was getting in deeper by the minute. "I'm real glad you came by, ma'm. Is there maybe somethin' I could do for you?"

"I was out for a stroll, saw the light and thought I'd come in and see how you're feeling. I didn't know you'd both be here. Mr. McGregor, your breathing difficulty is better?"

"Much better," James affirmed. "I never had such an attack before, but it's past an' now I'm feeling fine."

"Mr. Pepperdine?" she asked.

Hugh spread work-roughened hands atop the counter and beamed. "Summer complaint comes an' goes, ma'm. It was my own fault for not dosin' with coal oil and molasses. I know better, but sometimes when a man's real busy . . ."

She smiled. "I'm glad you're both recovered. I'd better get back now. Good evening."

They watched her pass beyond the doorway and turn northward. McGregor leaned and gazed at the empty doorway until Hugh asked irritably what he'd done with the bottle.

The gunsmith straightened up and wagged his head. "Hugh, if Joe Fogarty lets that one get away, he'd ought to be shot."

Beyond the doorway night had arrived. Someone over in Rusty's place was playing a banjo and singing. The banjo sounded fine, the singing sounded like a coyote with infected adenoids. Mary Ellen heard it too, on her way to the hotel where she sat down in the soft night and smiled about the two old men in the harness shop.

Distantly, a squealing horse overrode Sheridan's lesser night-time sounds after the banjo player stopped his racket. Mary Ellen had no way of knowing it, but that was Reg Lee's cranky gray mare, the one Reg had hoped very hard that runty little escaping raider had taken, and he hadn't.

Fogarty completed his final round of town over across Main Street and came ambling toward the porch. He did not see her sitting there until he was less then fifteen feet away and she spoke.

"Joe? How long would it take to get to the top of that blue ridge where the old Indian camp is? Up and back?"

He stepped onto the porch before replying. "Well, on horseback—and we really should take along a pack animal for grub and all—I'd say maybe a day out and a day back. Depending on how much time you wanted to spend up there gathering old In'ian stuff. To give you plenty of time—say three days. At the most four.''

He moved to a chair beside her and sat down. ''We'd want to head out early, an hour or two before sunup, otherwise we'd be traveling through the timber about sundown. It'd be better to have daylight all the way to the top.''

She was a good listener, particularly, as he'd eventually discover, when she'd already made her own reasonably accurate estimate of things. ''You don't anticipate any difficulty?''

He twisted to look at her. In overhang gloom she looked very young. He'd noticed that once before. ''I can't right offhand imagine what could happen, Mary Ellen. You're not worried about In'ians again, are you?''

''Not this time. I was worrying about something else—the people in town, if you and I went off together on horseback with a pack horse and were gone several days.''

He had to settle back before considering his answer. ''Well, I expect the ones that gossip would talk. They'd talk anyway. By now they're probably already at it because you and I've been buggy riding. The other folks . . .'' He knew about the others. They wouldn't gossip but they wouldn't approve.

She quietly said, ''Joe, will you marry me?''

He didn't move for three seconds, and then all he did was loosen slightly in the chair and stare the full length of Main Street. Eventually he grinned at her. ''Be right proud to, ma'm.''

She cocked her head, which was one thing about her he'd come to understand, and quickly made the correction. ''Mary Ellen. I've been screwing up my nerve for a week.''

She startled him again. ''I know, and not knowing how long that was going to take, I thought I'd do the unforgivable. I'd ask you.''

CHAPTER TWENTY-FOUR

Things Change.
People Most of All.

Two days later, when Joe went up to the hotel after sundown, he stopped on the porch to stare at that powerfully fragrant flourishing bush and shake his head. "Naw," he said, and pushed the door open. There'd only been he and Mary Ellen—and that damned bush out there when she'd proposed to him and he'd accepted.

It was all over town. People he knew only as acquaintances, such as the blacksmith's apprentice, were pumping his hand or thumping him on the back or grinning like tame apes as they warmly congratulated him on his upcoming marriage to that handsome nurse lady.

He hadn't been in his room ten minutes before the old gnome who owned the roominghouse came banging on the door, and when Joe opened it, the old man cackled like a demented rooster. "Best thing that ever happened to you, boy. Take m'word for it. An' ain't she purty, though? Slick as a calf and hung together just exactly right. Shake, Marshal!"

After Fogarty closed the door and began shedding clothes, he was still baffled at how thoroughly and swiftly the word had gone through town. He would willingly acknowledge at any time news never traveled faster than it did by moccasin

238

telegraph. In this instance, though, it seemed to him to have established some kind of record.

As he got into bed, the sound of music carried from Rusty's saloon. Some raffish wag was laboriously and with intentional loudness picking out the Wedding March with two fingers on Rusty's antiquated and off-key piano.

Somewhere between that noise and a damned horsing mare squealing somewhere down at the lower end of town, Fogarty fell asleep.

In the morning he was waylaid by Silas Browning out front of the corral yard before he'd got halfway along to unlock the jailhouse. Then he went across to the cafe for breakfast.

Silas had developed a high degree of dexterity with his crutches. As he swung out in front of Fogarty, he said, "Good mornin', Marshal. I been waitin' for you."

Fogarty suspiciously eyed the old man beneath his preposterous hat. "Why?"

"Well, some time before noon I'm sending a special down to Bordenton." Silas hitched closer and looked around before half whispering the rest of it. "Silver shipment from Pete's bank to the bank down in Bordenton."

Fogarty hadn't known. "How big a shipment?"

"Four crates. Don't worry, he went an' hired four gun guards to ride inside with the crates. What I was wonderin', Marshal, you fixin' to get married an' all, I could make a place for you inside too, so's you could go down there and talk to the minister about comin' up here for the marrying." Silas made a sly leer. "Maybe fetch him back with you."

Fogarty glanced down to where men were trooping into the cafe with its fogged-up roadway window, and over at his locked and dark jailhouse, then back to Browning, hovering on his crutches, still leering.

"Four gun guards," he said, "that Pete'll pay, and you'll do me the favor of letting me ride down yonder with those gun guards. Five guns if there's trouble, and somebody only has to pay four of them."

Silas popped his faded blue eyes wide open. "How can

you think such a thing? You'd ought to be ashamed of yourself. That there offer is my weddin' present in advance. Marshal, I got to say I'm real disappointed in you.''

Fogarty grinned. ''Who is driving the special coach, Jack Carpenter?''

''Well, yes, for a fact he is. I despise his bad habits and all, but when the chips are down, I got no better man to tool a treasure coach.''

''You ask Jack to hunt up the preacher for me down there and fetch him back when he returns. How much would you charge for that service, Silas?''

''Well now, Marshal, I couldn't hardly charge for somethin' Jack'll do on his own time, could I?''

Fogarty lightly rapped the old man on the shoulder and continued southward, but was waylaid again by Hugh Pepperdine leaning in his doorway, watching the sky brightening beyond town. Hugh said, ''I saw him ambush you out front of the corral yard. He didn't talk you into riding gun guard, did he?''

''No. Donner's got four men going with the special. They don't need me.'' Joe eyed the older man. ''You had breakfast yet?''

''Yep. Me'n James was first ones in for a change.''

After the lawman started on an angling course across Main Street, Pepperdine scuttled over to the gun shop, where McGregor was standing in his window watching the roadway. When Pepperdine entered, the gunsmith turned with raised eyebrows. ''He's not goin', is he?''

''Nope. Damned old Silas give me a bad scare, though. I would've sworn he'd have tried to weasel a free gun guard on that special.'' Hugh looked around the gloomy interior of the shop where sunlight wouldn't reach for another couple of hours. ''Where is he?''

McGregor didn't answer. He jerked his head and led the way to his storeroom, where the preacher was sitting on a chair reading a book about homeopathic diagnostic techniques. When Hugh walked in, the preacher smiled and arose. "This seems like an odd way for Marshal Fogarty to do things, but then you boys know him better'n I do. By the way, does Mr. Dennis know?"

Pepperdine smiled benignly. "Parson, don't you worry about a thing. Would you like a cup of coffee?"

"No thanks. Does the lady know about this?"

This time it was the gunsmith who replied. "She will as soon as we get you up to the hotel. Don't fret, parson, she's willing."

The minister leaned to put the book aside and straightened up. "It's kind of unusual, isn't it? Most often both the man and woman come to me ahead of time."

Hugh changed the subject. "Did you get any sleep on the stagecoach?"

It was the kind of question that would normally deserve a dour grunt, but the minister was a mild and obliging individual. "Not very much. It's been years since I've ridden a coach at night, and the road's not very good."

Pepperdine nodded sympathetically and glanced at Mc-Gregor, who hitched at his britches as he turned toward the door. "We'll go up the back alley, Reverend, an' cross over to the hotel from there."

The minister said nothing until the three of them were outside walking northward, then all he said was, "That's the biggest donation I ever received for marrying, gents."

McGregor noticeably winced, but Hugh Pepperdine didn't. "Put you to a lot of bother, parson, ridin' up here in the cold and dark from Bordenton. Anyway, we got a special reason for uppin' the ante a little."

Pepperdine halted near the end of the alley, left his companions, and went ahead to look over in the direction of the hotel. She wasn't on the porch. He frowned about that and walked out into plain view to look down toward Henry Pohl's cottage. If she was down there—damnation!

He returned, met McGregor's raised-eyebrow look and shrugged. They herded the minister across Main Street, over to the hotel porch, got him comfortably seated near the big smelly bush and walked a short distance away.

McGregor said, "Likely still in her room. It's pretty early."

Hugh did not think so. "Most likely down at Henry's place. You keep the old screwt settin' there quiet. I'll go down and see."

"An' if she's down there, maybe patchin' someone up?"

"I'll bring her back with me. James, while you're mindin' the preacher, keep an eye on the road for sign of Joe."

"How the hell are you goin' to get her away from down there if she's workin' on some sick person?"

Pepperdine eyed his shorter, thicker friend and smiled. "I'll tell her your asthmatics come back an' you need lookin' at."

Pepperdine left the gunsmith standing in place darkly scowling as he went briskly to the doctor's place and knocked. When Mary Ellen opened the door, he put on an ingratiating expression as he explained about McGregor having a relapse. She reacted more quickly than Hugh had expected. "Wait. I'll get some medicine and go with you to the gun shop."

"No ma'm. He's at the hotel . . . was up there visitin' someone when it come on him. You hurry, please?"

Mary Ellen disappeared back into the house and returned within minutes. What Hugh was sweating bullets about was that Henry might want to go along too, but a kind, or maybe a conniving, Fate interceded.

As she was closing the door before walking away with Pepperdine, someone called from southward and Joe Fogarty waved as he started toward them.

Hugh broke into a sweat, but after emerging whole from a lifetime of convoluted difficulties, he waved back at the marshal, as did Mary Ellen. Then Hugh took her in the direction of the hotel porch with a long stride.

She had to almost trot to keep up. If she thought anything of this, it was probably that Pepperdine's anxiety was for his friend. She said nothing until they reached the porch and she

saw McGregor sitting there with a man she recognized as
having come to Sheridan from down south for Matt Hampstead's funeral.

She nodded to the preacher, who started to smilingly arise
as she turned her back to him and leaned to look at Mc-
Gregor. James was sitting like a rock, glaring at the saddle
maker, but the moment she touched his forehead, the gunsmith pulled in a rattling breath.

She tapped McGregor's chest about the time he saw Joe
Fogarty coming toward the porch from down in front of
Browning's corral yard. His breath really did wheeze in and
out.

The minister was standing, watching everything with a
benign but puzzled expression. He stepped over to speak to
Mary Ellen, and Hugh abruptly said, "Ma'm, I think I can
get him down to his shop. I'll go real slow with him. Get
him into bed and put a pan of camphor oil on the stove. That
usually helps."

McGregor leaned to arise. He got upright with Hugh's
help, made a wan small smile as Joe Fogarty reached the
edge of the porch, and allowed himself to be led away under
Mary Ellen's solicitous gaze. She turned to Fogarty and said,
"That's about all I could have prescribed for him. Boiling
water with camphor oil in it."

Fogarty looked around where the pair of old men were
making their unsteady way toward the gun shop. "What's
wrong with him?"

"One of those sudden asthmatic attacks."

The minister also gazed after the pair of old men. "But he
was just fine an hour ago. Even fifteen minutes ago."

Mary Ellen nodded toward the preacher. "It can happen
that suddenly, Reverend."

"But we—"

Fogarty spoke while watching the old men disappear into
the gun shop. "He's always been hardy as a horse."

The minister edged closer. "Marshal . . . ?"

"Maybe I'd better go down there and make sure Mr. Pep-

perdine makes the right mixture of water and camphor oil,''
Mary Ellen said.

The minister cleared his throat. ''Ma'm? Miss Randolph?''

She faced half around. Joe was still frowning in the direction of the gun shop. He did not look around until the
minister said, ''This is unorthodox, you know. Not the marriage ceremony; that can be performed anywhere. In fact I've
wed folks in some very unusual places. But never before
when intermediaries arranged it.''

Mary Ellen and Joe stood in stunned silence.

The minister smiled benevolently at them. ''On the porch
here will be all right.'' He paused to look from one of them
to the other. ''Ordinarily the gent has someone stand up with
him and the lady has a bridesmaid. But like I said, I've—''

''Reverend,'' Mary Ellen said softly. ''I'd like you to clear
something up for me. Did Mr. McGregor and Mr. Pepperdine
arrange this? Did they bring you up here to marry us?''

''Indeed. They said you and Marshal Fogarty wanted it
like this.'' The minister looked back and forth at them. ''You
do want to be married, don't you? They sent word to me
down in Bordenton last night I'd be needed up here this
morning. . . . They paid the donation in advance. They said
that was their wedding present to you both.''

Mary Ellen turned toward Joe, who was staring at the
minister. He turned slowly to meet her gaze. Neither of them
said a word, and the minister's expression congealed.

At the lower end of Sheridan, a pair of riders were loping
side by side on a southwesterly course for the distant mountains. Reg Lee, who had rigged out the horses in haste for
them, leaned on a manure fork beside his dayman, scowling.
''Not what the hell do you expect those two old devils is up
to?''

''They was sure in a hurry,'' the hostler replied. ''Say,
you don't suppose they got a gold mine in them mountains
somewhere, do you?''

Reg snorted. ''They wouldn't know gold unless it was in

someone's mouth. They're up to something. That croaker sack was full of grub. They're not comin' back soon. Sure as hell they're up to something.''

The hostler had to squint to make out the distant loping horsemen. ''Did you hear what the gunsmith said as they was climbing astraddle?''

''No.''

''Didn't make a lick of sense, Mr. Lee.''

''Neither does them two old devils goin' off like this. I've known 'em both ten years an' more and never saw 'em in such a big hurry to leave town before. . . . What did the gunsmith say?''

''Well, it was somethin' about someone thinkin' twice before they give croton oil to anyone again. Somethin' like that . . . Mr. Lee, what's all that hollerin' up the road?''

Reg turned and limped alongside his dayman to the main roadway. Up at the north end of town people were congregating in front of the hotel porch. ''A shootin' maybe?'' said the hostler.

Lee threw him a fierce look. ''Did you hear any shooting? It's somethin' else . . . Gawddamn! You know who that is standing up there on the porch with the marshal an' the nurse lady?''

''Who?''

''That preacher who spoke over the lad's burial a few days back. Jesse . . . that's a marryin' goin on up there! I can't believe it. Nothin' was said to me. Everyone knew they was sweet on each other, but holy smoke, it's usually a couple months anyway before folks get married.''

''Let's go up and see, Mr. Lee.''

''You go. My foot's botherin' me and that's a long hike. You go, and hurry back here with what you find out.''

Epilogue

It was early springtime four years later that Rusty Morton picked up a bedraggled newspaper some passing peddler had left in the saloon and took it behind the bar to read, that the answer to the only remaining riddle was resolved.

He took the paper over to the harness works, showed it to Hugh, then recrossed the road to show it to McGregor. Pepperdine had read and reread the newspaper article but had not said a word. McGregor had something to say, though. "Too bad Joe don't come to the cafe any more to eat or you could show him that. He'd be interested." McGregor tightened the apron string around his middle before saying anything more. "Take it over to his house, Rusty."

But Morton didn't do that. He couldn't go waltzing all over town with his saloon untended and with customers likely to appear now that the day was well advanced, so he took the limp newspaper back with him to the saloon, and as evening arrived showed it to a number of his local customers.

They too thought someone should take the paper over to Marshal Fogarty's house, the one he and his wife had bought two years earlier. It was on the east side of town and out a little distance where there was privacy. Since it was quite a hike to the house, no one volunteered to take the paper. Also, this was their relaxing time, and Joe would see the paper anyway, sooner or later.

As Silas's top whip said, positioned comfortably against the bar, "What difference does it make anyway? Nothing's going to change in Sheridan."

He was right.

Joe Fogarty did not see the newspaper until the day after Rusty had shown it to half the town. He was at the jailhouse office brewing a fresh pot of coffee when Rusty finally went down there with the newspaper, which by now did not appear likely to endure much more handling.

He spread it on Joe's desk under the big lawman's quizzical stare and made a motion. "Read that. Look at that picture."

Fogarty went behind the table, leaned with a scowl, and continued to lean for so long, Rusty went over to a bench and sat down. When the marshal straightened up, gazing at Morton, the saloonman said, "Found the paper in the saloon yesterday. Couldn't believe my eyes. What'd they call him when he was in your jailhouse, Joe?"

"Billy Smith."

"Yeah. Billy Smith. Well now he's the terror of Lincoln County down in New Mexico and they call him Billy the Kid."

Fogarty sat down and leaned to reread the article and study the picture. "Got a little heavier but sure looks the same, don't he? Buckteeth, and he's got his head cocked a little to one side."

"Did you read about those killings?"

"Yeah. Rusty, I'm not surprised. I wonder what his name really is?"

Morton was arising as he dryly said, "I don't think I'd go down to New Mexico to ask him." From the door Morton also said, "Your wife ought to know."

Fogarty nodded without looking up from the paper. "So will Henry and Eleanor. You want the paper back?"

"No. Keep it."

"Thanks."

Rusty went briskly back up to the saloon. He had no customers, so he caught McGregor and Pepperdine drinking coffee at the gun shop and told them of Joe Fogarty's reaction to the news. They were only mildly interested, so Rusty suggested they might want to reread the article. He'd left it at the jailhouse with Marshal Fogarty. They could see it down there.

They did not go down there. They'd read the article once, but even if they hadn't, it would have done nothing to confirm the opinions they'd formed years earlier.

About the Author

Lauran Paine lives in Fort Jones, California. He is an accomplished western writer who has published dozens of books under various pseudonyms and his own name.

The
"WILD WEST"
according to
LAURAN PAINE